THE BED *She* MADE

ELICIA HYDER

For More Information:
www.eliciahyder.com

ISBN: 978-0-9964483-9-0
Forge Creek Press

For my husband, Chris…
the boy who *almost* got away.

And for my mom and dad…
who made my bed.

1

The Phoenix

"PLEASE, BRANDON," Marcus Garrett begged. "We're not going to tell anyone."

Brandon Stockport shook his head and pointed to the sign by the cash register. "Eighteen." He grumbled something under his breath as he pushed his black rimmed glasses up the bridge of his nose and leaned back over the skull he was etching on Marcus's shoulder.

Kara Robertson smirked from where she sat with her long legs crossed on a bar stool. "Geez, Brandon, for a tattoo artist you sure are a goodie two shoes. Journey's birthday is in, like, ten hours."

"I've got the most successful tattoo shop in town. I'm not jeopardizing it by putting ink on a kid," Brandon said.

Journey Durant laughed. "You've got the only tattoo shop in town."

Brandon stuck up his middle finger and wiped some oozing ink and blood from Marcus's skin.

Stockport Tattooing was one of many surprising new businesses for the quaint but growing town of Emerson, Georgia. Situated on Main Street in the heart of downtown, if there was such a thing, the shop seemed to be a block from everything important: the city high school, the police department, the courthouse, and the town's one and only bar, Barry's Bar & Grill. In a town where the biggest news story of the year was the county's ban on sagging pants, Brandon Stockport had every right to be worried about being put out of business.

Marcus looked over to where Journey was examining the tongue rings. "Do we have plans tomorrow?" he asked.

Kara's brow crumpled, and she tossed her blond hair over her shoulder. "Oh, I don't know. Just mine and Journey's *graduation.*"

Journey raised her hand half-way into the air. "And my birthday."

Marcus craned his neck to watch Brandon work. "I know that much. I mean, do we have plans for afterward? I know you guys don't want to go to that lame party that the school throws."

"We're going to Journey's lake house," Kara said. "Her parents are leaving for London tomorrow morning."

Marcus looked up with surprise. "London?"

Journey shrugged her shoulders and plopped down onto the barstool beside Kara. "Business," she said.

By American Southern standards, Journey's parents were perfect. They were staunch Republicans, successful small business owners, and devout Southern Baptists. Their busy schedules, combined with the increasing disconnection they had with their youngest daughter, allowed Journey freedoms that they didn't necessarily want to give but were forced to. They deeply loved her, and she knew it, but their customers needed their attention and Journey didn't want it. She hadn't been the least bit surprised that they were missing one of the biggest days in her life, and truth be told, she didn't really care.

She looked up to see Brandon and Marcus both looking at her with so much pity she wanted to run out of the shop. "Your parents are going to be in London on your eighteenth birthday and your graduation?" Marcus asked in disbelief.

She forced a laugh. "In their defense, they had a valid point when they said they weren't even sure I would show up for my graduation."

Marcus looked up at Brandon, his eyes begging for mercy. "C'mon, man. *Please?*"

Brandon let out a frustrated groan. He stared at her for a moment before throwing his hands up in defeat. "Oh, for Christ's sake... fine! What tattoo do you want?"

Journey smiled. Something good might come out of her parental issues after all.

She had been planning her first tattoo since her Uncle Ray had come home from the Navy with a pin-up on his forearm when she was seven. She had drawn out the design she wanted when she was thirteen and had changed it more times than she could count. She flipped through her sketchpad and pulled out the final draft of a colorful phoenix. She proudly slid the drawing toward Brandon.

He looked up from Marcus's arm. "You did this?" he asked.

"I did," she replied.

He turned and leaned over the drawing of the magical bird. "It's really good," he said, unable to mask the surprise in his voice. "Where do you want to put it?"

"On my ankle, going down onto my foot," she answered.

Brandon shook his head, still staring at the picture. "Damn, girl. I was expecting a butterfly or something."

Kara sighed and crossed her arms over her chest. "You don't know her at all then."

"You're going to be here for a while," Brandon said, turning back to finish Marcus's skull. "And it's not going to be cheap."

"It's on me," Marcus announced.

Journey looked up.

"And me," Kara added. "Happy Birthday, Journ."

Forty-five minutes later, as the tattoo gun buzzed against her skin, Journey decided that getting a tattoo was like having a sunburn and being drawn on with an Exacto knife. As Brandon completed the outline of the bird, she wondered if she could tolerate the pain for the next few hours. To help keep her distracted, Kara made faces behind Marcus as he relentlessly admired his new ink in the mirror.

Journey wasn't what anyone would've called a popular student in high school. From her short, randomly colored hair down to her combat boots, everything about her was different from the other small town kids who valued their GPAs, the homecoming court, and football. However, despite her individuality—which usually didn't bode well for high school girls—her eighteenth birthday proved that she had some amazing friends.

It all began halfway through football season her sophomore year when she walked into Geometry class to find the quarterback slumped over his desk. He'd never actually spoken to Journey before, other than to borrow a pencil or ask to share her book, but necessity didn't constitute a friendship. He was a junior, and all she really knew about him was his name: David Britton.

On any other day, she wouldn't have given him a second thought as she took her seat behind him, but that day he looked so pitiful and friendless that it was heartbreaking. She wondered if maybe someone had died or if he was having big problems at home. As the teacher took attendance, Journey scribbled a note to him.

Are you OK?

He looked surprised when she slipped the note under his elbow, but he opened it and wrote a reply before passing it back to her.

Rebecca dumped me.

When she read it, she rolled her eyes to his back. *You've got to be freaking kidding me*, she thought. Nevertheless, she responded.

Then she doesn't deserve you. ☺

She knew he would probably assume that she was flirting with him. Most of the girls at West Emerson High flirted with David Britton. He was the star of the football team and looked like an over-sized Ken Doll with perfectly groomed brown hair, a chiseled face, and chocolate brown eyes. To her surprise, he simply looked back at her and smiled. It was an honest smile—a grateful one.

An hour later when the bell rang, Kara, who had been her best friend since the fourth grade, was waiting for her at the locker they shared.

Kara was an individualist by genetics; she had reached six foot one by age eleven. Like Journey, she was a bit of a rebel. On the first day of high school, the basketball coach had called her 'a natural talent' upon meeting her in the hall and insisted that she join his team. With great offense, she fired back, "I will not be defined by a growth chart!" She never touched another basketball.

"Hey, do you want to come home with me after school?" Kara asked as Journey approached.

Journey gave a noncommittal shrug. "Maybe."

"Journey, right?" a male voice asked behind her.

She spun around to see David Britton. "Yeahhh," she said, drawing the word out till it sounded more like a question than an answer.

"Hi, Kara," David said like he had known her for years.

"Hey there," she replied with a polite nod before turning her wide, questioning eyes back to Journey.

Journey looked back at David. He rocked back and forth on his heels for a second and then lowered his voice so that only she could hear him. "I just wanted to say thanks for trying to cheer me up. No one has really said much since Rebecca and I split."

She offered him a kind smile. "They probably just don't know what to say," she suggested. "I doubt they mean anything by it."

He shrugged his shoulders. "I don't think they really care."

She thought for a second. "Then they aren't very good friends."

He let out a slight chuckle. "Most of them aren't," he agreed. "Are you looking for any new friends? You seem to be good at it."

For a brief moment she wondered why he was standing there, in his letter jacket, talking to her. She didn't think it was possible to make that big of an impression in just two scribbled sentences on a torn sheet of notebook paper.

She hugged her English book to her chest. "Sure. I'm always looking for new friends." She smiled. "As long as you're not always this big of a cry baby."

He laughed and looked at her with pleasant surprise in his eyes. "Do I look that bad?"

She laughed. "I thought someone had died."

He cast his eyes to her feet and laughed.

"Dave!" a voice boomed from down the crowded hallway.

The three of them looked up to see a pair of flailing arms in the air. Girls regularly blushed at the sight of Marcus Garrett, David's best friend. He was the football team's wide receiver and, like David, one of the most popular guys in school. He wasn't very tall, but what he lacked in height, he made up for in build. The rumor was that he had some Latino mix in his genes, so he was dark with a year-round tan and jet-black hair. However, he had the brightest green eyes Journey had ever seen. The year before, an infamous list had appeared in all the girls' bathrooms around school. Marcus was listed as 'Cutest Butt' and 'Most Beautiful Eyes'.

Until that day, Journey had never seen those bright green eyes up close, but there they were, taking a close inventory of her. He turned toward David and slapped him on the chest. "Coach Smith wants to see us before the end of the day. I told him I would let you know."

Journey wondered if she merited a proper introduction from one member of the jock squad to another. She was surprised when it seemed she did. David pointed at her. "Marcus, you know Journey, right?"

Marcus nodded his head. "Yeah, I've seen you around. Nice shirt."

She shifted awkwardly on her feet and wondered if he was serious or making fun of her black, vintage Metallica t-shirt. "Uh, thanks."

David nudged her with his elbow. "Are you coming to the game tonight?" he asked.

She nodded. "Yeah, I think so."

He flashed her a genuine smile. Marcus hooked his arm around David's neck and began pulling him backward down the hall. "Cool. I'll look for you!" he called out.

Journey and Kara stared after him for a moment before Kara peered down at her. "What was that all about?"

Journey shook her head. "I have no idea."

Brandon finally turned off the buzzing tattoo gun. "That's it. You're all done." He wiped a cool cloth over her throbbing leg and foot.

Marcus stepped over beside her and nodded with approval. "Wow."

Kara walked back inside from her fifth smoke break since they had arrived and joined them at Marcus's side. "Are you done?" she asked.

"Yeah," Journey said, wincing with pain as she stood. She stepped in front of the mirror on the wall and turned her leg in different directions to admire the work. "Oh Brandon, it's awesome!" She took a step closer to get a better look. It was exactly what she wanted.

Kara clapped her hands together. "It's beautiful!"

Journey spun around and wrapped her arms around Brandon's neck. "Thank you so much!"

He squirmed uncomfortably until she released him. "Fantastic. Now pay me and get the hell out of here before someone asks questions."

Journey laughed as he bent to cover her new ink with a sterile bandage.

Marcus pulled his wallet out of his back pocket. "You guys go outside. I'll be there in a second."

Obediently, Journey and Kara walked out into the bright Southern sunlight. Journey looked up at her friend. "Do you really like it?"

"I seriously love it," Kara replied. "I'm a little jealous.

When are you going to draw one for me?"

"Whenever you want."

Marcus walked out the door and slipped on his sunglasses. Journey grasped his arm and planted a loud smacking kiss on his cheek. "Thank you, Marcus," she sang in his ear.

He sighed and shook his head. "You'd better be thankful. I've never spent money like that on a chick before."

She tugged on his arm. "I love you. You know that right?"

"Yeah, yeah."

Journey was no longer awkward around Marcus. That all ended the day he broke down and confessed that he regularly visited the tanning salon, and he wore green contacts. She had laughed until he got up and left the room. The truth was, even Marcus was as insecure as the rest of them.

"Too bad Dave couldn't be here for my first tattoo," Journey said as they walked to Marcus's black truck.

"Is he coming to your birthday party?" Kara asked.

"Yeah, he'll be there," Journey answered. She slid into the middle seat between her friends and propped her throbbing leg up on the dashboard.

"Sore?" Marcus asked with a grin as he started the truck.

"Not unless I touch it." Journey laughed and squeezed his shoulder. "How's that arm?"

He yelped with pain. "Son of a...!" he shouted, shoving her into Kara.

She laughed as he threw the truck into reverse and pulled out onto the highway in the direction of Journey's house.

Her parents were having a barbecue in honor of her birthday and graduation the night before to ease the guilt they felt about their departing flight the next morning. Journey knew it had the potential to become a 'war of the worlds' type of event between Journey's motley crew and half of the First Baptist Church that her mother had no doubt invited. Sure enough, when they pulled in she saw that Steven Drake was waiting in his rebuilt, 1970s black Chevelle. Her pot-head boyfriend was parked right next to the preacher.

Marcus shook his head and put the truck in park. "I can't believe you're still with him."

Journey pointed toward Steven. "Look at him. Why wouldn't I be?"

Steven's black hair was still wet from the shower and it was pulled into a short ponytail. He was wearing her favorite dark blue jeans and a 50's style, navy mechanic's work shirt with the sleeves rolled to display his heavily tattooed arms. Journey's stomach still fluttered every time she looked at him.

Marcus rolled his eyes and yanked the key from the ignition.

Steven greeted her with a kiss when she slid out of the truck. The smell of his cologne nearly made her dizzy. The scent was the same one she had bought David for his birthday the year before. *I wonder if he knows that*, she thought.

Steven tugged on her belt loop with questioning eyes. "Did you get it?"

She smiled up at him and proudly propped her leg up on the fender of Marcus's truck. "Sure did," she said. Gently, she lifted the edge of the bandage. "My friends bought it for me for my birthday."

After examining it carefully for a moment, Steven tipped her chin up and lowered his lips to meet hers again. "It's sexy," he growled. He pulled back smiling. "Do you like it?"

"Oh yeah," she replied as she covered it back up.

"Journey, you're late for your own party!" she heard her mother call from the porch on the side of the house.

"We're coming, Mom!" she yelled back.

Randall and Carol Durant belonged on the cover of a Hallmark card—or maybe a Christian Life magazine. Carol's frosted blond hair was perfectly in place, and she wore an angel pin tacked to the front of her Sunday morning skirt suit. Randall matched his wife in pressed khakis and a summer sweater vest over a plaid button-up. There they were, stuffy and conservative, with smiles cemented in place, when Journey and her friends made it around to the back of the country house.

Randall's smile diminished momentarily at the sight of the questionable-at-best boyfriend whose finger was hooked in the waistband of his little girl's blue jeans. However, in true Durant patriarch style, he extended a hand to Steven, though Journey knew he was silently contemplating throwing the boy over the deck railing.

Carol stepped forward and embraced her daughter. "I'm glad you finally made it, dear," she said with a slight twinge of annoyance in her voice. She smelled of discount department store perfume and peppermints.

Journey wiggled free from her mother's arms and backed up into Steven. "Hi, Mom," she said.

"Everyone, this is the birthday girl!" Carol announced. "And this is her handsome boyfriend, David…"

"Steven," he corrected her.

Feigning embarrassment, she put a hand to her forehead and quickly laughed to cover her error. "I'm sorry, Steven. I lost my head for a second."

Journey gave an awkward wave to the crowd and then led her friends to the furthest point on the deck possible. "Sorry about that," she told Steven, dropping her head onto his shoulder and hiding her eyes.

He turned his head to playfully bite the bend of her neck. "I don't mind as long as it's not you saying it."

Steven Drake had attended their high school—when he bothered to show up. He was older than the rest of them, and he worked as a mechanic behind Barry's Bar & Grill where Journey was a part-time waitress. She had been crushing on him since her freshman year, and they had dated on and off after he dropped out. Since she started at the restaurant, he had made a regular habit of seeing her. She knew her friends didn't care much for him, but he was attractive, fun, and old enough to buy alcohol. He was able to get pot from his brother, and he had his own apartment. She found the element of rebellion he emanated to be intoxicating. And best of all, her parents hated him.

Journey looked up at Kara as she and Marcus joined them. "When is Justin coming?" Journey asked.

"He's supposed to be on his way," she replied.

Kara had begun dating Justin Kruse at the beginning of the school year, and their budding romance left a lot of holes in Journey's social schedule. She filled those gaps with Steven, Marcus, and mostly with David.

Much to the dismay of his parents, David hadn't made use of any of the scholarship money he had been offered and decided to work at the local hardware store after graduation in lieu of going to college or joining the military. Journey was happy about it though. She looked forward to spending the summer with him even more so than with her own boyfriend.

Steven didn't understand her close friendship with another guy, despite her attempts at forcing the two of them to be friends. However, he didn't usually complain much about it. Either he wasn't the jealous type or he just didn't care. Her friends suspected that he didn't care—about her—and it was a driving cause of tension between all of them.

"How ya doin', *Dave?*" Marcus teased, nudging Steven with his elbow.

Steven took a sip of his drink. "Kiss my ass, Marcus," he said with a smile.

"Where is David?" Kara asked, scanning her eyes around the crowded deck.

Journey shrugged. "I thought he would be here by now. He wasn't working today, but he said he had to run some errands with his parents."

"That's weird," she said.

"I thought so too. He'll be here sometime though," Journey said. "He'd better be anyway."

Steven discretely tipped a flask over Journey's glass of soda and winked at her. She giggled silently and sucked on her straw.

"I saw that," Journey's Uncle Ray said as he walked toward them. He was her mother's older brother, a retired Navy officer, and a fellow black sheep of the family.

She laughed. "Are you going to tell on me?"

He smiled and held out his glass. "Not if you share."

Steven laughed and passed him his flask. When Uncle Ray handed it back to him, Steven stood up. "Journ, do you want some food?" he asked.

"I'll fix it," she told him.

He shook his head. "It's your birthday. I'll get it."

She gave him a long kiss on the lips. "OK."

When Steven had gone, Uncle Ray bent and pulled Journey in for a hug. "Happy birthday, sweetie," he said as he slipped something into her hand.

She looked down at the $100 bill. "Thanks Uncle Ray."

"I know your parents are really sore about missing tomorrow," he said.

Journey just nodded politely, making it clear she had no interest in talking about her parents.

He cleared his throat uncomfortably. "Your aunt and I will be at your graduation. It's at five o'clock right?"

She nodded. "Yeah."

"OK. Well, I'm going to go and get some of that pig before it's all gone," he told her as he turned to leave.

She stuffed the money into her pocket, and Kara smiled at her. "It might not be such a bad thing that your parents are going out of the country. I wish my relatives would slip me some pity cash like that."

Journey smirked. "Ha, ha."

Marcus surveyed the older group gathered on the far end of the porch. "Do you know any of these people?" he asked. "It looks like a tent revival out here."

Journey looked around. "I recognize a few people from when I was a kid, and that woman in the polyester jacket always pats my hand and says 'I'm praying for you, honey' whenever she drops Christian tracts off at the bar. Other than that, no." She paused and grinned at Marcus. "I'm sorry there's not anyone worth flirting with."

"You think I'm that shallow?" he asked.

Kara and Journey answered together. "Yes."

"Did I miss much?" a voice asked from behind them.

They turned to see David smiling, dressed in a neatly pressed, dark brown button-up shirt and blue jeans. He had a fresh haircut, much shorter than Journey had ever seen on him before. It complemented him though and made him look much older than his nineteen years.

"Your hair is finally shorter than mine," Journey said with a smile.

He laughed and pulled her into a tight hug, lifting her off her feet. He pressed a kiss to her temple before returning her feet to the floor. "Happy birthday," he said.

"I'm glad you finally made it." She let her arm linger around his shoulders.

"Hey, hey!" another voice called from the steps.

Justin was taking the steps two at a time up to the deck.

He was the only other person in their group that matched Kara in height. He was thin and lanky with blond hair that always fell down into his eyes. Though he had been a running back for the football team and was attending one of the most elite motorcycle mechanic schools in the country, Justin could only be described as *adorable*; he looked like the lost member of a boy band.

Kara ran to greet him and exchanged the present he was carrying for her full plate of barbecue. She kissed him on the lips before he stepped over to give Journey a side-arm hug. "Happy birthday," he said. "Sorry I'm late."

Journey beamed up at him. "Thanks for coming."

Steven returned carrying two plates of food with napkins and two forks held in his mouth. "Need some help?" Journey asked, taking a plate and the forks from between his teeth.

"Thank you," he replied.

"Let's sit," Kara suggested.

David pulled a bottled water out of the cooler and sat down next to Journey.

She looked at him with questioning eyes. "Are you not going to eat?" she asked.

"No. I ate with Mom and Dad just a little while ago." He patted his flat stomach. "I'm still stuffed."

"Where have you been all day?"

"Just taking care of some stuff. Where have you been all day?" he redirected her question.

"Oh!" She squealed and turned around in her seat. She slung her leg over David's knees and reached down to uncover her tattoo.

David bent over her leg, resting a hand on her thigh as he inspected the artwork. He squeezed her knee. "It's beautiful."

She was beaming. "Thank you. Marcus had his shoulder done, too."

Marcus rolled his sleeve to show off his skull.

David nodded his head. "I think I'm going to get one next."

"What are you going to get?" Kara asked.

"Maybe an armband," he said.

Journey shook her head. "No. You have a great chest. A tattoo would look so good right here," she said, placing her palm over his heart.

Steven cleared his throat. "I'm still here."

She laughed and kissed his nose. "You have a nice chest too, baby."

Journey's mother was handing out glasses of sweet tea with neatly sliced lemons perched on each rim. She paused to laugh politely at something the preacher's wife said.

Justin pointed his fork at her. "Journey, are you sure you're not adopted?"

Journey took in the sight of her 46-year-old mother whose maroon skirt suit was a size too big, six inches too long, and ten years too old. Then she glanced down at her own tie-dyed tank top, cut-off jean shorts, and worn out flip-flops. That day, Journey's hair was platinum blond, with pink streaks in the front. She rolled her eyes and scooped up a heap of mashed potatoes. "I ask the same thing all the time."

As if on cue, Carol looked in their direction. "David!" Her mother nearly squealed with delight as she quickly crossed the porch, clapping her hands joyfully. "I was afraid you weren't going to make it!"

David stood and gave her a welcoming hug. "You know I wouldn't miss this for the world."

Every mother's dream, Journey thought. She knew it wasn't by mistake that her mother had messed up Steven's name during the introduction earlier. Carol had chosen David for her future son-in-law the very first time he had dropped

Journey off after school. No amount of arguing would ever convince Carol Durant that they were just friends.

"I like your new haircut. You look very handsome tonight." She placed her hand on his chest. "Journey, don't you think David looks very handsome?"

David flashed her a straight-from-the-dentist smile and batted his eyelashes dramatically.

Journey laughed. "Just dashing."

"Mrs. Durant, what do you think of Journey's new tattoo?" David asked.

Carol looked at her daughter with the same expression she had when Bill Clinton beat George Bush in the '92 presidential election.

"Oh yeah," Journey said to her mother. She stood and grasped David's arm for support as she held up her leg to remove the bandage.

Her mother looked at the tattoo sideways. "Why do you have a rainbow chicken on your leg?"

David choked back a chuckle.

Journey rolled her eyes and replaced the bandage. "It's not a chicken. It's a phoenix."

"A phoenix?"

"It's a bird that burns up and then is reborn from its own ashes," Journey explained.

Her mother stared at her like she had grown a third eye. "A what?"

Journey glanced up at David and sadly shook her head. "I'm definitely adopted."

Carol dismissed the conversation entirely. "Well, you just help yourself to anything you want, David. Our home is your home, you know." She turned on her heel and floated off to continue playing hostess-superior.

As soon as she was out of earshot, Justin's signature

snorting laugh triggered the rest of her friends into hysterics.

An hour later, Journey suffered through the obligatory 'Happy Birthday' song as Carol carried a chocolate cake to her table.

What to wish for? she thought.

She looked around the table at her friends and wondered what more she could want. She closed her eyes and blew out the candles.

I wish for everything to stay just the way it is.

When the party ended, most everyone went home. Her father retired to his recliner, David helped her mom clean up, and Steven sat on the porch playing with the new cell phone he had gotten Journey for her birthday. It seemed to Journey that Steven and David were trying to outlast each other as the night wore on. Finally, her parents went to bed, and David resigned himself to defeat.

He got up off the couch and pulled his truck keys from his pocket. "Well, I guess I'll see you guys tomorrow."

Journey stood up with him. "Are we still on for lunch with your parents?" she asked.

"Yeah, absolutely. Just come over whenever you drag yourself out of bed," he teased.

She hugged him. "Thanks for coming."

"I wouldn't miss this," he said. They heard chimes coming from the grandfather clock. He smiled down at her. "It's midnight. Happy birthday."

She giggled. "Thank you."

"Night Steve," he called.

"Bye Dave," Steven replied, not getting up from the couch or even looking away from the television.

Journey walked him to the front door. "Be careful driving home," she said.

He gave her a quick kiss on the cheek that made her

stomach tingle. "Bye girl," he whispered in her ear.

When he was gone, Steven met her at the door and hooked his arms around her waist from behind. "Wanna *smoke* with me before I go too, birthday girl?" He dangled a joint in front of her.

"Please!" She laughed and stumbled out of the front door with him.

2

No Sex, Drugs, or Rock and Roll

JOURNEY WOKE up the next morning to the smell of coffee and bacon. Birthdays and Christmas morning were the only times of the year that Carol ever cooked breakfast anymore.

Life hadn't always been so tense in the Durant household. Journey could still remember being walked to the school bus every morning, having her lunchbox packed with cute notes from her mother, and having help with her homework after school. Her mother had even been a teacher's aide for a while when she was in elementary school. All of that changed when her parents opened an antique and fine art store just after Journey turned thirteen.

Business was flourishing but at the expense of their once close-knit family. Suddenly, Journey was coming home to an empty house each day after school, cooking late dinners for her parents, and spending most weekends at home alone or pawned off on family members. With her parents always working and her sister, Elena, living in Tennessee, Journey became dependent on her friends for attention, conversation, and advice. Before long, Journey rarely came home at all.

By the time that the Durants sensed there might be a problem in their relationship with their youngest daughter, there wasn't much control they could regain. Though they tried for a while to pick up the discarded role of parenting, their curfews were broken, their lectures fell on deaf ears, and their prayers were mocked. Every attempt they made to reel their wayward daughter back in was too little, far too late.

After a quick shower and getting dressed in a pair of ripped blue jeans and debatably clean 'I Dress This Way To Bother You' t-shirt, Journey joined her parents for breakfast.

"Happy birthday," Carol said when she entered the kitchen.

"Thank you," Journey replied.

Her father didn't look up from the newspaper he was reading. "What time did your little friend leave last night?"

Journey poured herself a cup of coffee and took a seat across from him at the table. "Steven?" she asked as she helped herself to a biscuit.

"Yes."

Journey shrugged. "I don't remember, but it was well before the sun came up."

Randall's eyes rose momentarily. "You're still under our roof, young lady. Don't push it."

Journey rolled her eyes. "Right."

Carol awkwardly sank into the seat next to Journey. "You really like this boy, then?" she asked.

"Yeah, I do." Journey took a sip of coffee and turned on her new cell phone.

"He's a little rough around the edges," her mother said trying not to sound too negative. "He's certainly no David."

Journey rolled her eyes. "For the five millionth time, Mom —I'm not with David, and I'm not going to be."

"I've never seen him with any other girls except for you," she pointed out.

"Well, I've seen him with plenty," Journey snapped, though she knew *plenty* was an exaggeration.

The house phone rang and her mother got up to retrieve the cordless phone.

Her father put down the paper and picked up his coffee. "You're staying with Kara till we get back, correct?"

"Yeah, of course," she lied. They both knew better, but their relationship functioned best under plausible deniability.

After answering the phone, Carol extended the receiver to Journey. "It's for you."

Journey put the phone to her ear. "Hello?"

"Hellllooooooooo," a cheerful voice sang on the other end of the line. It was Journey's older sister, Elena, who had escaped the dead end town of Emerson and moved to Nashville. Elena proceeded to sing 'Happy Birthday' in her best Opera style voice.

Journey laughed when she finished. "Thanks," she said.

"Big day today?" her sister asked expectantly.

"Pretty big," Journey answered.

"Do you feel all grown up now?"

Journey glanced at her parents who were busy with their breakfast plates and the local news. "Um, no."

Both sisters laughed.

"I wish I was there today, kid," Elena said.

"I know. It's cool," Journey assured her.

"You're going to come and visit me soon, correct?"

Journey nodded. "You bet. Thanks for the card and the cash. Mom gave it to me last night."

"Oh yeah. How was your party?"

"Interesting," Journey replied.

Elena laughed. "I bet. Well, call me later, OK?"

"I will. I got a new cell phone."

"Nice!" Elena cheered. "I love you, sister."

"Love you, too," Journey said and disconnected the call.

After a few moments of silence, Carol finally spoke. "I really wish you were going to stay with your sister while we are out of town. We could give you gas money."

"I'm fine, Mom."

"No parties, promise?" her mother asked.

"And no Steven over here while we're gone," her dad added.

Journey smirked. "And no sex, drugs, or rock-and-roll. I got it."

Randall's coffee sloshed onto the white tablecloth when he slammed his cup down onto the table.

Journey dropped her fork onto her plate and pushed her chair back across the tile floor. "Guess what?" she asked, rising to her feet. "I just realized. I'm eighteen today. I don't have to listen to this anymore."

Her mother silently closed her eyes.

Her father's jaw was so tense Journey could swear she heard his back teeth cracking. "That's right." He let out a tight breath. "You're eighteen."

Journey looked at both of them. "Have a nice flight," she said with slicing sarcasm before she marched out of the kitchen.

After packing a suitcase for 'Kara's house', Journey drove the seven miles to David's. His white truck was in the driveway when she pulled in, so she walked into the house without ringing the doorbell. "Anyone home?" she called out from the foyer.

David's dad waved from the end of the hallway. Despite

that Dennis Britton had been out of the military for twenty years, he still looked like a tank and gave orders like a drill sergeant. He was a tough man, but he liked Journey.

He walked over and gave her a side-hug. "Hey girl. Happy birthday. Gail has prepared quite a feast for your big day."

"I'm looking forward to it." She politely slipped off her tennis shoes before stepping onto their new beige carpet.

"David is downstairs in his room. Go on down and tell him that lunch is almost ready," he said.

Journey turned toward the steps. "OK."

David practically owned the remodeled basement of his parents' house. He and his dad had worked for almost a year to finish it out into a living room, bedroom, and a bathroom just for him. He had his own television and stereo, and he had worked the summer before he graduated to buy a used pool table. His house had instantly become the hangout spot for all of their friends. Journey spent as much time there as she did at her own home.

When she entered the room, she noticed immediately that something was off. The photo that his mother had taken of the two of them together at his graduation the year before was missing from the entertainment center. She continued walking to David's half-open bedroom door. "Dave?" she called out as she pushed it open and stepped inside.

There was a suitcase on the bed.

He looked up and met her gaze with wide eyes as if he'd been caught in the middle of some terrible act.

Journey looked around the room at the dresser drawers standing open and empty. Half of his clothes in the closet were gone. She looked back at David who appeared to be scrambling to think of something to say.

"Geez, we're only going to be at the lake for a few days," Journey said. "Don't you think you're over-packing just a little bit?"

He took a deep breath. "I'm only staying tonight."

She laughed. "Well, then you seriously need to downsize."

He didn't laugh with her. He took a hesitant step forward. "I'm leaving tomorrow afternoon for boot camp."

Her head snapped up. "Boot camp?"

He nodded.

"You joined the military?" Her voice was trembling.

"The Army," he said. "About three weeks ago."

Journey couldn't speak. She had known for some time that his parents were pressuring him to follow in the footsteps of generations of Britton soldiers, but she didn't realize he was seriously considering it. She thought, surely, if he was going to enlist he would have at least mentioned it to her. Suddenly, she felt betrayed having not been privy to such important information. It had been nearly two years since they had passed that first note in third period, and suddenly she felt like she didn't know him any better than she had then.

Unable to fully process the information, and certainly lacking a response, Journey turned and walked silently out of the room.

"Journey!" David called and lunged in her direction.

She started up the steps taking them two at a time. He grabbed her around the waist and pulled her back down into his arms. "Will you stop for just a minute?" he almost shouted at her.

She punched him hard in the chest and pushed him away. "Don't touch me!" Angry tears filled her eyes, but she refused to break.

He looked shocked and hurt. *Good,* she thought as she resumed her march up the stairs.

She walked out the front door and slammed it closed behind her. She didn't care that she had yelled at him. She didn't even care that she had just left the birthday lunch that his mother had prepared for her. She couldn't bear to be in that house any longer and knew that she had to get as far away as possible before she became an emotional nightmare.

Maybe she'd been wrong about David the entire time. Obviously, she didn't matter to him as much as she thought she did. Maybe it was best that he was leaving.

The gravel shifted under her tires as she peeled out of the driveway and uncontrollable tears spilled out onto her cheeks.

. . .

David stared, motionless, at the front door.

"David, did Journey just leave?" his mother asked, coming down the hallway with a dish towel.

"Yeah, she's gone," he stammered.

Her eyes widened. "Gone?"

His dad walked in from the back porch to investigate the disturbance. "What happened?"

Gail looked at her husband and then back at her son. "Journey just about took the door off the hinges. David, what did you do?"

He was silent for a moment. "I didn't tell her about the Army. She came in and saw my stuff all packed up."

His dad folded his arms across his chest. "You didn't tell her?"

He shook his head. "I didn't know how."

His mother pointed out the door. "You'd better go after her."

"I can't. She's too mad. It will just piss her off more." He turned and walked to the living room and slumped down onto the sofa.

His mother followed him. "David, are you in love with her?"

He felt like the wind had been knocked out of him. He

just shrugged his shoulders and looked away.

She was quiet for a while. "You need to talk to her and tell her how you feel."

"I don't know how," he muttered.

"Come on, you talk to that girl more than you talk to everyone else in this world combined." She rolled her eyes before pointing out the front door again. "Go and find her."

David had no idea where Journey had gone. He got into his truck and drove through town thinking about what his mom had said. He knew she was right, but he also knew that Journey would never feel the same for him. Steven was her type, and even he never had her full attention. David knew he didn't stand a chance.

He decided to call Marcus because, lately, Marcus was the person she would run to when she was mad at him.

Two months earlier had been her senior prom. At the insistence of Kara, she had asked David to take her. It wasn't David's fault that the planning committee had scheduled the dance on April Fools' Day, but he was certainly to blame for everything that happened because of it…

He thought it would be funny to call Journey the night of the prom and tell her that he hadn't been able to leave work early enough to pick up his tuxedo and that he wouldn't be able to make it. He never believed she would actually fall for it. When she did, he received the worst verbal lashing of his life and she hung up on him. That's where he should have ended the joke, but he didn't.

Instead, he decided that he was going to pull off the April Fools' joke to end all April Fools' jokes. At Valentino's Italian Bistro, he sat with pride facing the door so that he wouldn't miss the look on her face when she walked in with Justin and Kara and saw him.

While he waited, he tried to picture her in a proper prom

dress. He liked it when she wore green, but she had turned up her nose when he mentioned it. Green brought out tiny flecks of emerald in her hazel eyes. Her blond hair would have a fresh batch of blue or purple highlights, and just for the occasion, she might wear some makeup. David didn't care if she wore it or not. He never thought she needed it.

He sat forward in his seat as the restaurant door opened. Justin and Kara entered. No Journey. *Uh oh.*

Kara's mouth fell open, and she put her hands on her hips. "Oh, you are *so* stupid."

Marcus had picked Journey up from Kara's that night and had taken her out to dinner. Afterward, the two of them went dancing at Barry's Bar & Grill. It was that same night that Steven had officially asked Journey to be his girlfriend.

To say David was stupid was the understatement of a lifetime.

Much like that fateful prom night where David was the fool, he was once again driving all over Emerson looking for his best friend. Marcus hadn't seen her, Kara didn't answer her phone, and Steven was at work. He drove by her work and by her favorite coffee shop, but she was nowhere to be found. He finally gave up and went home to finish packing.

. . .

Marcus hung up the phone and looked out of his window at Journey sitting on his porch in tears. Her hands shook as she drew a third cigarette up to her lips. He walked back outside and sat down on the step beside her. "That was him," he said. "He's looking for you, but I didn't say you were here."

She just nodded.

"Are you going to tell me what happened?"

She was quiet for a minute. "Did he tell you he was joining the Army?"

Marcus shrugged his shoulders. "He mentioned that he

was thinking about it."

She pulled her knees into her chest and cried. "Why wouldn't he tell me?"

Marcus knew how to handle girls but not in an emotionally-supportive type of way. He put an arm around her shoulders. He knew exactly why David hadn't told her about the Army. *He didn't want to deal with this*, he thought as she sobbed into her blue jeans. *Thanks a lot, buddy.* He could've knocked David's teeth out.

When David had first befriended Journey, Marcus couldn't figure out why. But as he got to know her, he began to appreciate that she was so different from the other girls—none of which he could just enjoy hanging out with. So, the summer before, when Justin had backed out of going with him to a Metallica concert in Atlanta, Marcus got her number from David and called her. He thought it was funny that she seemed so shocked when he offered her the extra ticket. She had even asked if it was really him.

"Why do you want to take me?" she had asked him.

"Because you might be the only person I know that likes them as much as I do," he said. "Do you want to go or not?"

Of course she had gone, and they had so much fun that he knew it made David a little jealous. There was nothing romantic there, although her unwillingness to be impressed with him became a challenge to try and gain her attention.

He didn't understand David. Obviously, the idiot was head-over-heels for her, but he never would make a move. He couldn't understand how David could leave her for guys like Steven to have.

"Happy freaking birthday to me," she sobbed.

"Come inside, and I'll get you something to drink. And don't you dare light another cigarette. I don't want to have to scrape your lungs off my steps."

She left her pack of cigarettes on the porch and followed him into the house.

Marcus wasn't proud of the fact that he still lived with his grandparents. But they had taken him in when his mother bailed on him as a kid, and he felt obligated to stay and help take care of them when they got older. They had built an extension onto their double-wide trailer for him to call his own, but he rarely had friends over. Only those closest to him were ever invited inside. Journey was one of the few regulars.

She stretched out across his black comforter, and he turned on MTV. "Want a Coke?" he asked as he walked toward the kitchen.

She hugged his pillow. "Sure."

When he returned, she was lying on her back staring at the ceiling. He handed her the drink and sat down on the corner of the bed facing her.

"Maybe it's time for me to move on," she said.

"From what?"

"From this place." She sighed. "I could go and stay with my sister for a while."

"You're going to leave the state because David joined the military and didn't tell you?" He laughed. "Get real."

"I'm serious. She's working for this big marketing company now and just bought a huge house," she said. "Hey! You could come with me!"

He nearly choked on his drink. "Yeah right," he said, lying down next to her. There was a blonde in a bikini staring down at them from a poster on his ceiling. "Where is Kara? Shouldn't the two of you be having a girl-crisis moment or something?"

"No idea. Trust me, I tried her before I showed up here," she said.

He raised an eyebrow. "Glad to know I'm second choice."

"Actually, you're third. I called my sister before you also," she added.

"Great," he groaned. "So, what do we do now? I'm not good at this whole 'supportive' thing."

She shrugged her shoulders. "You tell me that David is a jerk, and he doesn't deserve to have me as a friend."

He laughed. "David is a jerk and definitely doesn't deserve to have you as anything." He rolled over and looked at her. "Now, can we please watch a movie or something?"

3

THE RING

BY FIVE o'clock the sun was starting to set, and Journey was sweating underneath the weight of her blue cap and gown. Her eyes scanned the crowd for familiar faces during the valedictorian's speech. She saw Uncle Ray and Aunt Joan. Just behind them were David and his parents. *That damn haircut,* she thought when she suddenly put the new crew cut together with the joining of the military.

He caught her gaze, but she darted her eyes back to the stage.

Her thoughts were racing wild, so the speaker's voice was only an echo. Every few moments her ears would tune in and grasp a few random sentences from the speech. "…and we'll never forget these years of our lives…" *You can say that again,* Journey thought as her mind wandered back to David.

A little while later, her name was called, and she ceremoniously crossed the stage to accept her diploma. She heard Marcus's familiar whistle above the crowd, and she smiled for the first time all afternoon. It was her birthday and her graduation; by god, she was going to enjoy it.

. . .

Randall Durant didn't do anything half-assed, especially his mid-life crisis. On the day he turned fifty, he bought a lake house, a boat, and two jet skis without so much as consulting his wife. Everyone was sure it was the only time that Journey's mother had ever contemplated divorce—or homicide. Journey had her own room at the two-story, log cabin overlooking the water, but she rarely ever visited. At least not when her parents were in town, anyway.

Within an hour of the close of the graduation ceremony, David walked into the house and found it swarming with under-age drinkers.

Journey did an amazing job of avoiding David for most of the evening. She rode with Kara to the lake and then disappeared with Steven and a bottle of fruity wine to the hot tub for nearly an hour. During dinner, she immersed herself in conversations that didn't include him. As long as she wasn't looking directly at him, she seemed perfectly happy. Then, every once in a while, David would catch her eye and watch the life drain out of her. His stomach wrenched every time that it happened. He knew he was running out of time to make things right again.

As darkness fell, he sat nursing a beer with Marcus and Justin on the porch. Suddenly, Steven got up from his post at Journey's hip and went into the house. David knew that if he didn't take this chance that it might be the last one he got with her.

He pushed himself up off the porch steps and crossed the deck to where she sat with Kara. She looked up at him with glassy eyes. Maybe she'd had enough alcohol to forgive him. "Wanna walk with me?" he asked.

She hesitated for a minute and then fired back. "If you're going to try to explain to me why you didn't mention that you're running off to join the governmental circus, I don't want to hear it! I don't really care."

He paused, unsure of what to say next. Kara glared at him, and he realized he was in dangerous territory.

"Please," he finally muttered.

She looked at him with forced indifference. That brought him a tinge of hope. She was trying not to care. She stood up, and he led her down the steps to the path by the water's edge. She walked stiffly, hugging her arms though it wasn't even chilly. Maybe she was trying to restrain herself from hitting him. They walked in silence until the voices and the music from the house were only a distant hum.

"I owe you an apology," he said.

She smirked but said nothing.

"I'm sorry I didn't tell you about the Army," he continued. "I just didn't know how."

She stopped walking and looked up at him. "You say something like, 'Journey, just to let you know, I'm joining the Army.' Geez, David, it's not rocket science."

As she turned, she wobbled and lost her footing, nearly falling into the lake. David grabbed her and held her steady on the bank.

She was warm against his body and so close that he could smell her coconut shampoo. *Say something*, he told himself. As she tried to pull away from him, he tightened his arms around her.

"Let me go," she demanded.

There was enough light outside to reflect the tears sparkling in her eyes.

"Not until you listen to me," he insisted. "I didn't mean to make you this angry. I didn't want to tell you because I didn't want it to be real that I was leaving you."

"You didn't even warn me!" she said through a clenched jaw. She was trying desperately not to cry.

He clasped his hands around hers and pulled them to his chest. "Because I know this is something I'm supposed to do. And I knew if you breathed one word about not wanting me to go, I would stay here forever."

His words obviously caught her off guard. She looked at him wide-eyed for a moment as silent tears streamed down her cheeks.

He sighed and looked down at the ground. *Say it,* his mind urged.

"I would never stand in the way of your dreams," she said quietly.

He shook his head and touched her cheek. "You wouldn't have to." His fingers trailed down to her jaw. "One frown and I would have given it all up."

She finally softened. "How long will you be gone?"

He took her hand again. "I leave on Thursday for thirteen weeks. Then I'll be home for seven days."

"And then?" she asked.

He shrugged. "And then I don't know what will happen."

"Journey?" Steven's voice wasn't far away.

They looked back toward the house, and Steven was coming down the path. "Over here," she answered.

Missed your chance, David thought.

Steven jogged to catch up with them. "What's going on?"

Journey quickly wiped her eyes. "We were just talking. David joined the Army, and he was just giving me the details."

David watched as a possessive arm slipped around Journey's shoulders, and Steven's dark eyes danced with elation in the moonlight. "That's great, Dave!" He didn't even attempt to hide the joy in his voice. "When are you leaving?"

"Tomorrow," David said.

"Well, I think that is something we should be drinking a toast to!" Steven turned Journey back toward the house. "Let's go break open some champagne!"

David dropped his head and followed them.

Kara caught David's eye as he trudged back up the steps to the porch. Her eyes were strangely inquisitive. She glanced over at Steven and Journey and then back at him. He walked over and leaned against the railing near her.

"What?" he asked, desperate to know why Kara was suddenly so annoyed with him.

She pointed at him. "You're an idiot."

. . .

Journey's bedroom was a wreck when she awoke the next morning. She was fully dressed, sprawled across her comforter. Steven was shirtless and drooling on the pillow beside her. At least she had made it to her own bed. Her head was pounding, and her mouth was so dry she could barely open it. "Never again," she groaned as she slowly sat up.

She stumbled around the room for a moment before getting her bearings. Then she changed into some clean clothes and walked out of her room and down the hall to the kitchen. Kara was smoking a cigarette on the porch swing.

Journey poured a cup of coffee and walked out to join her. "Morning," Kara said, sliding over to make room.

"Have you been up long?"

Kara shrugged. "Long enough to know I won't make it through today without some coffee and pain killers."

"Yeah, last night is a little hazy."

"Do you remember talking to David?"

Journey thought for a second. "Yeah. That was before we cracked open that bottle of cinnamon schnapps. After that, my memory gets fuzzy."

"What did you guys talk about?" Kara asked.

"He apologized. He said that he didn't talk to me about it because he was afraid that I would talk him out of going."

"That's all?"

Journey shrugged. "Steven interrupted us."

"Steven's jealous," she said.

"I know, but I guess he has the right to be."

Kara shook her head. "I don't know why you and David aren't together. It's obvious to everyone—except the two of you—that you're in love with each other."

Journey rolled her eyes and took a long drag on her cigarette. "Whatever."

Journey wouldn't let herself fall for David or at least would never admit it to anyone if she had. That would be the fastest way she knew of to lose him. He'd once told her that he liked her because she was so different than all of the other girls he knew. Two years in, she wasn't about to become like all the rest.

A moment later, David appeared in the doorway. He walked across the deck and stretched out on the hammock across from them. "Have you forgiven me yet?" he asked Journey.

She shook her head. "No."

He smiled. "I figured as much."

"Hey Kara, can I have some of the painkillers you were talking about?" Journey asked. "I don't know what hurts worse, my head or my foot."

"Your tattoo?" David asked.

Journey nodded. "It hurts like hell." Kara handed her some ibuprofen pills, and she swallowed them with a gulp of coffee.

Kara motioned toward the house. "I'm going to go and take a shower before everyone else gets the hot water."

After she had gone inside, David reached an arm toward

Journey. "Come here."

She put her coffee down and walked to the hammock. She stretched out beside him. He dropped one leg to the porch floor and gently rocked them. She had been in the hammock with David a hundred times before, and she realized that this might be the last.

His hand brushed against hers and, without thinking, she wrapped her fingers around his. She heard him let out a deep, slow breath.

"I'm so mad at you," she whispered as she felt tears well up in her eyes again.

"I know," he replied. "But it won't be forever."

She shook her head. "It will be too long, David."

He looked over at her. "You could come with me."

She laughed. "I don't think boot camp is one of those things you can bring a friend to."

"I'm not talking about boot camp. I'm talking about after," he said.

She looked over at him. "What?"

He shrugged his shoulders. "Who knows where they might send me? Maybe California or Florida or even Hawaii. You could come, and we could get a place together off-base somewhere."

"You're serious, aren't you?"

He nodded. "Yeah, I am."

She thought for a moment. "What about Steven and your string of girlfriends? Don't you think things could get complicated?"

"I can handle complicated. It's just something to think about." He shifted awkwardly in the hammock and retrieved something from his pocket. He held out a small box to her.

"What is this?" she asked.

"It's your birthday present. I was going to give it to you

yesterday, but you not speaking to me at all kinda put a dent in that plan," he said.

She took the box and flipped open the lid. Inside was a simple, silver ring. She pulled it out and slipped it on a finger. It slid right off. She gave him a curious look.

"It's a thumb ring," he informed her, taking it and sliding it on her thumb.

"Oh," she said. "Thanks."

"Read the inside," he added.

She slipped the ring back off and tilted it in the sunlight to read the inscription inside. *My best friend, Forever.* She smiled and put it back on her thumb before meshing her fingers with his and squeezing his hand. He squeezed back and rested his head against hers.

After a few moments of sweet silence, she peered up at the blue morning sky. "Best friends forever? What are you? A girl?"

He burst out laughing, and as he rolled to tickle her, he flipped the hammock.

4

The Summer of '99

JUNE 4TH, 1999

Journey,

The first week here has been hell. I'm exhausted, and I have muscles that hurt that I didn't know I had. Even my damn elbows hurt! They are so tough on us. One thing is for sure—I'm going to have the body of a god when I get done.

No one here knows how to speak at a normal level. They yell to wake us up, they yell to tell us to eat, and they yell to tell us to go to bed. I've learned new curse words I didn't even know existed. I thought I was prepared for this since my dad has grilled me since I was a kid, but wow, I was wrong. This is ridiculous. We've already had guys talking about suicide to try and get out of here. Like jumping out of windows and stuff. Yeah, it's THAT bad.

The only personal items I was allowed to keep when I got here were two pictures; one is that picture of me and you. Everything else is in storage. So, you were right... I over-packed.

Every second of every day is planned out, not leaving much time to write. This is the first time I have been allowed to write since I got here. But I promise to write every chance I get. This is my new address for the next few months, and I expect you to use it a lot! And I should get to make a phone call soon, so keep your cell close.

Well, they are getting ready to shut the lights off on me, so I have to cut this short. Write back when you get a chance. I can't wait to hear from you.

Luv ya girl,
David

. . .

Marcus was busy robbing a hooker on his Grand Theft Auto video game while Journey searched through the classified ads on his bed. "Are you ever going to go home?" he asked while swerving his controller trying to knock the hooker out of his way.

Journey didn't look up from the newspaper. "Are you getting sick of me?"

"Yes," he said and then muttered a few obscenities at his television.

She playfully kicked him in the back from behind.

His thumbs furiously pounded the game controller. "Seriously, have you even talked to your parents since they got back from London?"

"Nope," she said letting the word dramatically pop off her lips.

He just shook his head.

Journey sat up on her knees. "Listen to this. 'Charming cottage on Olaca Lake Road. Two bedrooms, two baths. Utilities included. Rent $800.'"

He didn't look back at her. "You don't have $800."

She pinched his side, which she knew he hated, and he squirmed out of her reach. "You could move in, and we could be roommates."

"No thanks," he said.

Journey put him in a choke hold from behind. "Why not?"

He laughed. "Because you're a train wreck."

She bit his ear, and he yelped with pain.

"Damn it! You got me killed!" He slammed the controller down on the bed and used a quick, high school wrestling move to flip her over onto her back. He studied her face for a moment. "I can't live with you," he finally said, holding her down by her shoulders.

Her bottom lip poked out. "Why not?"

He pressed her upper body harder into the mattress. "Because I'm starting the police academy next week, and your boyfriend is a drug dealer."

She frowned. "He's not a drug dealer."

Marcus rolled his eyes and let her go. "You live in Fantasyland."

"Well, if he's a drug dealer, he's got to have plenty of money then. Maybe I should live with him." She stuck her tongue out at him.

He watched her mouth for a second and then pulled his eyes up to meet hers. "I love you, but you can be as dumb as a box of rocks sometimes."

. . .

June 10th, 1999

David,

Sorry I haven't been able to write sooner. I hadn't been back to

Mom and Dad's till today, but they called and told me on my voicemail that I had a letter waiting from you. Do you see how much I love you, punk? It got pretty ugly when I showed up. I grabbed some more stuff and am going to stay with Steven for a few days. I think we are going to rent a house together. It's got two bedrooms and a great big deck and a pretty big backyard. I think it will be the perfect place for your welcome home party!!! We'll see. Write to me at Kara's or Marcus's for the time being.

I'm working full-time these days and it sucks. But I'm a grown-up now, and I need the money. Things aren't the same without you here. It's kinda thrown me for a loop. I'm not sure what to do with myself now. I don't have anyone to go with me for ice cream runs at 2 AM and as hard as I try to talk Steven into all-day movie marathons at the theater, he just won't go for it. I even get sad every time I see the stupid Dallas Cowboys' logo. So, I guess it's obvious that I miss you too!

How are things there with you? I'm sure it's unbelievably hard, but I KNOW that if anyone can do it, it's you. So hang in there and don't try to jump out of any windows, K? I can't wait to see this god-like body when you get home.

Marcus said to tell you 'hi,' and so did Kara. They ask about you all the time. I'll definitely start planning a party for you. It will be the blowout of the century.

Write back soon. And I'll keep my cell phone on.

Love,
Journey

Ps. Marcus joined the police academy and bought a crotch-rocket. Say a prayer for all the innocent pedestrians of Emerson.

. . .

Journey had planned to wait until her parents were at work to go home and pack all of her things, but when she pulled her white, beaten-up hatchback to the front door, her father's truck was in its normal spot. She looked over her shoulder at Steven. "Crap."

Steven studied the house for signs of life inside. "I thought you said no one would be home."

The front curtains shifted as she killed the engine. "I didn't think anyone would be."

Steven groaned as he angled out of the car.

Journey took a deep breath and used her key to open the front door. Her father was standing in the foyer, next to a small stack of boxes and trash bags. Journey's mind danced with confusion. "What is this?" she finally asked.

"Your clothes." There was no emotion in his voice. "We've already cleaned out your room."

Her eyes widened as she pushed past him toward the stairs. "You *what?*" She took the steps two at a time until she reached her bedroom, and she jerked to a stop when she stepped through the door. Everything was gone: her posters, her pictures of all her friends, even the five foot tall stuffed rooster that David had won for her at the fair. Gone. The sheets were stripped from the bed, and the closet was bare.

Her father was standing rigid with his arms folded over his chest when she turned around.

"What the hell did you do?" she shouted at him, her fists clenched at her sides.

"You don't live here anymore." He held tight control of his voice. "Go get your stuff downstairs and leave. I don't want to see you—or him—here again."

Journey stood there in stunned silence. "You're serious? You're kicking me out?"

His blue eyes were empty as he stared at her. He started to turn away slowly. "You've been gone for years."

. . .

June 17th, 1999

Journey,

I'm happy to report that I haven't jumped out of any windows just yet. But, god, this place is miserable. I'm so ready to be done with this shit, but don't worry, I'm not suicidal. I miss having someone—anyone—to talk to. I hate almost everyone here, except the guy who was assigned as what's called my "battle buddy." We have to look out for each other and stay glued to each other's hip all day and night. I guess I got lucky because he's actually a really cool guy. He's right up your alley—covered from head to toe in tattoos. I know you're busy, but god I miss you.

So, Marcus got a bike? Have you ridden on it yet? Don't let him drive like he does in a car with you on the back of that thing. Tell him I said it's cool, but a Harley would've been better.

Did you get moved in the new house? I can't wait to see it. I may kick Steven out when I get home and move in myself.

Less than 2 months to go until I'm home. I'll be home on Friday, August 6th. I can't wait! I'm just going to show up at your door without warning. I miss you so bad. Write back soon. I check the mail every day for a letter from you. Tell the gang I said hello.

Luv ya,
Dave

. . .

June 22nd, 1999

Hey woman,

Hello? Are you alive? Is Marcus giving you my letters? I haven't heard from you in a looooooong time, and I'm starting to get a little worried. My mom sent me a letter and said she ran into your mom at the grocery store. She said that you stormed out a week ago, and they haven't heard from you since. You're so damn dramatic. Call your mother. I know you think she's a quack, but she's just worried about you. And to be honest, you do seem to be going off the deep end a little. Don't be pissed. You know I love you.

I get ONE phone call this weekend and YOU ARE IT. Answer the damn phone or I'll go AWOL just to kick your ass.

Dave

. . .

David picked at the peeling paint beside the payphone while the phone rang over and over. "C'mon. Pick up," he muttered to himself.

Finally, the call went to her voicemail. He dropped his head against the wall. At least he got to hear her voice on the greeting. "Hey, it's Journey. I'm probably digging around trying to find my phone right now, so leave me a message, and I'll get back with you as soon as I find it." *Beep.*

He sighed. "Hey Journ, it's Dave. Well, this is my one phone call. I was really hoping to talk to you. I probably won't get to call again, but if you see a weird number pop up, please answer it. Don't bother calling back. This phone doesn't receive calls. I miss you."

He slammed the phone back onto the receiver and cursed under his breath all the way back to his barracks.

. . .

Journey rolled over in bed. "Was that my phone?"

Steven groaned and rolled onto his back, stuffing a couple of pillows behind his head. "Yeah, I killed the call. Whoever it was can leave a message."

She snuggled up to him and could still smell a hint of his

cologne from the night before. She breathed in deep and smiled as she drew circles on his bare chest with her finger. He reached for his pack of cigarettes and a lighter on the nightstand. He lit one and ran his hand down her back.

"I don't want to go to work," she whined. "I'm so tired. You keep me up too much at night."

He let out a deep breath of smoke and laughed. "I'm sorry?" he said more as a question than an apology.

She giggled and threw her leg over his and sat up on his hips. She took his cigarette and inhaled a long drag. "No you're not."

He laughed and shook his head. "You're right. I'm not."

He reached back to the nightstand and opened the drawer. He pulled out a tiny blue zip lock bag with white powder inside. "This will help you get going if you want it." He held it between his fingers in front of her.

She took it from his grasp and studied it for a moment. She returned it to the nightstand. "I think I'm good."

He took back the cigarette, puffed on it, then stamped it out in the ashtray and smiled. "Don't say I didn't try to help." He reached up and hooked his finger in the collar of her t-shirt, pulling her down for a long slow kiss.

. . .

July 4th, 1999

David,

I am SO SO SO SO SO sorry that I missed your call. I was asleep after staying up late the night before. I am absolutely sick over missing the chance to talk to you. Please, please, please call me back. I promise I will answer. Absent-minded Marcus forgot to give me your letters until he got the second one. I really, really need to talk to you. Things have been so crazy around here the past few weeks. Your mom was right. I did storm out of my parents' house... but only because they kicked me out. I guess they just saved me the trouble of packing since I was there to get my stuff anyway, but still...

Steven and I got that house I told you about, so we've been busy moving in. Well, at least he has been busy. I don't have any stuff anymore. My parents trashed it all. Ugh. I have some of my clothes and my car, and that's it. Anyway, it's nice to be out on my own now without having anyone to answer to. It was such a drag, you know?

Enough about me. How are you??? It's only like a month till you're home. I can't wait! I hope it's getting easier there for you. Note my new address, and write me back soon!!

Luv you tons and tons,
Journey

Ps. Happy 4th! I'm going to miss watching the fireworks with you at the lake this year!!

. . .

July 10th, 1999

Journey,

It was awful when you didn't answer the phone. Not to sound like a big, damn baby, but I really need to hear your voice. Between being homesick and worried about you, I'm getting a little desperate and needy for your attention. I'm so glad I got your letter. I don't think you know how much I miss you... definitely much more than you miss me. Ha. Ha. I'm joking. (Sort of.)

I hope you got things straight with your parents. I'm glad you moved out though. I think it was time. I just hate you're living with Steven and not with me!!! Speaking of... It looks like I will be in California for a while for more training before I get assigned to my unit. Have you thought any more about moving with me when I get my orders? You know I would be great to live with... especially now that I clean like a soldier! Anyway, think about it and let me know.

I love you.
David

. . .

Kara was having a late lunch at the bar while Journey dried and stacked beer glasses one on top of the other when the front door opened, and Steven stormed in. He ripped off his sunglasses, and Journey could see trouble in his dark eyes.

Kara bumped him with her shoulder when he got to the bar. "Why the long face, grumpy?"

His eyes shot down at her. "Can you give us a minute?" he said through a clenched jaw.

Her eyes widened with concern, and she cast a questioning glance at Journey.

Journey nodded as she dried her hands. "It's OK. Give us just a second."

Carefully, Kara picked up her cigarettes and rose from her seat. She cautiously studied Steven as she angled around him toward the front door. No one was allowed to smoke in the bar before 8 PM, so she stepped outside to the sidewalk.

Steven was quiet for what felt like an eternity. Journey stepped closer to where he stood motionless, and fuming, across the bar. "What's up?" she asked a little hesitantly.

He pulled an open envelope out of his jacket pocket and slammed it on the counter before pushing it toward her. She recognized the military seal, and her eyes shot up at him as her mouth dropped open. "You opened my mail?"

"You're thinking about moving in with him?" he shouted.

Journey snapped the letter out of his reach. "How dare you go through my things?"

"So, it's true?" he barked.

She stuffed the letter into her apron. "It's none of your damn business!"

He gripped the bar until his knuckles turned white. He twisted his head toward her in frustration. "None of my business? He misses you and loves you and wants to live with you, and it's *none of my business?*"

They were drawing stares from the few patrons around them. She lowered her voice and cut her eyes at him. "I will talk to you about this when I get home. I'm at work now, and I suggest you go somewhere and cool off for a while."

He pounded his fist against the wood and then pointed an angry finger at her. "This isn't over."

He stalked out, without pausing to acknowledge Kara who was watching from the window. She hurried back inside. Journey watched Steven cross the street, and when he was out of sight, she pulled the envelope out and opened it.

Kara slid back onto her barstool. "What was that about?" she asked.

Journey nodded to the paper. "He read my letter from David." Journey's eyes scanned the letter before passing it to Kara.

Kara read a few lines out loud as Journey returned to drying glasses. "*I just hate you're living with Steven and not with me... It looks like I will be in California for a while... Have you thought any more about moving with me when I get my orders?*" Kara paused. "Are you thinking about moving to California?"

Journey laughed. "No. This is the first I've even heard about California. I mean, David mentioned us moving together when he gets his orders, but I don't think he's serious."

Kara scanned the letter again. "Sounds like he's serious to me."

Journey shrugged her shoulders. "He's just homesick. He's not serious."

"Are you sure?" Kara asked.

Journey was pretty sure. She finally sighed. "No wonder Steven is so pissed."

Kara pointed in the direction of where Steven had just stormed out. "Yeah, but that was over the top. I thought for a second he was going to come over the bar after you."

Journey thought so too, but she kept it to herself.

When she clocked out a six, she drove the four miles back to her house. Steven's car was in the driveway. She cautiously opened the front door, and he met her in the foyer. His eyes were bloodshot, but she knew it wasn't from being brokenhearted. The haze of marijuana floated around the room. He silently pulled her into his arms and pressed his lips against her hair. After a long silence, he finally whispered, "I'm sorry."

With her face against his chest, she let his apology linger before finally looking up at him. "You scared the crap out of me today."

He sighed and dropped his forehead gently against hers. "I know. I'm sorry. I just love you so much, and I completely lost it."

She pulled back. "You what?"

"I love you." He studied her stunned expression before laughing. "You know I love you. Why do you look so shocked?"

"Because you've never said it before," she stammered.

He grasped her face between his hands and covered her mouth with his. When he finally broke the kiss, he studied her lower lip. "Well, I do."

"I love you, too." She poked him in the ribs. "But stop going through my crap."

He laughed and grasped her wrist to pull her close again. He lowered toward her ear. "I'm not going to lose you," he said in a whisper so calm it made her spine tingle.

. . .

July 22nd, 1999

David,

I got your letter. I'm sorry I've been so MIA lately. I've just been so busy. I hardly see anyone anymore... It's pretty sad. I'm still keeping my phone close so I don't miss you if you call.

Funny story... Steven intercepted your last letter, and he completely freaked out. However, he did finally tell me he loves me. It only took him five months and being threatened by the thought of me running off with you. He's been boyfriend extraordinaire ever since. No more wishy-washy man for me. He's so attention needy now that it's almost exhausting. He didn't take too well to the idea of me and you talking about moving away together. And California? You know how much trouble I get into in Emerson. I would be in jail within a year! Haha.

Nevertheless, I'm counting the days till you get home. I might just have to kidnap you while you're here and keep you all to myself. I miss our all-night talks... we have so much to catch up on!

I hope things are getting easier for you. I ran into your mom at the restaurant the other day, and she said that it has been really rough, but that you're doing well. I kinda got the impression that you sent her there to check in on me? :)

I've got to run to work, but I'll write more soon. Come home already!

Love,
Journey

. . .

August 2nd, 1999

Journey,

I know what you mean about missing our talks. I don't have anyone here that I can talk to really. I mean we cut up about guy stuff, but nothing really important. I'm hoping that you'll have some time off from work and school while I'm home so we can really catch up. I'm planning on moving in for the whole seven days! You can tell Steven to go ahead and get used to the idea.

I can't wait to be home. I think the waiting is going to kill me. I wish you could be here for my graduation, but I know you have a lot of responsibilities now. I know one thing… As soon as I get into town, I'm dropping my stuff and coming straight to you. Forget everything else.

This will probably be the last letter I will have time to write. We have our big final training coming up, and I will be gone for three days, stuck in the middle of nowhere and sleeping on the ground. Say a prayer for me.

I love you more than you know.

Love,
David

5

BLOW

STEVEN PROTESTED the idea of a surprise welcome home party for David at his own house, but Journey knew he wouldn't actually do anything to stop her. Their small house was already packed with people forty-five minutes before David even arrived. Most of her guests were happy with the keg of beer on the deck, but a few—primarily Steven and his friends—were hunkered down with a bong in the back bedroom. Journey was so anxious to see her best friend that she walked down her gravel road alone to intercept him.

She was sitting by the row of mailboxes with a beer in her hand when the familiar front fender of David's white pickup truck came into view. He honked the horn, and she jumped up with a smile so wide it hurt her face. Before he could even slow the truck to a stop, the driver's side door was open. She scrambled toward him and spilt her beer.

Without a word, he scooped her up in his arms. He lifted her feet off the ground and squeezed her so tight she thought her ribs might break. Finally, he pulled back enough to look at her and gently returned her to her feet. "You're real," he choked out. His face was streaked with tears, but he was laughing.

Journey dug her fingers into David's hips as he held her. She didn't realize until that moment, when she felt tears threatening to spill out, just how much she had missed him. She threw her arms around his neck and squeezed him again.

"You ruined the big entrance I had planned!" He laughed. "I was coming to you!"

She tugged playfully at his belt loops. "I couldn't wait anymore."

He reached down and pushed her bangs behind her ears. "Your hair," he said. "I've never seen it so long!"

She smiled. "I haven't cut it out of protest since you've been gone."

He laughed and shook his head. "Whatever."

She took in the full sight of him. He was tan, and she could tell through his 'Go Army' gray t-shirt and jeans that he had probably put on twenty pounds of solid muscle. David had always had a good build, but this was a significant improvement. "So, this is what the body of a god looks like, huh?" she asked.

He winked. "It's worth seeing me naked. I promise."

She laughed and tears finally escaped down her cheeks as he pulled her close again.

She took a deep breath and let it out slowly, closing her eyes to seal the moment in her memory. "I've missed you," she finally breathed into the soft cotton of his shirt.

His fingertips trailed down to the small of her back and then carefully up her sides. He studied her eyes for a long moment before sliding his hands along her jaw and tilting her face up toward his. His gaze fell to her mouth, and he bent toward her. The moment that his lips brushed hers, a car pulled up blasting its horn behind his truck.

Journey recognized the sound of Justin's snorting laugh before she even saw who was in the car. They both spun around to see Kara standing up out of the sunroof, flailing her arms like a madwoman.

"You're back!" she cheered.

David laughed. "I'm back!"

She blew him kisses with both hands. "Didn't mean to interrupt!" She giggled. "We'll see you at the party!"

David laughed as they pulled around his truck. "Party?"

Journey gave him a guilty smile. "You know I don't need much of a reason to throw a party. And this day"—she placed her palms on his chest—"is certainly a reason to celebrate."

She stretched up on her tiptoes and gave him a quick kiss on the lips before bounding around to the passenger's side of the truck.

. . .

David didn't know half the guests at his homecoming party, but Journey had gone all out with the preparation. There was food from her work and a keg on ice outside. It was obvious that the party started long before his arrival. Steven's car was in the driveway, but he was nowhere to be seen. David wasn't complaining though. He was hoping to steal a moment with Journey and continue what had almost happened in the driveway.

Just thinking about it made David start to sweat. She looked amazing with denim shorts hanging off her hips exposing just enough of her hipbones to make his brain go blank. He couldn't help but imagine what might have transpired had they not been ambushed by their friends and had returned to an empty house. Instead, he was being whisked around rooms full of semi-drunken party-goers with his life-of-the-party best friend. All he wanted to do was get her alone.

"Brit-ton!" Marcus's voice boomed from behind him.

David turned around as Marcus walked through the front door. The two old friends met in the middle of the room and clapped each other on the back. "So good to see you, man," David said when they stepped back from each other.

Marcus grabbed David's bicep and laughed. "Look at you, G.I. Joe!"

David laughed. "That's what a half a million push-ups will do to you."

He felt Journey slide under his arm and lock her arms around his midsection. The corner of her perfect mouth tipped up into a smile. "I like it."

"I'm glad you came home, Dave. Maybe you can talk some damn sense into the young one here," Marcus said, playfully poking Journey in the stomach.

Journey allowed David's hand to slide down to that tantalizing bare hipbone, making it nearly impossible for him to keep up with the conversation. He looked down at her. "I hear you've been a pain in the ass all summer."

"Me?" she whimpered, batting her eyes at him.

Suddenly, the chatter died in the house. The three of them looked around the living room, and David quickly saw the reason for why it seemed all of the oxygen had left the building. Steven was glaring from the opening of the hallway. Journey quickly unwrapped herself from David's torso as Steven crossed the room.

Do I say hello or just punch him in the face? David wondered.

Steven curled his arm around Journey's shoulders and offered his free hand to David. "Welcome home, Dave."

David was a little surprised, but even though Steven

seemed calm and his words were courteous, he knew 'welcome' was a stretch. They clasped hands.

"Congrats on the place, man. It's great," David said, unable to think of anything else to say that wouldn't end with one of them bleeding in the front yard.

As if sensing the tension, Kara grasped David by the front of his t-shirt. "Come smoke with me. I wanna hear all about the gas chamber."

The volume in the room returned to normal when David went outside with his other friends. Once they were clear of all the hostility, David laughed with relief. "Thanks," he said to Kara.

She handed him the beer she was holding. "Don't mention it."

"What the hell was that about?" David asked, rubbing his eyes.

Kara laughed. "You're not stupid. You know what that was about."

Marcus slapped David on the back. "You're on his home turf now, brother," he said. "Things have changed since you've been gone."

David motioned back inside. "Is he high right now?"

Justin laughed. "You didn't smell it? Hell, Journey probably is too."

Kara shook her head. "Not today. She wouldn't with David here."

"You're kidding?" David asked.

Kara, Justin, and Marcus all shook their heads.

"She's kinda lost it in the past few months," Kara said.

It was hard for David to believe what he was hearing. "Is she just smoking pot or what?"

Marcus shrugged his shoulders. "I don't know. I asked around at the station, and Steven only has a couple of misdemeanors: minor possession and an assault charge from high school. But I heard a rumor they are trying to pop his brother with some of the local coke distribution around here. That dude has a list of priors as long as my arm."

David's stomach turned.

Kara reached over and squeezed his arm. "Sorry to rain on your party."

"No, I'm glad you told me," he said. "I'll talk to her."

Marcus sighed. "Just don't expect too much. Shit goes in one ear and out the other with her lately."

David lit a cigarette and leaned back against the railing. He knew Journey had tried marijuana; most of his friends had. The only reason he, himself, hadn't is because he had always wanted to be in some form of law enforcement. Until then, he had never given it much thought because hard drug use was rare in Emerson.

He watched Journey through the window as she turned up the stereo and began to dance around what would've been a dining room if they owned a table. She caught him staring and beckoned for him to come inside.

He shook his head. "No. You come out here," he mouthed.

She bit her lower lip, shook her head, and continued to dance in front of the sliding glass door. She ran her fingers through her hair, leaving it wild and messy. It was about to make him crazy.

She had changed so much in the past year. She had always been a little wild—she had even gotten David drunk for the first time in high school—but this new level of dysfunction started around the same time she got the job at the restaurant. All of her new friends were older and none of them seemed to have any goals in life whatsoever. Then, when she met Steven, it was all over. David never felt more like an idiot than when he thought about not making a move for her before Steven did.

An hour later, Steven and his friends moved to the garage to play darts, and before Journey went out to join them, David took her by the arm. "I think I'm going to take off. I really don't need to stay out too late my first night back."

She pouted. "I don't want you to leave."

"I don't want to either, but I have to."

She held his hand all the way to the front door. "It's so good to have you back," she said.

He shook his head and smiled. "You have no idea."

Journey carefully scanned the room before turning back to him and lowering her voice. "Steven and the guys from his work have a racing team. They have a car that races every Saturday night about an hour away from here. I usually work, but I didn't tell him I took tomorrow night off." Her hazel eyes were sparkling with a mix of moonlight and mischief.

"Are you asking me to sneak out with you?" he whispered, trying to stuff his laughter.

She giggled and clasped his hands in hers. "Yes! It will be just like old times!"

He thought for a second and grinned. "Except then you were sneaking out of your parents' house, and now you're sneaking out of your own."

She pressed a finger to her lips. "Shhhh…"

"Of course I will," he said. "What time?"

"He always leaves here at four. So, I'll meet you at your house at five," she said.

He nodded, barely able to contain the smile that was threatening to erupt on his face. "Five," he repeated. He pulled her close and kissed her forehead before releasing her. "I'll see you tomorrow."

· · ·

There wasn't enough Xanax in the world to help Journey get to sleep that night. She tossed and turned, continually replaying the events of the evening in her mind. She couldn't believe how painfully hard her heart pounded each time she thought of the way David held her in his arms. And she wasn't stupid. She knew that he was going to kiss her in the driveway. She also knew she would have let him.

She tried and tried to convince herself that he was simply caught up in the moment of being back at home and seeing her for the first time, but she knew that wasn't true. She wondered what might have happened if he had never joined the military or if she had never met Steven.

She glanced over at her boyfriend who had passed out beside her. He was beautiful, on the exterior. He was exciting. He was dangerous. But her mother had been right: he was no David. However, they did live together, and she really didn't have anywhere else to go. She couldn't go back to her parents' house, and despite what David had dreamed up, she couldn't tag along with him in the Army. She had never felt so confused or so *stuck* in her entire life.

. . .

The next day, Journey noticed a 'for sale' sign posted at the end of the Britton's driveway when she pulled in. David was sitting on the front porch steps wearing jeans, a Dallas Cowboys t-shirt, and black sunglasses.

She smiled and got out of her car. "What's with the sign?" she asked pointing.

He stood up. "They're downsizing," he said. "They say they don't need the space anymore."

She nodded. "Makes sense."

He reached for her hand and led her inside.

Gail came out of the kitchen to greet her. "Journey!" she cheered, crossing the room and pulling her into a tight hug.

"Hey," Journey replied. She pulled away and looked down

at David's tiny, white-haired mother. "I'm really sorry about running out on my birthday."

Gail shook her head. "It's OK, honey. It wasn't your fault." She glared over the top of her glasses at David. "It was my son's fault."

Journey laughed, and David just dropped his head.

Gail winked at her. "We'll reschedule."

Journey smiled and followed David downstairs to his room. It was even more packed up than the last time she had seen it, but that made sense if the Brittons were moving. The walls were bare, and a dusty cover was over the pool table.

She scrunched up her nose. "This is so weird."

He nodded in agreement. "I know." They entered his bedroom, and he sat down on the edge of his bed. "What do you want to do tonight?"

She rocked back and forth on her heels and stuffed her hands in her back pockets. "I don't know. What do you want to do? You're the one on vacation."

He studied her for a minute, and she was glad she had dressed up a little. She was actually wearing boot cut jeans that didn't have holes and a brand new pink jersey shirt that hung off one shoulder.

He reached out, hooked his finger in her belt loop, and pulled her between his knees. He wrapped his arms around her waist and nuzzled his face against her stomach. She ran her hands over the soft bristles of his short hair, and he let out a slow deep sigh. His warm breath penetrated the thin fabric of her shirt.

She closed her eyes and desperately tried not to let her knees buckle.

After a long silence, he looked up at her and smiled. "This is it. This is all I wanna do."

She softly laughed and looked around the room. She knew

that if they didn't get out of there very soon, things were going to get infinitely more complicated. "I say, we go get in your truck, pick up some take out from Lottie's Diner, and have dinner up at Look Off Rock," she suggested. "Then maybe go catch a movie later."

"Or…"

In one smooth motion, he had her flat on her back on the bed. She sucked in a deep breath while she took in how his triceps flexed as he held himself up over her. She forced out an awkward laugh, so as not to lose her head. "Or maybe we need to go get you a girl," she said with wide eyes. "Apparently, you have been estrogen deprived for too long."

Her words knocked the life right out of his eyes. He went from seductive to embarrassed with a blink. Swiftly, he pushed himself away from her and turned his back.

She clambered to her knees and put her hands on his shoulders. "Dave…"

He shifted away from her touch and stood up. "No, it's cool." When he blinked again the embarrassment was replaced with indifference. "You're probably right," he conceded, shaking his head. "Let's get out of here."

The silence in the air was palpable on the ride to Lottie's Diner. Journey had no idea how to recover from the scene that had just imploded in his bedroom. His face was set toward the road, his hands not wavering from the steering wheel. Journey clung to the handle on her door like it was a lifeline. She wanted to jump out of her window. And when they pulled into the parking lot, everything went from bad to infinitely worse.

Rebecca Ashburn—David's ex-girlfriend from high school —was walking to her tiny, blue sports car.

Journey watched David lower his sunglasses, checking to be certain it was her as he pulled into the space next to her.

When he stepped out of the truck, Rebecca's eyes lit up at the sight of him.

"Oh my god!" she squealed as he slammed his door closed.

Journey darted her eyes away as they embraced. "You've got to be kidding me!" she raged as she wrenched her door open.

They were still clinging to each other laughing when Journey walked to the front of the truck. She didn't want to be anywhere near them, so she leaned against his front fender.

Rebecca had been the captain of the dance team and the cheerleading squad during high school. Her short white party dress showed off her perfectly tanned gymnast legs. She was just as disgustingly perky as ever.

"Well, hi there Journey!" Rebecca sang when she registered Journey's presence.

"Hey," Journey grumbled. She pointed to the diner. "I'll let you two catch up. I'll be inside."

Neither of them even responded. David didn't so much as glance in her direction as she walked away.

After ten long, angry minutes of waiting on the joyful reunion to subside, Journey called Kara from her cell phone. When Kara picked up, Journey asked, "Where are you?"

"Leaving my mom's," she answered. "What's up?"

"I need a ride."

. . .

It wasn't until Kara pulled up behind Rebecca's car that David realized how badly he had screwed up. He intended to just make Journey a little jealous—not make her leave.

Journey flashed him a tight smile when she walked back out of the diner and gave him a little wave. "I'll see ya, Dave. Good to see you again, Rebecca."

Instinctively, he wanted to chase after her, but he didn't want to do that in front of the girl who had broken his heart so badly two years before.

Rebecca placed her hand on his forearm drawing his attention back. "Do you need to go?" she asked.

He watched Journey duck into the passenger's seat of Kara's car. "No, I'm good," he said.

He left with Rebecca's new phone number, which he knew he would never dial, and returned home to an empty driveway. He sat there with his motor running until he realized that if he didn't make things right with her immediately, it might never happen. He threw the truck into reverse and sped down the road.

Her car was in front of her house, and he spun up gravel as he peeled into her driveway. He walked inside without knocking and found her sitting on the kitchen counter with a smoking joint in her hand. She didn't speak, and she didn't take her eyes off of him as she took in a long drag. He crossed through the haze of sticky sweet smoke and took the joint from her fingertips. He snubbed it out in a butter dish.

"What the hell are you doing?" he shouted.

She pushed herself off the counter and attempted to blow by him. He didn't budge, cornering her against the cabinets. "What do you care?"

He threw his hands in the air. "What do I care?" he bellowed. "You're all I care about!"

She nodded with a dangerously fierce glare. "Oh really? You have a fascinating way of showing it!"

He let out a slow deep breath to steady his voice. "You're driving everyone away. You're ruining every relationship around you."

She jabbed an angry finger in his chest and narrowed her eyes. "*We* don't have a relationship!"

"Oh, I'm well aware!" He picked up the joint from the dish and slammed it into the sink. "What are you doing to yourself? The drugs? The parties? The douchebag boyfriend?" When he realized his arms were pinning her in the corner, he pushed back on his hands and stepped back slowly. He shook his head. "You've got to make a decision."

She folded her arms across her chest. "Are you giving me an ultimatum?"

He nodded. "Yep. You can't have me and this life both. I won't sit here and watch you destroy yourself."

She dropped her head, silent for a moment. Finally, she slowly crossed the room toward him and stopped at his side. He stared at the floor but could see her face turn toward him out of the corner of his eye.

Her voice was a low hiss. "Get out."

. . .

By the time Steven came home a little after midnight, she had successfully finished off what was left of the beer keg, and she had smoked all of the cigarettes and pot in the house. The TV was blaring, but she was staring at the little blue bag of powder on the coffee table in front of her.

He walked cautiously around to face her. "Hey babe," he said. "What are you doing?"

She nodded to the bag. "Teach me."

He dropped his keys on the couch and sat down next to her. "Bad day?"

She turned her bloodshot eyes to meet his but didn't answer.

Steven pulled out his wallet and retrieved a dollar bill. She watched him roll it into a tight straw. He picked up the blue bag along with the dirty mirror upon which it rested and dumped out a small pile of soft white cocaine. Carefully, he chopped it up with a credit card and lined up three small rows on the mirror glass. Without hesitation, he offered her the dollar straw and held out the mirror balanced on his palms.

Ten minutes later, everything was numb.

6

Come and Get Me

NOTHING WAS the same after David left town, except that Journey continued to spiral out of control. She rarely saw Kara. She saw even less of Marcus. She and Steven still lived together, but his enchantment over her was dwindling. She was snorting coke to get up in the morning and washing down Xanax with beer at night to fall asleep. The days blurred into weeks and the weeks into months, and by December, Journey wasn't having fun anymore.

Snow was coming down hard outside of the bar when Steven showed up around eleven on a Friday night. He rarely came to see her at work anymore. She carried a plate of food to a nearby table and then walked to the door. She wiped her hands on her apron.

"Hey," she said.

He shuddered and dusted some snow off his black coat. "What time do you get off?" he asked.

"In about an hour. We are closing early because of the

weather. What's up?"

He nodded toward the window. "It's snowing. I thought I would give you a ride home."

She narrowed her eyes and examined his pupils. "Are you high?" she asked.

He laughed and kissed her. "You're my girlfriend. I worry about you."

She wanted to ask 'since when?' but thought better of it.

"Give me your keys. I'll drop your car off at the house and get my truck," he offered.

She handed him her keychain. "Be careful," she said.

He gave her a quick kiss and turned to leave. "I'll be back."

She watched him walk back out into the snow, puzzled by his sudden concern for her well-being. After a moment, she shrugged and went back to work.

Forty-five minutes later, Steven returned and drank a beer at the bar while she cleaned up. As she wiped down one of the dining tables, one of the newer waitresses, whose name Journey could never remember, called to her from the back room. "Journey! Phone call!"

Journey walked to the back room and picked up the phone that was laying on her boss' desk. "Hello?" she asked.

"Journ, it's Marcus."

"Hey?" she replied as a question. He had never called her at work before.

"Hey," he said. "Sorry to bother you at work. Have you been there all day?"

"I came in at two," she replied. "Why?"

She could hear his police scanner in the background. "Where is your car?" he asked.

"At home, why?"

"We just got a report of an accident involving a car that sounded like yours. I'm just checking on you," he said.

"I'm fine. My car is at home. Steven is here to drive me since it's snowing," she said. "Is that it? I've got to close up here."

"Yeah, that's it. Glad it wasn't you. Be careful tonight. The roads are getting really bad," he said. "See you soon?"

"Sure," she answered. She told him goodbye and hung up the phone.

When she walked back out, Steven looked up. "Everything OK?"

She nodded. "Yeah. You about done with that beer? I'm almost finished."

Steven's new 4x4 truck was parked in the lot next to his Chevelle. Knowing his job at the auto body shop barely paid enough to cover their rent she had, unfortunately, asked him how he could afford another vehicle. His answer was 'some side work' and a wink. She knew then that he didn't mean oil changes.

She shook the snow out of her hair when she settled in the passenger's seat. "Why did you leave the Chevelle here?" she asked.

He put his truck in reverse. "Didn't want to risk putting it in a ditch," he replied.

She raised an eyebrow. "But my car is OK to put in a ditch?"

He nodded and laughed. "It's not a Chevelle, babe."

She reached across the cab and slapped him on the arm. "Jerk," she said.

He tugged on her pant leg. "Slide over here."

Obediently, she slid into the middle seat beside him and fastened her seatbelt. "You're being very weird tonight, Mr. Drake."

He leaned over and kissed her lips. "What can I say? I'm in love."

She laughed as he pulled out of the parking lot. "Pssshhh, whatever."

· · ·

Snow always had a crippling effect on the entire town of Emerson. It was two days before the bar opened back up, and Journey returned to work on Sunday.

Kara showed up at lunchtime and took a seat at the bar. "Slow day, huh?" she asked, looking around at the empty restaurant.

"Yeah. I've had two tables in two hours, including you." Journey pointed at her. "I expect a damn good tip."

Kara sipped her water. "What did you do yesterday?"

"Slept. You?"

"Justin and I went sledding at Mom's," she said.

Journey nodded. "Nice."

"Anything new with you?" Kara asked.

Journey leaned against the bar. "Nah. Other than Steven has been really freaking sweet to me lately. It's creepy."

Kara laughed. "Your boyfriend being sweet shouldn't be creepy. It should be normal."

"He even came and drove me home in the snowstorm the other night to make sure I was safe," Journey added.

Kara made a puppy dog face. "Aw, that is sweet. I didn't think he had it in him."

Journey laughed. "I didn't either."

"It's probably a good thing that he did," Kara said. "A lot of bad accidents happened that night."

Journey shrugged with indifference. "I don't watch the news."

Kara crossed her arms on the counter. "Oh, so you haven't heard about that 4-wheeler accident? It was so sad. These two girls were on a 4-wheeler, that went off the road. It flipped, and the girl on the back broke her neck and died."

Journey made a sour face. "That's awful. How old was she?"

"Like sixteen," Kara answered.

Journey shook her head. "That's sad. Right here at Christmas time too."

"*And*, they were sisters," Kara said.

Journey poked out her bottom lip. "Oh, man."

Kara just nodded. "Speaking of sisters… have you talked to Elena?"

"No," Journey replied. "But she should be coming into town soon for Christmas."

"Are you going to see your parents?"

"Nope." Journey was anxious to change the subject. "We should hang out more. I really miss you."

Kara tilted her head and smiled. "I miss you too."

"And Marcus," Journey added. "I haven't seen him since he graduated from the police academy."

"He misses you too," Kara said. "He asks about you every time I see him. You should go over there sometime."

Journey nodded. "Yeah, I know."

The 4-wheeler accident certainly was all over the news. Over the next few days, Journey saw the story at least six times, and she never turned on the television at home. It was because of the publicity that Journey knew exactly who the young brunette was that showed up at her front door four days later. Julie Kennedy was dressed in a simple black dress and flat shoes. Her eyes were puffy and smudged with mascara. Journey curiously opened her front door to the timid young woman.

"Can I help you?" she asked.

The girl looked carefully around. "Is Steven home?"

Journey was surprised. "Uh, yeah. Come on in."

Julie carefully stepped through the door. "Thanks."

Journey ushered her into the living room. "You're Julie, right?"

Julie pushed her hair behind her ears and nodded. "Yeah."

Journey was unsure how to adequately say anything else. Julie had been driving the 4-wheeler when her sister, Marci, had died. Obviously, she had just come from the funeral. "I'm really… really sorry for all you're going through," Journey finally offered, stumbling over almost every syllable. "I'm Journey. Steven's girlfriend."

Julie nodded. "I know who you are. It's nice to meet you."

Journey motioned toward the hallway. "He's in the shower. I'll tell him you're here."

Julie sniffed "Thank you."

Journey walked into their bathroom. "Hey," she called out as she closed the door behind her.

Steven pulled back the shower curtain. "What?"

"You know the two sisters in that 4-wheeler accident?" she asked.

"I heard something about it on the news. Why?"

"That girl Julie is sitting on our couch," Journey said. "She's asking for you."

Steven looked away for a moment. "Oh yeah. Can you do me a big favor?"

Journey's eyes were wide.

"I know you hate this shit, but she's looking for some weed. I've got a small bag in my sock drawer. Can you give it to her? Just tell her it's on the house… you know, 'cause of everything," he said.

Journey was confused. "Do you know this girl?"

"Just business, babe," he replied and pulled the curtain closed.

Journey walked out of the bathroom and retrieved the stash from his sock drawer. She carried it back to the living room where Julie was still quietly waiting with her hands in her lap. She stood up as Journey approached holding out the bag. "He said to give this to you and to tell you not to worry about it. It's on him," Journey said.

Julie opened her mouth to say something but, apparently, changed her mind and closed it. She accepted the bag. "Uh, thanks. I really appreciate it."

Journey stuffed her hands into her pockets. "Sure. I hope things get better."

"Yeah," Julie mumbled. She turned to leave, and Journey walked with her to the front door. She stopped before leaving and turned back around. "Can you please ask Steven to call me?"

Journey found it an odd request. "Sure. Does he have your number?"

She just nodded.

"No problem," Journey said.

Julie gave half of a polite smile. "Thanks," she said and walked out.

Journey waited at the door and watched her car disappear down the driveway.

"Did you take care of it?" Steven asked, buttoning his jeans as he walked into the room. He hadn't put on a shirt, and Journey noticed he was running out of skin on his upper body for any more tattoos.

"Yeah. She wants you to call her."

"K," he answered, pulling his wet black hair into a short ponytail.

He walked toward the kitchen, but Journey stayed frozen in her place. "That was really freaking weird," she said.

He shrugged and pulled open the refrigerator door. "People like to get high when they're sad. I don't see what the big deal is."

Journey let out a deep breath. "I guess it's just because it's *sooo* sad, and it's been all over the news, and then *bam!*, she's on our couch."

He shrugged again and took a big gulp of milk out of the half-gallon jug. "Small town," he said after he swallowed.

"I wonder why she wants you to call her," Journey said.

Steven laughed as he closed the refrigerator. He came into the living room and slipped his hand behind her head. "Let it go, babe," he said and kissed her lips.

. . .

Journey was at work on Monday night when Julie walked in the front door. She looked lost and like she hadn't slept in days. Journey was certain that she probably hadn't. Several people turned to stare at her. Journey walked over, approaching her cautiously. "Hey Julie," she said.

"Hey," Julie replied nervously.

"Are you here to eat?"

Julie shook her head. "No. I'm really sorry to bother you. Do you know where I can find Steven? I went by your house again, and no one was home." She was wringing her cold hands.

Journey really had no idea where her boyfriend was. "He worked today, but he usually gets off at four. I have no clue where he was headed tonight. I'm sorry. Want me to give him a message?"

"Just ask him to call me, please," she said, turning to leave.

Something about her demeanor caught Journey's attention, but she wasn't sure what it was. "Is something wrong?" Journey asked.

Tears slipped down Julie's cheeks as she glanced back at Journey. "Yeah. Everything."

Steven was already in bed watching television when Journey got home that night. She walked into their bedroom and dropped her purse and keys on the dresser.

"Hey. How was work?" he asked.

She groaned. "Slow." She unbuttoned her uniform and deposited it on the floor. "Oh, did that girl, Julie, get ahold of you?"

He changed the channel on the TV. "Yeah, she's been blowing up my phone all day. I talked to her a couple of hours ago."

"She came to the bar looking for you," Journey said. She pulled on Steven's discarded t-shirt to sleep in.

"Yeah, she had just left there when I talked to her. That chick has lost it," he said, shaking his head.

Journey nodded and went to the bathroom to brush her teeth. "I'm sure she has. Hell, I would too. What did she want so bad from you?" she asked before she stuck her toothbrush in her mouth.

"Freaking pills, man," he said. "She sounded crazy though, and I told her no. She needs help. Bad. Like, the kind of help that I sure as hell can't give her."

Journey finished brushing and rinsed out her mouth. She went back to the bedroom and pulled the covers back before sliding in next to him. "Were you worried that she might O.D.?"

He shrugged. "I don't know, but I didn't want it on my head if that's what she had in mind. I'm telling you, she was out of her head. I'm surprised she's not been back over here."

Journey was cold, so she cuddled up next to him and tangled her feet with his. He yelped and jerked his feet away. "Your feet are like ice blocks!"

"For supposedly being such a bad ass, you're a pretty big sissy," she teased.

"What'd you call me?" he asked, raising his voice a little.

She smirked at him. "A sissy. What are you gonna do

about it?"

He threw the remote on the floor and rolled over on her, tickling her sides. "Take it back," he demanded.

"Sissy," she repeated, laughing.

"Take it back!"

"Sissy!" she screamed.

They wrestled till they were both panting. He finally pinned her down and began kissing her. As soon as he got the t-shirt off over her head, their doorbell rang. He collapsed on top of her in frustration. "You've got to be kidding me," he groaned.

Journey laughed. "You called it."

He pushed himself up, and the doorbell rang again. "I hate crazy chicks," he grumbled.

Journey decided she had better go with him, so she got up and pulled on the first pieces of clothing her fingers found on the floor.

There was a loud pounding at the door that caused Steven to freeze. "That's not the girl," he said, zipping up his pants. "That's the cops. Do you have anything on you?"

"I've got a gram in my nightstand," she answered.

"Is that it?" he asked a little desperately.

"Yeah," she answered.

He pointed to the bathroom. "Flush it. Now."

She was surprised. "You don't have any?"

He shook his head. "No, I'm clean."

. . .

Marcus had heard the call come over dispatch about sending someone to Journey's address. He quickly volunteered to take the call. He couldn't believe he was getting ready to question her about a disappearance. He rapped his fist on the door again and heard Steven yell, "I'm coming!"

A moment later, Steven wrenched the door open wearing

just a pair of torn blue jeans. He was smoothing out his hair with his hands.

Curtis Martin, Marcus's partner, spoke first. "Steven Drake?"

"Yeah," Steven answered.

Marcus took half a step forward and looked at his partner. "I've got this," he said.

Curtis nodded.

Marcus turned to Steven. "Hey Steve. We need to talk to you and Journey. Is she here?"

Journey stepped out of the hallway in an oversized t-shirt and jeans. She offered him a small wave, and he returned a slight nod. He knew he had to be professional.

"What's this about?" Steven asked.

Marcus looked back at him. "Can we come in?"

"Do you have a warrant?" Steven asked quickly.

Journey slapped him on the side. "Of course you can," she said, pulling the door open further.

Marcus caught Steven's angered expression. He looked at him, and finally Steven stepped out of his way.

Journey nervously nibbled on a fingernail. "What's going on, Marcus?"

Marcus pulled out a pad of paper from his shirt pocket. "Do either of you know Julie Kennedy?"

Journey shrugged her shoulders. "Steven knows her a little bit, and I just met her a few days ago when she stopped by here."

Steven cast her a menacing scowl that Marcus immediately noted.

"How do you know her?" Marcus asked, looking at Steven.

Steven folded his arms across his chest. "She's a client," he said. All three of them looked up with surprise. A thin smile spread across Steven's lips. "I change the oil in her car every

3,000 miles."

Marcus almost laughed.

Journey sat down on their sofa. "Is something wrong?"

Marcus shifted on his feet. "She's missing and, as far as we can tell, Steven was the last person to talk to her on the phone, and you were the last to speak to her in person."

Journey swallowed hard. "I think she might be suicidal, Marcus. You've got to find her."

He nodded. "I'm hoping you both can help us do that."

Steven spoke up. "We don't have to tell you anything."

Marcus leaned toward him. "Why wouldn't you? We are looking for an unstable, missing kid."

"Because it's not my damn job," Steven snapped.

Journey reached toward him, but his eyes widened with a silent warning. He shook his head slowly, not breaking eye contact with her.

Marcus could tell she was deeply concerned, and he wondered how much she really knew about her boyfriend's involvement. He knew her well enough to know that if she could help him find a suicidal girl, she would. However, Steven was doing everything short of duct-taping her mouth closed.

"Steven, I'm going to need you to step outside with me," Marcus finally said. He looked at Journey. Her eyes were wide with concern. "I'm going to let you talk to my partner. This won't take long."

Marcus followed Steven out onto the front porch. "Are you arresting me?" he asked.

"No. I just want to talk to you," Marcus answered. "How well do you know Julie Kennedy? And don't give me a bullshit answer that you would give your girlfriend."

Steven leaned against the porch rail. "I already told you. I met her at the shop. Her whole family comes there. I don't see her out much."

Marcus could tell from Steven's demeanor that he was probably telling the truth. "When was the last time you saw her?"

Steven thought for a moment. "Maybe a week and a half ago. I ran into her at the mall."

Marcus pointed back inside. "But I know she was just here a few days ago."

Steven sighed. "Just because she stopped by doesn't mean I saw her. I was in the shower. Ask Journey."

"And what did she say to you on the phone today?"

Steven was losing the little bit of patience he had. "All I can tell you is that girl was out of her damn mind on the phone."

"What do you mean by that?" Marcus asked, scribbling in his notebook.

"She was really upset about her sister, and she just kept saying she wanted to make the pain stop," Steven said.

Marcus slowly cast his gaze back at Steven. It was unbelievable how much he hated the guy. "And why would she want to talk to her mechanic so badly? Are you moonlighting as a therapist now?"

Steven shrugged. "I guess I'm just a good go-to guy," he answered with a smirk.

Marcus wanted to permanently remove Steven's smart ass mouth from his face.

"Did she give you any idea where she was going?"

Steven shook his head. "She didn't say a word about it."

Marcus studied Steven's face for a moment. "Where were you on Friday night last week? The night that it snowed?"

Steven shifted his weight from one foot to the other. "I was at Barry's Bar with Journey, waiting for her to get off work so I could drive her home," he answered.

"What time did she get off?"

Steven thought for a moment. "Around midnight."

Marcus made a note to ask Journey the same question and then snapped his notebook closed. "I appreciate it. I hope that if you hear from her, you will call immediately," he said, handing Steven a business card with the police station information on it.

"Yeah," Steven agreed, flicking the card in his fingertips.

Marcus looked inside to see if Curtis and Journey were finished talking. They were.

They walked back in the house, and Journey stood up.

"We may need you to come down to the station tomorrow to answer some more questions," Marcus said.

"Sure," Journey answered.

Journey followed him outside, but Steven stayed at the front door. When they were a few feet away she touched his arm. "Marcus?"

He looked down at her. "Yeah?"

"You need to find her fast," she said with serious concern.

"Do I need to know anything else?" he asked again.

She shook her head. "No. You know I would tell you. She's just really messed up."

Marcus looked back to see Steven fuming under the porch light. Marcus didn't want her to go back into that house; he seriously contemplated kidnapping her right then. He looked down at her. She didn't look well. She was too thin and had dark circles under her eyes.

Marcus lowered his voice even more. "Get out of here, please," he begged. "Go to your parents. Hell, come to my house. Things are about to get bad, hun. I don't want you in the middle of it."

She squeezed his arm. "Call me tomorrow," she said and turned back to the house.

Marcus watched Steven's angry eyes follow her all the way back to the house. He couldn't force himself back into his squad car until they went inside and Steven slammed the door. If it hadn't been for a missing girl, he would've sat in the driveway all night just to make sure Steven knew he was watching.

"What did you get?" Curtis asked, snapping him back to reality.

Marcus shook his head and got in the passenger's seat. "Not much. He said he was at the bar last Friday."

Curtis nodded. "Girlfriend confirmed it. She said he drove her home in his truck because of the snow."

Marcus thought for a second. "In his truck," he repeated. Marcus looked at his partner. "When I drove by there that night, Steven's Chevelle was parked at the bar. She said her car was at home."

Curtis shrugged. "She drove his car to work."

Marcus shook his head. "She wouldn't dare."

. . .

"What did you tell him?" Steven angrily demanded after he slammed the door behind Journey.

Startled, she backed up into the wall away from him. She held up her hands in defense. "Nothing!" she insisted.

He closed the space between them. "Did you tell him that she was coming around looking for drugs?"

She shrank back as far from him as she could and turned her face away from his raised fist. "I swear I didn't. You know I wouldn't!"

"*Do I?*" he shouted so close she could feel his hot breath on her skin.

She was trembling for the first time ever in front of him. His fury radiated off the walls. She took a few slow, deep breaths. "Please calm down," she whispered.

He slammed his finger into her breast bone. "You don't talk to the fucking cops. I don't care if it's one of your boyfriends or not. You don't open your damn mouth! Do you understand?"

She flinched. "We haven't done anything wrong!" she cried.

She was sobbing uncontrollably.

He finally released her arm and grabbed her face desperately instead. "I did it!" he snapped. "I was messing around and swerved toward them as a joke! Your car slid on the ice. I didn't mean to, and I didn't hit them, but she went off the fucking road and flipped!" His eyes were wild with panic.

The information slammed into her brain like a freight train. "But… it was an accident," she stammered.

"But I ran, Journ. I had about eight grams on me and an ounce of weed that I was taking to Julie that night. I fucking ran!" His hands were trembling.

It suddenly registered with Journey: he had been in her car. Someone had described it, and that is why Marcus had called her at work the night of the accident. She had never told Steven that Marcus had called.

"You can't talk to them, Journey," he repeated, dropping his head against her shoulder.

"Shhh…" she consoled him, running her fingers through his hair. "Let's go to bed. We will figure it all out tomorrow."

. . .

After a restless night, Journey woke up alone in her bed to the sound of her cell phone ringing. Steven had left for work two hours before, and she was going to be late for her lunch shift if she didn't get moving soon. She pulled the phone to her ear. "Hello?"

"Hey, it's Marcus."

"Hey," she said.

"Are you OK?" he asked.

Journey groaned and pulled the blue comforter up to block the chill in the room. "Didn't sleep much, but I'm OK. Have you found Julie?"

"No," he replied. "They are still searching for her." He cleared his throat. "I'm having a hard time trying to do my job and protect you at the same time, Journ. You need to get out of that house. A lot of bad shit is getting ready to land on Steven. I don't want the fallout to be on your head too."

"Thanks for worrying about me. I'm OK," she replied. "I've got to get ready for work."

"You can probably expect some visitors today. Just a heads up," he said.

"Thanks Marcus," she said and disconnected.

She pulled herself out of bed and trudged to the bathroom, carrying her cell phone in case there was any news. She turned on the shower and pulled off her t-shirt. She paused in front of the sink to brush her teeth, and her reflection in the mirror was startling.

There were five distinct finger markings on the top of her right arm from where Steven had grabbed her the night before and held her against the wall. Her chest tightened, and her knees began to shake. Unstoppable tears spilled down her cheeks, and she melted to the floor.

She reached for her phone and redialed Marcus's phone number. When he answered, all she could say was "come get me."

7

Daddy Issues

JOURNEY WAS still at the police station when they brought Steven in in handcuffs. She was sitting at an empty desk with her fingers curled around a terrible cup of black coffee.

Steven's eyes found her as he was led into the room. "You fucking bitch," he hissed. He struggled against his restraints, and she cringed as he lunged in her direction. "I'm going to rip off your head and piss down your throat!" Two more officers jumped to restrain him. He continued to spew obscenities at her as they dragged him down the adjoining hallway.

Marcus walked out of a nearby office and put his hand on her shoulder. "You OK?" he asked.

She was trembling, but she nodded and squeezed his hand.

"Come on," he said. "The investigators need to talk to you some more."

Steven was charged with vehicular manslaughter, reckless endangerment, leaving the scene of a crime, obstruction, and making false statements. Marcus had urged Journey to press

85

assault charges also, but she didn't want to have to spend any more time in court than she already had to.

"You did the right thing," Marcus had assured her.

She knew that, but it didn't help calm her nerves as she sat beneath the sour glow of the halogen lights.

The sun was going down outside. "What happens now?" she asked.

Marcus sat down on the edge of the desk in front of her. "He will go before the judge in the morning to have his bond set. He will probably bond out in the next couple of days and wait for trial."

The information made her spine tingle.

"You can't go back to your house," he said.

She already knew that. Her eyes stung with impending tears. "Where am I supposed to go?"

He shifted uncomfortably. "You're going to be pissed off."

She stared blankly at him.

He nodded behind her, and she turned to see her parents in another room talking to the police chief.

She sank down further in her chair. "What the hell, Marcus?" she groaned.

He leaned toward her. "They're worried about you. We're all worried as hell about you." He put both hands on her shoulders. "It's only temporary. I just need to put you somewhere safe till we see what Steven is going to do."

"You're worried he might come after me?"

He shrugged his shoulders. "He's facing a lot of time. And especially until we find out what happened to Julie…" His voice trailed off.

"Do you think he might have killed her?" she asked.

He shook his head. "Not really, but I want to be cautious until we know for sure. She could positively I.D. him as driving your car, and while I don't *think* he killed her, I know even the sanest people do desperate things," he said. "And there is also his brother to worry about."

Journey had only met Brian Drake once, and he had left a chilling impression. She knew that Marcus's concerns were valid. Still, the last place in the world she wanted to be was back under the roof of her parents.

As if reading her mind, Marcus spoke. "You can either go with your family or I will keep you here."

She scowled at him. "You would put me in jail?"

"Yes," he answered quickly. "I've only got one of you, and I'm done watching you slowly kill yourself."

She stood and put her arms around his neck. "I love you," she said. "I hate you right now too, but I love you."

He ran his hand up through the back of her hair and pressed a kiss to her temple. She relaxed for the first time in two days. When he released her, he wrapped his hand around hers and pulled her up. "Let's do this," he said.

When they entered the room with the police chief, Carol immediately ran to embrace her daughter. Journey stood awkwardly with her hands at her sides. Her mother had been crying. Her eyes were puffy and red. Randall, whom she could see over her tiny mother's shoulder, was rigid and cold. He didn't even look at her. Instead, he reached his hand toward Marcus. "Good work, son," he said.

"Thank you, Mr. Durant," Marcus replied.

The chief slapped Marcus on the back. "The new kid is making a name for himself quickly around here. We're all very proud of him."

Marcus laughed and shook his head. "I can't take credit for this one. Journey walked in this morning and closed the case. Not me."

Journey's mother examined her face. "Are you hungry?" she asked. "We brought you a chicken sandwich."

"Thanks," Journey mumbled accepting the bag of fast food.

She felt Marcus's hand at the small of her back. "I'll pick you up tomorrow and take you to get your car and your things."

She turned to look at him and nodded her head. She was so exhausted she could hardly stand. "Thank you," she said.

He winked a sky blue eye at her, and she smiled remembering the crazy green contacts that she had finally convinced him to stop wearing.

The drive home was painfully silent. She sat in the backseat of her parents' Cadillac with her head resting against the ice cold window. Christmas lights streaked in a blur as they drove past all of the decorated houses.

Unsuccessfully, she tried to remember the date. Christmas could only be a few days away. She and Steven hadn't even put up a tree.

Less than twenty-four hours before, she had been freezing him with her feet, and suddenly she was on her way to the last place on Earth she wanted to be.

Her sister's car was in the driveway when they pulled up in front of the Durant house. Journey hadn't been home since she had left six months before. A Christmas tree was lit up in the front window. Elena stood at the door, and Journey's heart leapt at the sight of her. Journey had barely talked to her big sister since her exodus from the family earlier that year.

Elena rushed to embrace her. "Thank God, you're safe." Her sister sighed. "You look like hell."

Journey smiled and ran her fingers through her hair which had been dried by the cold winter air that morning. "I've had a rough day," she said.

"I'll bet," Elena agreed.

They went inside, and Journey gave her mother and sister

the condensed version of the week's events. Her father was absent for most of the evening. Journey assumed he was busying himself with work that didn't need to be done in an effort to avoid talking to her.

Much to her surprise, there were no lectures, looks of disgust, or I-told-you-so's through the course of the night. Before retreating to her bedroom, her mother paused and kissed Journey on the top of the head. She told her how much she loved her and how thankful she was that Journey was home.

Once Carol had gone to bed and Journey was alone with her sister, Elena slid close to her on the sofa. "Be patient with Dad. He's processing through all of this the best he can."

"He hasn't even acknowledged that I exist," Journey pointed out.

Elena shrugged her shoulders. "This is harder for him than you realize," she said.

Journey just nodded.

"Where is David with all this going on?" Elena asked, looking around as if she expected to find him hiding in a corner.

Journey's eyes closed. She rolled her head sideways to look at her sister. "I really don't have the desire or the energy to get into all that tonight. Can I have a raincheck? I'm so exhausted."

Elena squeezed her knee. "Sure. Tomorrow, maybe." She stood up and offered Journey a hand and helped pull her to her feet. "Go get some much-needed rest, sister."

They embraced.

"I've missed you," Journey said.

"I've missed you too, kid. I'm so glad you're home."

Journey walked upstairs to what used to be her bedroom and surveyed the empty space. Her heart sank even further as she stood in the emptiness of what used to be her life. In stark contrast to the bare walls and empty closet, her bed was perfectly made. It looked so warm and inviting that her whole body relaxed at just the sight of it.

Her dad's voice startled her from behind. "I had told myself, when we started hearing of the trouble you were in, that you had made your bed and now you had to lie in it."

Journey turned to see tears falling down his strong and age-lined face.

He sucked in a quick breath to stifle a whimper. "But tonight, *I made your bed*," he said, his bottom lip beginning to tremble. "And I want you to lie in it."

She had never seen her father cry.

All at once, Journey's resolve shattered. "Daddy," she wept and fell into his open arms.

He held her tight and let her cry. He gently stroked her hair and rubbed her back. When she finally pulled away, he looked down at her with all the tenderness any father could give. "No matter where you go or what decisions you make… you will always be my little girl."

She wiped her nose and hugged him again. "I'm so sorry, Dad."

"I am too," he said. "We'll get through this together. I promise."

8

NOTHING BUT THE TRUTH

ON CHRISTMAS Eve, a team of volunteers found the body of Julie Kennedy less than a mile from her house and partially buried in the snow. She had a self-inflicted gunshot wound to the head. The coroner reported that the .22 caliber bullet lodged in her brain, and she died an excruciating two hours later.

In exchange for her parents' promise to help her pay for college, Journey checked herself into a thirty day rehab program in Tennessee. When she graduated from the program in February, her parents, Elena, Kara, and Marcus were all there cheering for her. Marcus carried with him the news that Steven Drake had gone before the grand jury, and they decided to let his case go to trial. Steven's lawyer had advised against taking a plea agreement, and they agreed to wait for a trial date. Journey would have to testify in court. She dreaded it like the end of the human race.

Everyone decided it was best for Journey to spend the

spring and summer in Nashville with Elena since Steven was out on bond. She enrolled in a few undergraduate classes which would keep her busy but allow flexibility for her to be in Georgia for court proceedings. When she wasn't in class, she worked part-time at a department store. She still enjoyed the party life from time to time, but, like the tattoo on her leg, she realized she had been reborn from the ashes once and had no desire to go up in flames again. She stopped using drugs completely.

On a Friday late in March, Journey walked outside to the smoking section of her small community college and saw Marcus crossing the parking lot. Not caring that she was making a scene, she squealed and took off in a sprint toward him. His face broke into a smile, and he opened his arms. Marcus picked her up and spun her around before returning her feet to the ground.

"What are you doing here?"

He laughed and shrugged his shoulders. "I was in the neighborhood."

"Big damn neighborhood," she said laughing. "Why didn't you tell me you were coming?"

He draped his arm over her shoulders as they walked back to the picnic tables. "I wanted it to be a surprise."

"You succeeded," she said.

He reached into his back pocket and pulled out a folded manila envelope and frowned. "I do have some business." He handed it to her. "It's a subpoena. The court date is Monday, June 5th."

She groaned and sank back down on the tabletop. She pulled out the paperwork and looked it over. "How long do you think it will take?" she asked.

He stuffed his hands in his pockets. "There is no telling," he replied. "A few days or maybe a few weeks."

"Ugh." She let out a puff of air. "At least it will be over, right?"

He nodded. "Yes."

She held up the envelope in her hand. "You didn't have to bring this to me, did you?"

He smiled. "Technically, you still live with your parents in Georgia so delivering it wasn't really out of my way." He winked at her.

She stood and put her arms around his waist. "How long can you stay?" she asked, looking up at him.

"Well, I don't have to be at work till Monday," he said.

She squeezed him. "Yay!"

He nudged her with his shoulder. "Go get your crap. Let's get out of here."

She laughed and stumbled back a couple of steps. "Are you encouraging me to skip school, Officer Garrett?"

His lips spread into a thin smile. "I like it when you call me that."

She stretched up on the tip of her toes and kissed his cheek. "I'll be right back," she said.

Later that night, they rented movies and ordered pizza. Elena got home after a work dinner and was only mildly surprised to find Marcus there. Marcus, always the ladies' man, greeted her at the door and offered to take her briefcase.

She kissed him on the cheek and gave him a friendly side-hug. "I didn't know you were coming," she said, genuinely delighted to see him.

"I didn't even tell Journey," he told her. "I hope you don't mind."

Elena shook her head. "Of course not. I meant it when I said you are welcome anytime you want to come. You don't need an invitation."

Journey's entire family credited Marcus for single-handedly

pulling Journey out of the viper pit and setting her on the road to redemption.

He carried her briefcase to the kitchen and motioned to where Journey sat on the couch with the pizza box in her lap. "We ordered a pizza if you're hungry."

"No thanks," Elena said. "I already ate. I hope you'll both forgive me if I just retreat to my room. This has been a week from hell at work."

Marcus waved her away. "Don't worry about us."

Journey looked over her shoulder as Elena passed behind her. "Hold up a sec. I have news," she said.

Elena leaned against the back of the couch. "What news?"

Journey's bottom lip poked out. "Marcus came to tell me I have court on June 5th."

"June 5th," Elena repeated.

Marcus sat back down next to Journey. "Yeah," he confirmed.

Elena nodded. "Hey, look on the bright side. At least you'll be at home around your birthday."

Marcus slapped Journey on the knee. "That's right."

Journey hadn't considered that. "That certainly is a plus."

Elena squeezed her shoulder. "I would love to talk more about this tomorrow. My feet are killing me, and I have to get out of these shoes."

Journey patted her hand. "No worries. Go to bed. Love you."

"Love you, too," Elena replied, heading toward her bedroom. "Marcus, I'm glad you're here."

"Thank you, again," he called after her.

She closed the door, and he picked up another piece of pizza. "It's scary how similar and how different the two of you are at the same time," he said. "She was wearing high heels, Journey. And a suit!"

Journey elbowed him in the ribs. "Shut up. I own heels."

He laughed. "Hooker boots don't count."

She giggled and put her feet up on the coffee table. "What movies did you get?" she asked.

He had picked out the movies while she went next door to get the pizza.

He stretched to where he had stacked the DVDs on the table. He held them up. "I got *The Sixth Sense* and *Fight Club*."

She scrunched up her nose. "Not *Fight Club*."

He went slack-jawed. "What? Chicks love *Fight Club*!"

She shook her head. "I saw it with David, and I don't want to think about David."

His expression was vacant. "You still haven't talked to him or heard from him?"

She shook her head. "No. Have you?"

"No," he said through a mouthful of pizza. "Have you tried?"

She shifted uncomfortably on the sofa. "I tried his cell a few times, but his number is disconnected."

"What about his parents?"

"They moved," she said.

He thought for a second. "What if you wrote to their address? Maybe the post office would forward your letter."

She bumped him with her shoulder. "I told you, I don't want to think about David."

He nodded and dropped *Fight Club* back on the table. "*The Sixth Sense* then?"

"Is it scary?"

"Yep," he answered.

She laughed. "Then I'm sleeping with you tonight."

He rolled his eyes. "Don't you always?"

She hadn't spent the night with Marcus since she had left her parents' house and had no other place to go the summer before. That seemed like another lifetime.

He got up and put the movie in the DVD player. Then he stretched out on his side across the couch, settling his feet behind her back. He tugged on her sleeve. "Come here," he said.

She kicked off her shoes before lying down beside him and relaxed against the warmth of his chest. He pulled the blanket off the back of the couch and draped it over them before curling his arm around her waist. Thirty minutes into the movie, she was sound asleep.

. . .

Journey became more and more nervous the closer they got to Steven's trial date. By her birthday weekend, she had practically given herself an ulcer with worry. Marcus had driven to Nashville to pick her up and bring her home, insisting that her car shouldn't be seen around town. He told her that he wasn't as worried about Steven as he was about Steven's brother. Journey couldn't argue; Brian Drake made Steven come off like a Boy Scout. He scared the absolute bejeezus out of her.

She thought it was sweet of Marcus to be so concerned. He had even offered to stay over at her parents' house, just so she felt safe. She had declined, however, knowing that although her father might be a conservative Baptist deacon, he kept a small arsenal locked up in his gun safe.

For her birthday, her mother had offered to cook dinner for Journey and invite her friends over, but Journey quickly shot down the idea and went tubing with her friends instead. She knew a party at her parents' would be too painful of a reminder of David's absence since he had been present there the birthday before.

David was still nowhere to be found. Marcus had driven by and confirmed that his parents had, in fact, sold their house and moved, but no one knew where. Following Marcus's suggestion, Journey had sent two different letters to their old address and both had been returned as 'undeliverable' with no forwarding address. She was beginning to lose hope that she would ever be able to apologize for how she had acted toward him.

The trial began on Monday morning, and Journey was scheduled to testify for the prosecution early in the process along with two other witnesses. Journey sat in the crowded courtroom sandwiched between Marcus and her father. She looked around and then leaned over to Marcus.

"Steven's mother is here, but Brian isn't," she said.

"I'm sure Steven's lawyer advised him not to be here. It wouldn't help his case at all," Marcus replied.

A moment later, the door opened, and a man with a comb-over and a pot belly stuffed into an expensive suit entered the room. Steven followed close behind, but Journey almost didn't recognize him. His hair was cut neatly like a politician, and he was wearing a suit that didn't quite fit. He scanned the room, and his eyes fell on her briefly before his lawyer instructed him to sit down at a small table. Journey shivered, and her father reached over and squeezed her hand. Steven didn't look in her direction again.

After forty-five minutes of legal jargon and opening arguments by the prosecution and the defense, the first two witnesses, a man and a woman, were called to testify. Their stories were almost identical. They had both described seeing Journey's white hatchback swerve in the direction of the 4-wheeler and then speed away. The man identified Steven as driving the car, and the woman gave a heart-wrenching account of how Marci Kennedy had died in her arms on the side of the snowy gravel road. Journey felt like she might throw up.

When Steven's oompa-loompa lawyer finished his weak cross-examination of the woman, the prosecution called Journey to the witness stand. She swore to tell the truth, the whole truth, and nothing but the truth before sitting down and spelling her name for the clerk. The prosecuting attorney, whom she had met with a few times, gave her a reassuring smile. Journey was careful to keep her eyes on him and to not glance in her ex-boyfriend's direction.

"Miss Durant, can you please describe, for the court, your relationship with the defendant?" he asked.

Journey clenched her hands together in her lap. "I was Steven's girlfriend. We started dating in April of last year and lived together from June until the end of December when he was arrested."

The attorney leaned casually against the panel wall in front of the jury. "Can you please tell the court about the night of Friday, December 10th?"

Journey nodded. "I was working the night shift at Barry's Bar & Grill on Main Street. Normally, the bar closes at 2:00 AM on Friday nights, but it had started snowing really hard around 9:00 PM, and Barry decided to close early at midnight. Steven came by around eleven and told me that he would drive my car home and return with his truck to give me a ride in the snow."

The lawyer stopped her. "Was this unusual behavior for Mr. Drake? Did you think he might have an ulterior motive in taking your car? Perhaps to deliver drugs to…"

Steven's lawyer stood up and shouted, "Objection. Leading the witness, your Honor. My client is not on trial for drug charges."

"Sustained," the gray-haired male judge ruled.

The prosecutor held up his hands in surrender. "Let me rephrase." He turned back to Journey. "Was Steven Drake the type of boyfriend who regularly picked you up during bad weather?"

"No," she answered. "I was surprised."

The prosecutor seemed satisfied. "So, the defendant came to your work at 11 PM and picked up your car. Then what happened?"

"He came back about forty-five minutes later and waited for me to get off work. Then we went home."

"What time did you go home?" he asked.

"At about ten after midnight," she answered.

He turned his palms face up. "So, just to clarify, Steven Drake was in possession of your car at the time of the accident at 11:20 PM?"

Journey nodded her head. "Yes."

"When did you first hear about the Kennedy girls' accident?" he asked.

Journey shifted in her chair. "One of my friends is a police officer. He called me at work before Steven and I left the bar to make sure I was OK. He said that a car that fit the description of mine had been involved in an accident, but he didn't elaborate. The next time I heard about it was when I returned to work on Sunday."

"What was your involvement with the victim's sister, Julie Kennedy?" he asked.

Journey shrugged. "I had never met her before she showed up at mine and Steven's house a few days after the accident."

"Why was she at your house?"

"She asked to see Steven, but he didn't come out to talk to her. He asked me to give her a bag of marijuana that he had in our bedroom," she said nervously. "I did but only because he told me to. He said he wasn't going to charge her for it."

His eyebrows rose with fake surprise. "Charge her for it? So, Steven Drake was a drug dealer?"

Journey nodded. "I believe so."

"Objection, the witness is speculating!" Steven's lawyer shouted.

"Your Honor, the witness is attesting to the character of the man that she lived with and why he might have been present on the road the night of the accident. And since both of the other people who can attest to his involvement with the Kennedy girls are dead, I ask that you allow this testimony," the prosecutor insisted.

The judge nodded. "Overruled, but watch yourself counselor."

"Miss Durant, do you believe that Steven Drake is a drug dealer?"

"Yes, I do," she answered.

"Do you believe that Steven Drake intended to use your car to deliver drugs the night that Marci Kennedy was killed?"

"Yes," she stated.

He held up his hands and walked toward the audience. "Why?"

Journey shifted in her seat. "Because Steven told me that he did."

There was a shift in the air in the courtroom. People began to whisper.

"Steven Drake *told you* that he was at the scene of the accident," the lawyer clarified. "Can you please tell us what he said?"

Journey cleared her throat. "The night that the police came to question us when Julie disappeared, the police officers separated us, so Steven didn't know what I had told them. He wanted to know if I had told them that Julie was asking him for drugs. When I began to question why he was so worried, he had a meltdown. He told me that he had caused the accident. He said that he was messing around with them and swerved toward them as a joke, but my car had slid on some ice. He said he saw the 4-wheeler flip, but that it was an accident. He said he panicked because he had a lot of drugs in his possession and he ran."

The prosecutor raised his eyebrows. "Steven Drake admitted that he was guilty of vehicular manslaughter and leaving the scene of an accident?"

"Objection!"

The prosecuting attorney gave her a small wink. "I retract the question, your Honor."

. . .

No one was surprised that Steven Drake was convicted on all charges. The jury had only spent thirty minutes deliberating at the conclusion of the trial, and Marcus said that he heard that most of the deliberation was on whether or not Steven had wasted his own money on his worthless lawyer. Steven was taken into custody and booked into the county jail to await sentencing.

On the day her parents were supposed to drive her back to Nashville, Marcus showed up and tried to talk her into staying. "There's no reason for you not to come home now," he said as they sat on the bed of his truck in the driveway.

She took a deep breath and looked up at the clear, blue sky. "Yeah, there is," she said. "I need a fresh start. I need to get away from everything here for a while. Maybe forever."

His shoulders sank a little, but he nodded. "You do have a lot of history here." After a long silence, he wrapped his hand around hers. "Just so you know, I really wish you would stay."

She smiled and rested her head against his shoulder. Being with him would be so easy, but it also wouldn't be fair. Because of David, she could only see a fiery ending to any kind of relationship with Marcus, and she loved him too much to lose him too.

9

THE LITTLE SPOON

WHEN HER sophomore year of college ended, Journey returned to Emerson and found her parents' driveway full of familiar vehicles. Over the front door was a huge sign that read, "HAPPY 21ST BIRTHDAY!" She laughed and got out of her car in time for a small welcoming party to run out the front door.

Kara was the first to reach her with wide arms. "Happy birthday!"

Journey laughed and took a step back. "Thank you," she said.

Justin stepped over and wrapped an arm around Journey's shoulders. He squeezed her until she grunted for release. "You don't know how glad I am that you're back."

Kara posed with a hand on her hip and glared at him. "He keeps hoping that your commitment issues will rub off on me, and I'll let him off the hook about getting married."

Journey's mouth fell open a bit. "I don't have commitment

issues!"

There was a brief exchange of wide eyes and awkward glances before the entire group burst out in unison laughter around her.

She covered her red face. "Shut up!"

"I would like to testify against the accused." Marcus's hand was raised in the air as he stepped around Kara and Justin.

It had been a while since she had seen him without his cop uniform. For most of her weekend trips home, he was working, and he hadn't had time to visit her at school all year.

When Steven was sentenced to four years in the state prison, the media turned Marcus into somewhat of a superhero in Emerson. He had quickly advanced through the ranks at the police station and made detective in less than three years. At the same time, he completed a bachelor's degree in criminal justice.

That night, standing her parents' driveway, he looked almost edible in khaki shorts and a button-up blue striped shirt. He scooped her into his solid arms and lifted her feet off the ground.

"Welcome home, stranger," he said with a smile that sparkled in the moonlight.

She gave him a friendly peck on the lips and blew out a slow sigh. "Marcus."

His head tilted to the side. "Are you ready for the best weekend of your life?"

Journey smiled as he carefully lowered her back to the ground. "I've been marking the days off on my calendar." Emerson was just a pit stop to meet up with her friends before heading to Charleston for the weekend. Her Uncle Ray was graciously allowing them to celebrate at his beach house.

Journey's parents were next in line to greet her, and they both hugged her at the same time. Randall Durant planted a kiss on the top of her head. "Welcome home, sweetie. Did you have a good trip? Any car problems?"

She shook her head. "It was uneventful." She kissed his cheek and then hugged her mother again.

Carol jerked her thumb toward the house. "I made everyone lunch so you can eat before you get back on the road. We'd better get to it before you lose too much daylight."

At around seven o'clock, the four of them arrived at the beach house on the Isle of Palms, just outside of the city. Marcus carried his bag and Journey's inside. "Where are we sleeping?" he asked when she opened the front door.

"Kara, you and Justin can have the master. Marcus and I can take the other two rooms," she said as she led them all inside. She pointed down the hallway and looked at Marcus. "We're on this side of the house."

When they reached one of the bedrooms, he looked at her sideways as he deposited her suitcase onto the bed. "You know you're going to wind up in my room," he teased. "You always do."

She laughed. "You have a girlfriend now," she said. "I wouldn't feel right about it."

"Destiny isn't my girlfriend."

Journey's brow crumpled. "Destiny? Geez, I didn't know her name was Destiny. Is she a stripper?"

He rolled his eyes and turned on his heel. "She's not a stripper."

Journey followed him across the hall. "What does she do?"

He was quiet for a moment. "She's a dancer."

"Ha!" Journey laughed. "I knew it!"

He looked over his shoulder at her. "She's not a stripper, and she's not my girlfriend."

Journey smiled and leaned in the doorway. "*Surrrre*," she said, dragging out the word to mock him.

Marcus reached for the door and pushed it closed, forcing Journey into the hallway. "Sorry, no girls allowed in my room."

"Marcus is dating a stripper!" Journey sang through the house.

There was a band playing on the rooftop of Coconut Joe's when they arrived. Kara and Justin sat down at an empty table, but Journey walked straight to the railing that overlooked the beach. Marcus followed. The sun was setting behind them and casting a sparkling golden glow over the waves. The cool ocean breeze blew her hair back off her shoulders, and she could already taste salt on her lips. She stretched her arms high over her head. "This is awesome! Our whole group back together again."

Marcus leaned on the rail next to her and adjusted his black sunglasses. "Yeah, all except Dave, I guess."

Journey's heart took an unexpected nose dive, and she dropped her hands like she had been punched in the stomach. Marcus didn't notice; there was a blonde in a bikini on the beach.

Journey sighed. "Yeah, except for Dave."

David had never been far from Journey's thoughts, but the U.S. going to war in the Middle East erupted him back to the forefront of her mind. She had never forgiven herself for pushing him away like she had. She tried a few times to look him up online but never found any trace of him. For a while she had even continued to write letters to his old address without any response. David was a ghost, and Journey had all but given up the hope of ever finding him again. She could barely even tolerate the sound of his all-to-common name, much less the memory of their days together before she so definitively destroyed it all.

However, she was lucky enough to still be loved by some of the most amazing friends on the planet. She looped her arm through Marcus's and rested her cheek against his shoulder. "I've missed you, Marcus."

He leaned over and pressed his lips against her temple. "I've missed you, too."

"Journey!" Kara called out.

The two of them turned to see Kara holding up a bottle of tequila.

"It's birthday time!" she cheered.

. . .

Two hours and half of the bottle later, the birthday girl was no longer able to sit completely vertical in her chair. She dug her fingernails into Marcus's arm. "I wanna go on the beach!"

He laughed and nodded his head. "OK, I'll get the check and we—"

Journey cut him off. "Kara!" she screamed. "Let's go play on the beach!"

Kara was dancing with Justin, but she spun around when she heard Journey yell. "Yes! The beach!"

Marcus laughed as he watched Kara try and run back to the table. Her sandal caught on a plank on the floor, sending her sprawling forward. Justin caught her before she hit the ground. She pushed his hands away and laughed all the way back to her seat.

Journey stood up too fast and wobbled. Marcus jumped up to steady her, but Kara grabbed her arm. "Let's go swimming!" she shouted.

Marcus caught Justin's eye and pointed at them. "Please go with them while I pay the bill!"

Justin nodded. "I've got this."

Leaning on each other for support, the two drunken girls staggered across the rooftop and knocked over a table and a tiki torch. Justin had to stop and pick up the burning lamp before it started a blaze, but the girls kept going toward the stairs.

"Shit!" Marcus said. He waved his arm and caught the attention of their waitress. He shoved a hundred dollar bill into her hands. "Keep the change!" he called as he ran toward the steps.

He caught up with the two of them just as Journey missed the top step completely. He was able to jerk her back into his arms before she plummeted down the stairs. He blocked Kara's path with his leg. He let out a deep sigh as Journey giggled in his grasp.

"Maybe it's time to go home," he suggested.

"Noooooo!" she protested. She pointed back toward the ocean. "It's my birthday, and I wanna go to the beach!"

He groaned. Finally Justin caught up with them and took hold of Kara's hand.

When they finally made it down the twenty-seven harrowing wooden steps to the ground below, Marcus released his hold on Journey. She took off in a sideways sprint almost in the direction of the beach. Kara followed after her, screaming like a banshee.

"This is going to be a long night," Justin said.

Marcus laughed as Kara fell on top of Journey, and they both landed laughing in a sand dune. "Maybe we can get them to walk some of it off," he wondered out loud.

Justin sighed as they began to walk toward them. "I dunno. Kara's already reached the point where she keeps calling me 'bitch'."

Marcus rubbed his hands down his face and laughed.

The girls were heading toward the water, and Journey stripped her t-shirt off over her head. "Uh oh," Marcus said and took off in a jog.

He picked up her shirt but couldn't catch her before she dropped her jeans shorts to the sand and kicked off her flip-flops. He scanned the area for onlookers or worse, the police. Her arms were flailing over her head as she ran into the waves. At least her rainbow bra and panties could almost pass as a bathing suit. Kara ran into the water fully dressed. Marcus folded his arms over his chest as Justin joined him at the water's edge. "Damn it."

Justin just laughed.

"Marcus!" Journey yelled from where she had waded out to waist deep water. "Come swim with me!"

He shook his head. "No! And stop yelling!"

"I won't! Not until you come get me!" She started slapping the water with her hands. "Marcus! Marcus! Marcus!"

Kara pointed her long finger at Justin. "You too, you little bitch!"

Marcus doubled over laughing and grabbed his knees for support.

Justin shook his head. "We'd better get out there before someone calls the cops."

Marcus groaned and unbuttoned his shirt. "I'm going to get fired." He pulled off his tennis shoes and socks and tucked his wallet and keys into his shoe. He walked into ankle deep water and held up his arms. "OK, I'm in!"

Journey was slinging her wet hair back and forth. "No! Come here!"

"You come get me!" he called back to her.

She laughed and started sloshing toward him. When the water was shallow enough, she started to run. When she was close enough, he grabbed her around the waist and carried her out into the ocean. She squealed in his ear till they were both knocked down by a wave. She splashed her way toward him in the water when he came up laughing.

He wiped salt water off his face. "I'm in. Are you happy now?"

She looped her arms around his neck, and her body bobbed in the surf against his chest. She tossed her head back. "I'm deliriously happy!"

The way that the water drizzled down the smooth skin of her neck was making Marcus dizzy. He took a deep breath and closed his eyes. "Can we please go home now before you get us all arrested?" he asked.

She kissed his cheek. "Yes. We can go home now. Will you carry me?"

He sighed. "Only if you put your clothes back on."

"Deal."

When they reached the beach, he put her arms into his shirt and buttoned the buttons. Justin was dragging Kara in from the water. Marcus put his shoes back on and then turned his back toward Journey. "Hop on," he said. "Let's get out of here before you change your mind."

When they got back to the car, he buckled Journey into the passenger's seat, and Justin and Kara got in the back. Journey turned sideways in her seat toward him. "You're so pretty, Marcus."

He laughed and rolled his eyes.

When they got back to the house, Journey spilled out of her door before he could get around to her. "Hey Kara," she called out. "Let's go jump in the pool!"

"Oh yes!" Kara agreed.

Marcus shook his head. "No swimming."

Kara pulled on his arm. "What if it's skinny dipping?"

He paused to think about it. Just then, Journey sat down in the middle of the sidewalk for no reason at all. "Definitely no swimming," he repeated. He stretched his arms down toward her. "Come here."

Journey slapped his hands away and staggered to her feet. "I can walk," she argued.

She took one step and then nearly fell over laughing. Without a word, he bent over, grabbed her around her hips, and slung her over his shoulder. She laughed and pounded her fists on his back. "I can walk!" she squealed.

"I don't want you to break your neck trying to get up the steps," he told her as he followed Kara and Justin to the front door.

Once inside, he carried her to her room and deposited her on the mattress. He looked down to where she was sprawled out. "You're not going to be sick are you?"

She shook her head. "No."

He looked at her wet hair and then at the bathroom. He knew she needed a shower before bed, but he decided he didn't have the honorability or willpower to supervise. He looked at the alarm clock. It was almost one in the morning. He pointed at her. "Go to bed."

"Where are you going to sleep?" she asked.

"In the other room," he replied.

She held out her arms toward him. "No, sleep with me," she slurred.

That's not a good idea, he thought to himself. "No, you sleep in here. And maybe I'll make breakfast for you in the morning."

She smiled and closed her eyes. "I haven't had Marcus-pancakes in a long time."

Marcus unzipped her suitcase. Lying on top was an old, familiar Metallica t-shirt. He held it up. "Is this my shirt?"

She giggled. "Not anymore."

He laughed and pulled her to her feet. "Can you get changed or do you need help?"

She smacked his hand again. "I can do it," she said.

He breathed a sigh of relief. He nodded toward the hall. "I'll be in my room if you need me."

"Mm-kay," she said.

He watched for a moment as she fumbled with the buttons on his shirt, and then he smiled and slowly backed out of the bedroom. Before bed, he forced himself into a cold shower. When he got back to his room, Journey was under the covers.

An irrepressible smile crept across his face. "Are you lost?"

"You can't go to sleep without me," she said.

He walked over and pulled the covers back. She was wearing his shirt and not much else. "Scoot over."

She rolled onto her side with her back to him. When he stretched out next to her, she looked back over her shoulder. "I get to be the little spoon."

He laughed and curled his arm around her. Her body was warm against his, and their legs tangled together under the blankets.

She's drunk Marcus, he silently reminded himself.

He moved his lips against her ear. "That was one of my favorite shirts," he whispered.

She giggled. "It's been one of my favorites for five years."

Her hair fell away from her neck exposing a small patch of creamy skin just below her ear. Unable to stop himself, he kissed it. She tasted like the sea. To his surprise, she sighed and nuzzled back into him. As if on its own accord, his hand crept up under the t-shirt to her bare stomach.

"Journey?"

No response.

He sat up a little and leaned over to see her face. "Journ?" he asked again.

Nothing. She was asleep.

He groaned and fell back onto his pillow.

. . .

The distant sound of a phone ringing jarred Journey from a hard sleep. She opened her eyes and had to think for a second to determine where she was. She was alone in a strange bed, in a strange room that smelled like maple syrup and bacon. She sat up and saw Marcus's clothes from the night before scattered across the hardwood floor.

Oh crap, she thought, quickly picking up the edge of the blanket to make sure she was dressed. *Cotton panties, check. T-shirt, check.*

She laughed with relief before swinging her legs off the edge of the bed. Marcus's suitcase was open on the floor and a pair of black gym shorts was laying on top. She bent to retrieve them and thought her brain might explode. She gripped her forehead and winced with pain. She pulled the shorts on, rolling them at the waist three or four times to make them fit better and then walked barefoot out of the bedroom. She shuffled down the hallway toward the sound of her friends' voices.

Justin and Kara were at the kitchen breakfast bar eating pancakes. Kara cocked her head sideways and took in Journey's attire before smiling wide.

"Shut up," Journey said as she walked to the coffee pot and picked up an empty mug.

"I didn't say a word," she said.

Justin laughed. "Looks like your evening got interesting."

She held up her middle finger in response.

Marcus walked in from the balcony, snapping his cell phone shut. He saw Journey and smiled. "Morning."

She sipped the black coffee. "Morning."

He put his phone down on the counter.

"Looks to me like someone had a good night," Kara teased.

"Marcus, tell them nothing happened," Journey instructed, leaning against the counter.

Marcus playfully slipped his arm around her waist and pulled her close. "Baby, you were spectacular."

She shoved him, and they all laughed. Marcus handed her a plate.

She held the plate close to her nose and took a deep whiff. "Mmm, pancakes."

"Hurry up and eat. I wanna get out on the beach before we have to head home," he said.

She looked around at all the food. "Did you go shopping?"

"Yes. I've been up since seven." He pointed to the clock. "It's almost lunchtime. I'm going to go get my swimming trunks on." As he passed, he smacked Journey on the butt.

She rested her plate by Kara who was still laughing. "Shut up!"

Later that day Journey stretched out on a beach towel in the sun next to Kara. Out in the water, Marcus and Justin tossed a football. Journey smiled. "This has been a really great birthday."

Kara grinned. "Including last night?"

Journey rolled her eyes. "We fell asleep together. That is all."

"Could've fooled me by that outfit you were wearing when you came stumbling out of Marcus's bedroom," she teased.

"Let it go," Journey said.

Kara reached over and smacked Journey on the back of the head.

"*Ow!*" Journey shot her friend an ugly look. "What the hell was that for?"

"You're such an idiot!" she shouted. "What's the matter with you?"

Journey rubbed the back of her head. "What are you talking about?"

"You know what I'm talking about." She pointed out to the water. "I'm talking about you and Marcus."

"What about me and Marcus?"

"Look at him," she said. When Journey didn't obey, Kara reached over and forced Journey's head in Marcus's direction. "Look at him."

"OK! OK!" Journey glanced out into the water. Marcus was in black and blue swimming trunks that hung low on his hip bones. Each dark tattoo on his perfectly tanned skin accentuated a different muscle group.

Kara laughed. "You look like you could eat him for lunch right now!"

Journey cocked an eyebrow at her. She knew Kara had a point that she was slowly getting to.

Kara took a deep breath and pulled off her sunglasses. "Journey, I sat back and watched you do the same damn song and dance with David for years." Journey flinched, but Kara didn't stop. "I know you don't like talking about David, but you were too stupid to admit how you felt about him and look where it got you! You're still cringing at his name years later. Now you're doing the same damn thing with Marcus, and I'm not keeping my mouth shut this time!"

Kara's intervention was much more dramatic than Journey had expected, but she knew Kara was right.

"He's been in love with you for years and whether or not you want to actually admit to it, you love him too. We all know it." She shoved Journey again in the shoulder. "Don't screw this one up."

Wow, Journey thought.

Kara finally pointed at her. "You know I'm right."

For a long time Journey was silent. She watched Marcus doubled over laughing at something Justin was saying. By the way Justin kept cupping his hands at his chest, she could only assume he was talking about boobs. Journey loved it when Marcus laughed.

"But what if it doesn't work and I lose him?" Journey

finally asked, not meeting Kara's eyes.

"You don't know that's what will happen," Kara replied. "But we all know that you two can't keep this crap up forever. He will eventually get serious with someone else, and you will really lose him."

"But what about David?" Journey asked. "Being with Marcus seals that forever. I can't go back from that. And I don't know what happened to him, Kara."

Kara sighed. "Journey, you've searched for David for years and have found nothing. If David wanted to find you, it wouldn't be that hard. The truth that you need to realize is… he hasn't even looked for you."

If Kara had just punched her in the face, it couldn't have hurt any more than her words. But Journey refused to cry. Kara put a gentle hand on her forearm. "David's gone. It's time to move on. It's time for you to be happy."

. . .

Journey couldn't shake her conversation with Kara for the rest of the day at the beach. That afternoon, they made the drive back to Emerson. She said goodbye to her friends when they all arrived back at her parents' house. Marcus was the last to leave.

"You've been really quiet the whole way back," he said. "Is everything OK?"

She hooked her thumbs in the belt loops of her blue jean shorts and smiled. "Yeah, I'm just tired and probably still a little hungover."

He reached out to her. "Well, come here." He pulled her into his arms. She took a deep breath. He smelled like cool cologne and sunshine.

She looked up at him. "Thank you, Marcus." The corners of his mouth tipped up into a smile. "Thank you for everything you've always done for me," she added.

He looked stunned for a moment and then finally cracked a smile. "You don't have cancer or something do you?"

She laughed. "No. I'm just feeling really loved."

He pulled her close again. "Well, you are." He kissed her on the top of the head. After a long while, he released her. "I'd better see you in the next couple of days. No sneaking back to Tennessee without saying goodbye like you sometimes do," he said, pointing at her.

She laughed. "I promise."

He opened his door and climbed into the seat. She started toward the house, but then stopped and looked back at him before he closed his door. "Marcus?"

He held the door open and looked out at her. "Yeah?"

She opened her mouth to speak but couldn't find the words. "Nothing. Never mind. I'll talk to you tomorrow."

He looked at her sideways for a second, then laughed. "OK. Later," he said and shut his door.

Journey went inside and sat on her bed in silence for a long time. She absentmindedly twisted David's ring around her thumb. Finally, she pulled it off and looked it over. *My best friend, Forever*, she read on the inside of the band.

"What are you doing?" she asked out loud.

Immediately, she pushed herself off the bed, grabbed her keys, and bolted out the front door.

Marcus's new house was only about five miles away from her parents' home. The light was on inside when she pulled into his empty driveway and parked her car in front of his garage. With one last deep breath, she wrenched her door open, crossed his yard, and took his front porch steps two at a time till she reached the door. She almost hesitated but pressed the doorbell anyway. A moment later, the door opened and he was standing before her.

He looked at her and then around the yard in confusion.

"Journey? What are you doing here?"

She looked up, breathing hard, with sweat beaded on her forehead. "I'm complicating our friendship."

She grabbed his shirt and kissed him.

. . .

It took a moment for Marcus's brain to catch up with what was happening. One minute he was checking his voicemail, and the next, Journey was molded against his body with her mouth fiercely on his. He moved his hands up her body to her bare arms that held him still.

Yes, this is really happening, he decided.

He pulled back and studied her golden eyes for a moment. She looked absolutely terrified and absolutely desperate for him at the same time. Her fingernails scraped the back of his neck. Her lips were parted, waiting for him to say or do something… anything.

A million thoughts raced through his mind.

In one swift motion, he closed the door and pressed her back against it. His fingers tangled in her hair as he tasted her lips again. This moment had been his favorite fantasy for years, and he couldn't get close enough fast enough.

He lifted her off the floor, and she tightened her legs around his waist making it easier for him to walk, carry her, and toss her shirt across the room all at once. The moment that he laid her down onto his bed, he knew it was exactly where he wanted her to be for the rest of his life.

10

THE MAGIC WAND

JOURNEY RETURNED to Nashville as she had planned, though Marcus tried his best to talk her out of going. She had made a commitment to Elena's office for a summer internship, and she had a lease on an apartment that she didn't want to break. And, as much as she was enjoying being with Marcus, she didn't want to jinx it by moving too fast. He understood, but he certainly wasn't happy about it. She promised that at the end of the summer they would reevaluate her living situation, and she would seriously consider moving back to Emerson. In the meantime, he visited whenever he had time off.

On Friday morning, Journey's cell phone rang as she walked out of her apartment. It was Marcus. "Hey," she answered.

"Hey," he said. "I just wanted to tell you good morning before work."

She smiled. "Thanks. I'm headed there now."

"I'll be on my way tomorrow by three o'clock," he said as she got in her car.

Her eyes widened. "You're getting off early?"

"Yeah. I switched my shift so I could get on the road earlier," he said.

She started her engine and backed out of her space. "I can't wait to see you," she told him.

"Me too," he said. "Have you made any fun plans for us this weekend?"

"Yes," she replied. "But it's a secret. You'll just have to wait and see."

"Does it involve me getting to see you naked?" he asked.

She laughed as she waited at the light to exit her apartment complex. "I'm sure you will find a way to work that into my plans."

"Well, make sure we aren't too busy," he said. "I have a surprise of my own."

She was wondering if he was making a sex reference when the traffic light turned green. "I can only imagine…" she began just when the front fender from another car slammed through her passenger's side door.

. . .

The line went dead in Marcus's hand. Having heard the sound of clashing metal a few times in his reckless driving youth, his heart began to pound. He dialed her number again. It went straight to voicemail. "Hey, it's Journey. I'm probably digging around trying to find my phone…"

He shouted a few obscenities and dialed her again to no avail. He pulled his truck over to the side of the road and called Elena. She answered on the fourth ring. "Hello?"

"Elena, hey it's Marcus," he said, trying to slow his breathing.

"Hey, what's up?" she asked.

"Are you home?"

She hesitated. "Yeah. Getting ready for work. What's going on?"

"I need you to drive to Journey's apartment. I'm afraid there's been an accident," he said, using all of his cop skills to try and remain calm.

Elena didn't have that ability. "What?!"

He took a deep breath. "I was on the phone with her while she was driving. I heard something that sounded like a crash, and the line went dead. I can't get her back on the phone."

Elena was fumbling around so much Marcus knew she might drop and break her phone at any second. "I'm grabbing my shoes!" she shouted.

"Elena, I need you to calm down. The last thing we need is for you to have a wreck," he said, forcing his words out slowly.

She was breathing into the phone. "I'll call you back."

The line went dead, and Marcus slammed his fist into his steering wheel.

. . .

"Ma'am, are you OK?" Someone was shouting at Journey when she floated back to consciousness. She was in her driver's seat holding the airbag that was deployed from the steering wheel and staring at her apartment building. Her car had been spun completely around. Sunlight glimmered off the glass shards that surrounded her. Somewhere, rubber was burning.

She blinked her eyes and focused on the red-haired man at her window. He had more freckles than God should've put on anyone. "I think so," she stammered. "What happened?"

"That car ran a red light and hit you," he said. "Sit still. We've already called 911."

Journey didn't have any choice but to sit still. The passenger's seat was pinning her against the steering wheel. She blinked again and realized she couldn't see—or feel—her right arm. Everything went black.

The next time she came to, she could feel hands on her. "I think she's waking up," someone said. "Journey! Can you hear me?"

Journey's eyes slowly came into focus. A paramedic was kneeling beside her open door. Her neck was in a brace. She could see her sister standing behind him with her hands in the prayer position. Elena's face lit up when their eyes met. The whole car shuddered, and a jolting pain shot through her. She cried out.

The paramedic had one hand behind her head. "Look at me, Journey," he instructed.

She focused on his face. "What's happening?"

"Your arm is pinned under the steering wheel and the dashboard. We are working on getting you out of there. Just stay with me," he said.

She cried out again as more pieces of the car shifted. Desperately, she prayed to pass out again, but the black veil never came. After what seemed like an eternity, she felt her shoulder move as pain seared through her chest. "Good, good," the paramedic said. "Try not to move. We are going to get you out."

A team of uniformed men lifted her onto a waiting stretcher. Journey stretched out her left arm toward Elena who took hold of her hand. "I'm here," Elena assured her.

"How bad is it?" Journey asked, feeling her entire body begin to tremble.

Elena shook her head. "Not too bad," she said forcing a smile. Journey recognized the fear in her eyes.

They lifted the stretcher into the back of an ambulance. Pain radiated down her right side, and she could feel the pain in her arm. At least she knew it was still attached; she hadn't been so sure that it was before. Elena climbed into the back of the ambulance with her.

"Is anyone else hurt?" Journey asked.

"The guy that hit you was taken to the hospital while they were trying to get you out, but he was talking, so I think he's OK," she replied.

Journey tried to nod, but her head was stabilized. She heard a phone ring, and she remembered Marcus and panicked. "Elena, you have to call Marcus. He's probably freaking out."

Elena squeezed her hand. "Marcus is already on his way here."

"On his way?" Journey asked. "He has to work. Call him, and tell him I'm fine and not to come."

Elena laughed and rolled her eyes. "*Right*. Your boyfriend called the police department and got the play-by-play before I even got here. He's probably closer to the hospital than we are." She made a sour face. "Mom and Dad are coming too."

Journey felt tension in her chest. "How bad am I?"

The paramedic feverishly worked to insert a catheter into her good arm to start an IV. He didn't look old enough to be an emergency worker. He finally met her gaze. "We don't see anything life threatening," he said and patted her left shoulder. He grimaced a little. "I can tell you that your right arm is definitely going to need some attention."

Journey groaned with pain. "I can tell you that too."

"Do you know if you're allergic to any meds?"

"I'm not."

"I'm starting you on some morphine now. They will check you out at the hospital, and then we'll know more," he said.

Journey's teeth began to chatter. "I can't stop shaking."

"That's normal," he said. "It's adrenaline."

The shock had completely worn off by the time they reached the emergency room. Even with the morphine,

Journey's whole body was throbbing with unimaginable pain. They wheeled her inside and parked her behind a thin curtain. Nurses fluttered around taking her vital signs and asking her so many questions that her head was starting to spin.

A female in a long white coat walked in. She was in her early forties and had her brown hair pulled back in a tight bun. She adjusted her glasses and touched Journey's good arm. "Ms. Durant, I'm Dr. Stahl. I would ask how you're feeling, but I think I can guess that one for myself."

"Yeah." Tears were leaking uncontrollably from her eyes.

"We are going to start with some routine tests. I want to do a full CT scan because of the severity of the accident before we do anything else, but I'm going to go ahead and increase your morphine," she said. "Are you allergic to any medications?"

"No," Journey answered.

"Are you, or could you be, pregnant?"

Journey didn't think so. "Anything is possible, I guess."

"OK," Dr. Stahl said. "I'm going to let Nina, your nurse, draw some blood, and then we'll get you up to radiology. Can you tell me about your pain?"

"I'm really sore all over, but my right arm..." Journey's voice trailed off.

The doctor nodded. "Oh, it's broken. I don't need a machine to tell me that. You have an open compound fracture that is going to require surgery. We've got it packed and stabilized right now. Are you especially hurting anywhere else?"

"My head," Journey replied.

Again, the doctor nodded. "You definitely hit your head. They tell me you lost consciousness a couple of times." The doctor gently touched Journey's skull. "Is it just pain or do you feel pressure?"

"Just pain, I think."

"How is your vision? Is it blurry at all?"

"No," Journey answered.

"What about dizziness? Confusion? Or difficulty thinking?"

"No," Journey said while the doctor flashed a light in her eyes.

Dr. Stahl nodded. "I think it's probably just a mild concussion, but like I said, we will do a full CT scan and rule out anything major."

"Thank you," Journey told her.

The doctor winked an eye and left the room.

While the nurse was drawing blood, Elena's phone rang. "It's Marcus."

"Can you hold it to my ear?" Journey asked.

Elena answered the call. "Hey Marcus. Hang on. She wants to talk to you." Elena held the phone to Journey's ear.

"Hey," Journey said.

"Oh my god," he panted.

"I'm sorry. I know I scared the hell out of you."

"Are you freaking kidding? You're apologizing? I'm just so glad to hear your voice. How are you? What's going on?"

"I hurt so bad," she softly cried.

He groaned. "I'm so sorry."

"But I'm not dying, and they gave me morphine. My arm is definitely broken, and I hit my head. They are doing a bunch of tests, and I'm going to have to have surgery. Please slow down on the road. I know you're flying down the interstate right now," she said.

"Ehh," he said. "Ninety-eight isn't too bad."

"Marcus," she scolded.

"I'll probably be there in about three and a half hours," he said. "I'm so glad you're OK. I love you."

"I love you, too."

A few minutes after she said goodbye to Marcus, the doctor returned with the nurse who was holding a couple of IV bags. "Well, slight change of plans," Dr. Stahl said, walking to the edge of the bed. "There's no easy way to say this but… your pregnancy test came back positive."

If Journey hadn't been lying down, she would have fainted. "What?"

"Seriously?" Elena asked.

The doctor nodded. "Looks like it. So, before we do anything, I want to get an O.B. down here to check you out. Then we can decide what to do from there. In the meantime, I'm going to give you morphine because it's good for you and relatively safe for your baby."

The words 'your baby' hung in the air like hot, damp laundry.

The doctor held up her hands as if to cheer. "Surprise!" she said awkwardly. She gently pinched Journey's toe. "Try not to freak out too much."

Another female doctor came in a little while later and introduced herself as Dr. Woods. She was younger and prettier than Dr. Stahl. She had a kind face. "I'm an obstetrician," she explained. "I hear this is a big day for you."

"Understatement of a lifetime," Journey said.

Dr. Woods sympathetically patted her hand. "I've had patients find out in worse ways." She smiled. "Do you remember the first day of your last period?"

Journey thought for a second. "I got pregnant on the night of May 27th." She and Marcus had gotten a little carried away that first night together and didn't bother with protection.

The doctor and Elena laughed.

Dr. Woods made some notes on the clipboard she was holding. She thought for a few minutes. "It's still going to be really early to try and see anything on an ultrasound. So, I'm not going to waste time with that before they address your obvious injuries. Do you know if you had any trauma to your pelvis or abdomen?" Dr. Woods lifted her shirt and pressed around gently on her midsection.

"I don't think so," Journey said. "My right knee hurts like hell, but that's the closest to my stomach."

The doctor pulled Journey's shirt back down. "I don't see anything alarming. With your injuries, you don't have any option but to have surgery. You have a big risk for infection right now. With it being so early on in the pregnancy, we will just have to wait and see. I won't lie; the trauma might terminate the pregnancy, if it hasn't already. Or, your baby might be perfectly fine in there." She squeezed Journey's hand. "We just need to wait. I'll schedule an ultrasound post-op and tell radiology to take the necessary precautions while they do the CT scan."

"OK," Journey said. "But the medicine…"

"The morphine is fine. At this point the stress on your body from the pain would probably be worse on the fetus," she said.

Journey suddenly realized how instantly concerned she was.

She looked at her sister. "Don't tell Marcus. I don't want him to know until after the surgery."

. . .

Marcus had been making the 336 mile trip to Nashville from Emerson for the two and a half years Journey lived there—and every weekend in a row for the past month—but he had never made it there in less than four hours. He arrived in time to wait out the last half hour of Journey's four hour surgery. He and Elena were waiting in the patient room, where they would move her after clearing her from the recovery room, when her parents walked in.

Marcus stood when they entered. Elena went to hug them, and Randall extended his hand to Marcus. "Son," he said by way of a greeting.

"How is she?" Carol asked.

Marcus looked at Elena to see if she would answer or if he should.

She spoke first. "She's in the recovery room. They came out and told us that the surgery went well, but they had to put in two titanium plates and twelve screws. Both of the bones in her forearm were completely broken."

Her mother groaned.

"Her shoulder was dislocated also, but they were able to reset it without surgery," Elena added.

"And nothing else was broken?" her father asked.

Marcus let out a deep breath and shook his head. "No. Thank God. They said she's really banged up though."

Elena shuddered. "It took them about forty-five minutes to get her out of the car."

Randall blew out a long puff of air, and Marcus clapped him on the back.

"I'm glad you're here," Journey's dad told him.

Marcus was surprised. "Of course." He gestured down at his gym clothes and laughed. "I was on my way to work out."

Carol smiled and hugged him. "You sweet boy."

Just then, two nurses rolled Journey's bed into the room. His chest tightened when he saw her. Her right arm was hidden by blood-stained wraps and splints. The right side of her face looked slightly burned, her eye was black, and a gash on her forehead was butterflied shut. The rest of her was covered by a sheet. Marcus stayed out of the way while the nurses got her settled, and when they finished, he was at her side.

Her eyes were barely open, but she smiled when he came

into her view. He took hold of her good hand and leaned down close. "Hey," he said. "How do you feel?"

"Like I've been hit by a car," she whispered.

"Your mom and dad just got here," he told her.

"Hi honey," Carol said over Marcus's shoulder. He ushered her parents forward realizing he was probably being rude. Her mother sat down on the edge of her bed, and Randall leaned over and kissed her on the uninjured side of her forehead.

The nurse laid what looked like a game show buzzer on Journey's chest. Marcus knew it was a pain medicine pump. "Journey," the nurse said. "Don't forget when the light is green you can push the button for more morphine."

The light was green.

Carol picked up the pump. "Here, let me help you…" she began.

Journey pushed the button back down. "Mom," she choked out. "I need a minute alone with Marcus please."

Carol looked surprised but nodded. "Of course, honey," she said, stepping away.

Elena touched her mom on the shoulder. "Let's give them some privacy."

The three of them backed toward the door, and Journey weakly reached toward her boyfriend. "I need to talk to you," she said.

He curiously stepped toward her and took her hand. He made a skeptical face. "If you're breaking up with me, you've got terrible timing."

He could tell she wanted to laugh, but it hurt too much.

He gestured toward the morphine pump. "You know that little button will help, right? You're finally able to legally get high and not be in trouble for it."

She nodded. "Yeah, but that's what I need to talk to you about."

He was confused, but he kept quiet.

She gently squeezed his hand. She took a labored breath and struggled to open her eyes wider. "I'm a little pregnant," she finally said.

"You're what?" he asked, certain he had misheard her.

"They did a pregnancy test and it came back positive," she explained.

Marcus suddenly felt dizzy, so he sank down beside her on the bed. "Ummmm… OK. Wow." He rubbed his face, and she tugged on his hand.

"Are you freaking out?"

He laughed. "Trying not to." He took a few deep breaths and tried to bring his priorities back into focus. She was the woman that he loved. She was hurting. And he was certain that she was probably a lot more freaked out than he was. He decided to try and lighten the mood. "Was this the surprise you had planned for me?"

Again she tried to laugh. "No. I had no idea. I got tickets to the Patriots-Titans game for us on Sunday. Surprise."

He pushed her hair back gently. "I don't think we are going to make the game."

She smiled.

He shifted in his seat. "What do you mean by 'a little pregnant'?" he asked. "Isn't it kind of an all or nothing sort of thing?"

"The doctor said that I may or may not be pregnant. It's really early, and with the car accident and everything…" her voice trailed off, and he noticed tears in her eyes.

He understood. He leaned down and kissed her softly on the lips. "Hey, hey," he consoled her. "We'll figure this out."

He wiped away a tear as it slipped back onto her pillow. Her poor face looked so painful, and he wished there was anything he could do to make her feel better. He placed his hand on her stomach. "Can I tell you a secret?"

She looked at him with questioning eyes.

He bent toward her and lowered his voice. "I hope you are pregnant."

She laughed through her tears. "Whatever."

He shook his head and rubbed her midsection. "I'm serious. You're still a flight risk. If you have my baby you'll never be able to get rid of me."

She laughed again and winced with pain. He suddenly realized why she wasn't taking the morphine. "The doctor said I should, but I'm trying not to take it," she explained.

He picked up the button and pressed it. He couldn't stand seeing her in so much pain. "If you can't rest and get well, that isn't healthy for the baby."

She obediently nodded. "Elena knows, but I don't want to tell Mom and Dad till we find out for sure what's going."

Marcus started laughing. "I wish I had brought my body armor. Your dad is going to kill me."

. . .

Marcus spent the night at the hospital with Journey, while her parents went home to sleep at her apartment. They offered to bring her some of her things and, though she felt very awkward about it, she had to ask them to bring some of the clothes Marcus had left there over the past month as well. She realized that no matter how old she got, she would probably never stop fearing their disapproval. They weren't surprised, however, and agreed to bring them anything they needed.

Before her parents returned in the morning, Dr. Woods came in to check on her. "Knock, knock," she said to announce her presence at the door.

Journey looked up from the bed as the doctor came into the room. "Good morning."

"You look much better today," Dr. Woods said as she

approached the bed. It was then that she noticed Marcus, and she paused hesitantly.

Journey nodded. "It's OK. This is my boyfriend, Marcus Garrett. He knows."

Marcus extended his hand.

She accepted it and smiled. "I'm Dr. Woods. Journey's obstetrician." She turned her focus back to Journey. "It looks like everything went well with your surgery. How are you feeling?"

"Sore," Journey answered.

The doctor nodded. "I'm sure." Just then a nurse wheeled in a large computer-shaped device. "I want to go ahead and do an ultrasound this morning if that's OK."

Journey nodded. "Sure."

"Do you want me to stay?" Marcus asked.

"Yes. You caused this," Journey said, winking at him.

The nurse began hooking up the odd machine. Dr. Woods filled out something on a clipboard. "This is a transvaginal ultrasound. Have you ever had anything like this done before?"

Journey shook her head.

"It's going to be a little awkward," the doctor said and held out what looked like a giant magic wand.

Journey raised an eyebrow. "Are you casting a spell on the baby?"

Dr. Woods smiled, and Journey blushed when she explained how it was used.

Marcus looked down at her with wide blue eyes. "Is it wrong that I'm a little turned on right now?"

Journey, the doctor, and the nurse all laughed.

A few moments later, the doctor switched on the machine. Between the pain of moving her legs at all and the ultrasound gizmo, Journey was quite… uncomfortable.

After a few seconds, Dr. Woods turned the cart a little so Journey could see the fuzzy black and white screen. The doctor pointed to a black blob in the middle of all the white fuzz. "This is called the gestational sac. It's where the fetus grows." She moved the wand around a little and pressed a button on a keyboard with her free hand to enlarge the picture. Then she pointed to a tiny little bean shape on the edge of the blob. "Do you see that?"

Journey nodded.

"That is your baby," she said. "And this tiny blinking light is the baby's heartbeat."

Journey sucked in a deep breath and held it. Marcus's grip on her hand was making her fingers go numb. "It's alive?" Journey asked.

The doctor nodded and smiled. "Very much so. The heart rate looks wonderful. Maybe a tad bit slow, but that's probably because of the morphine," she said.

Marcus kissed Journey's hand and laughed. "No way!"

"This little guy isn't out of the woods yet," she explained. "But this is much better than I expected. We will keep an eye on it while you're here, and as soon as you're released you'll need to follow up with myself or another O.B. immediately."

More uncontrollable tears fell down Journey's cheeks. She was so happy and terrified that she felt a little queasy. She looked at Marcus in disbelief. "We're going to have a baby."

He leaned over and pressed his lips to hers. "We're going to have a baby."

11

THE BIG DAY

JOURNEY PUT her hands on her hips in front of the full length mirror of her new master bathroom and groaned. "This is such a cliché."

Her mother laughed behind her. "I think *cliché* is the closest I'm ever going to get to *traditional* with you," Carol said as she clasped a simple diamond solitaire necklace around Journey's neck.

Journey smoothed the soft white fabric over her nineteen-week baby bump. The dress was short and sleeveless. It was fitted at the top and then fell loose just below the silver sash that crowned her growing tummy. Her mother, dressed in a lace covered skirt suit, smiled over her shoulder. She pulled Journey's gently curled hair back into place, flowing down her back. "You really do look beautiful."

Journey turned to survey her right side more closely. "Do you think I should wear the shawl?" she asked as she studied the bright pink scars that hideously decorated her arm.

Carol shook her head. "Not at all. No one will even notice."

Journey doubted her words but appreciated the sincerity in them. She reached up and squeezed her mother's hand that rested on her shoulder. "Thanks, Mom."

"Your groom looks pretty handsome as well," Carol said, urging her in the direction of the window.

Journey peeked out to see Marcus laughing with his partner, Curtis Martin, on the back patio. He had sunglasses resting on the top of his head, and he was holding a beer bottle in his hand. He wore a light gray suit and white shirt that was unbuttoned at the top. Journey had disallowed him from wearing a tie. His black hair was cropped short on the sides but a little messy on top. He had just a hint of a five o'clock shadow. The ceremony hadn't even started yet, and she was already looking forward to the wedding photos of him. He was still one of the most beautiful men she had ever seen in person. How on earth they wound up together continually baffled her.

Elena stuck her head in the bathroom door. "You about ready?"

"Just need to get my shoes on," Journey answered.

"Do you need help?" her mother asked.

Journey shook her head. "No, I can do it."

Carol kissed her daughter's cheek. "I'll see you out there, Mrs. Garrett," she said with a sweet smile.

Her mother and sister left her alone to tend to her silver sandals. She sat down at the vanity and bent to strap them around her ankles. Her phoenix tattoo was still bright with color. She still loved her tattoo as much as the day Marcus and Kara had bought it for her. That birthday felt like it was part of a different lifetime. As she ran her hand over the colorful ink, the light from the window bounced off her thumb ring, and her heart twinged with a familiar pain.

Journey's life was full and happy. She had recently moved into Marcus's big, beautiful home near the river. They had just found out that week that they were expecting a baby girl. She was the envy of every girl in Emerson, marrying the most sought-after bachelor in the tri-state area. And while Journey had never been the type of girl who dreamed about her wedding day, if she had, this wedding would've been her dream. Most of all, she was moments away from walking down the makeshift aisle in her backyard to marry a man that she truly loved and respected. But in that instant, the glimmer of sunlight off a scuffed and tarnished silver band ushered in David Britton's memory like an uninvited, belligerent in-law.

She couldn't help but wonder where he was and what he had become. She wondered if he, too, had fallen in love with someone else. She wondered if he was happy. She wondered if he ever thought about her. As desperately as she didn't want it to, her heart ached for that irrevocable moment in time when she knew she had chosen wrong. She took a deep breath and repeated Kara's words in her mind. *He hasn't even looked for you…*

Journey took a deep and labored breath. For the first time since David gave her the ring, Journey purposefully slipped the band off of her thumb. She traced her finger over it for a moment, read its heartfelt—but false—inscription one last time, and then placed it in her vanity drawer. As she slowly closed the drawer, she silently vowed to finally put David Britton to rest and stop ripping off the metaphorical scab on the wound that his sudden departure had left behind.

She straightened the new ring that was on another finger. It was an antique diamond engagement ring from the 1920's. It had belonged to Marcus's grandmother who passed away the year before. His grandparents had been married for fifty-two years.

There was a light knock on the bathroom door and her father, in his best Sunday suit, stepped inside. "They're playing your song, sweetheart."

She dabbed carefully at her eyes with a tissue, then smiled and stood up. She picked up her flowers. "I'm ready."

12

Laying Eggs

MARCUS WAS desperately trying to be a good husband when he insisted on taking Journey out to dinner for Valentine's Day, but in the last days of her pregnancy, it seemed that no matter how hard he tried, he couldn't do anything right. Dinner ended early with a to-go bag and his profuse apologies to their waitress. Journey's mother had encouraged them both to spend time together before the baby came, but lately he was becoming more and more afraid that spending time together might get him killed.

"I told you that Chinese food in bed would have been much more romantic," she told him as he helped her get out of the car when they arrived back home.

He held her hand as she waddled through the garage. "Have I told you lately that I'm really ready for you to not be pregnant anymore?"

"You did this to me," she grumbled.

"I know. You won't let me forget." He held open the door

for her. "You look pretty, though."

She groaned. "I'm as big as the broad side of a barn."

"A very pretty barn," he said with a wink before locking the garage door behind them.

She held up her middle finger and eased her swollen body into a chair at the breakfast table. "You know what I think?" she asked.

He looked over at her. "That all men should be castrated and/or burnt at the stake?"

"Besides that," she answered. "I think women should lay eggs."

He laughed while shaking his head. "Lay eggs, huh?"

She nodded and rested her hands on her huge belly. "Yes. I'm not sure how all that works, but I wanna sign up for that kind of childbirth. Do you know how much easier that would be?"

He nodded and washed his hands at the sink. "I'm sure it would be much easier."

She moaned and kicked off her shoes onto the tile floor. "Did you know that a very common pesticide has been known to actually transform male frogs into female frogs that can lay eggs?"

He looked at her sideways as he took the food containers out of the bag. "I'm not sure I even want to know how you came across that information."

She shrugged. "I read it."

"Are you planning on poisoning me?"

"Not today, honey," she said.

He cocked his eyebrow, noting that she didn't laugh. He placed her chicken parmesan on the table in front of her and bent to give her a quick kiss on the lips. "I would lay eggs for you if I could, baby."

Journey shifted awkwardly in her seat as he retrieved two

glasses from the cabinet. "Your daughter won't get her foot out of my damn ribcage." She looked down at her stomach. "Please get out of me!"

He tried really hard not to laugh. "What do you want to drink?"

"Vodka."

He laughed. "Water? Is that what I heard?"

"You asked what I wanted," she reminded him.

He looked at her, waving the empty glass in his hand.

She sighed. "Chocolate milk."

He looked at her $35 fine Italian dinner and laughed. Chocolate milk seemed to be her drink of choice that month. He poured her glass full, got water for himself, and sat down across from her. "Happy Valentine's Day, wife," he said, holding his water up for a toast.

She clinked her glass with his. "Happy Valentine's Day, husband."

She drained half the glass before she put it down. "I'm sorry I've been such a witch to you lately."

"You're fine." He smiled before devouring a forkful of lasagna. "You're carrying another human around inside of you. I think that would make anyone grumpy."

She ate five bites and half of her slice of garlic bread before pushing the plate away. "It's really delicious, but I have no room for food."

He reached over and squeezed her hand. "It's OK. How about a hot bath?"

She laughed. "My lower back has been so sore for the past few days that a bath sounds like heaven, but I don't think I can get in and out of the bathtub."

He stood and offered his hand to her. "Come on. I can handle that part."

She hoisted herself up onto her feet and then squatted

down to pick up her shoes before he could stop her.

"Journey, let me…"

She interrupted him, laughing hysterically.

"What is it?" he asked, pulling her back up to standing.

She cradled her belly still laughing. "I peed a little."

He laughed and kissed her forehead. "Come on. Let's get you in the bath, Mrs. Garrett."

When they made it to their master bedroom down the hall, she sat on the king sized bed while he went into the bathroom and started running hot water into the tub. "Do you want bubbles?" he called to her.

"No," she replied. "And not too hot, please, or my feet will swell even more. My tattoo on my ankle is starting to look pregnant."

When he went back to the bedroom to help her out of her clothes, she had reclined back on the bed. All he could see was her belly and her legs. He covered his mouth, so as not to laugh out loud and incite her wrath. "Come on, Mama," he said, reaching for her hands.

"You're gonna have to pull me up."

He laughed. "I know."

He helped her sit up, and she slowly stood. The moment she was vertical, she bent at the hips and cradled her stomach again. "Uh oh."

His head snapped up. "What is it?"

"Either I peed my pants again, or my water is leaking."

"Your water?" he asked.

She nodded and tried to straighten. Before she could get fully vertical, she whimpered again. "Yep. I definitely think my water broke."

He looked down at her pants and saw they were wet down the inside of her legs. His chest tightened, and his hands began to sweat. "The baby is coming?"

She was pinching her knees together. "I think so. Help me get to the bathroom so I don't ruin the carpet."

"Forget the carpet!" he shouted. "We've got to get to the hospital. We can take the squad car! I'll turn on the siren and…"

"Marcus!"

He snapped to attention. She was laughing.

"Deep breaths," she said. "Get me to the bathroom, and then call the doctor."

She was so calm it frustrated him. He gripped her arms and helped her shuffle to the tile bathroom. "Help me into the shower," she said.

He panicked. "We don't have time for a shower!"

"Marcus! I'm going to sit on the seat in the shower while you call the doctor and bring me some dry pants," she told him.

With one sweep of his hand, he gathered all of the shampoo and soaps off of the shower seat. He helped her sit down and dropped the bottles into the tub behind him before shutting off the running bathwater.

He patted himself down. "Crap. My phone is in the kitchen. Are you going to be OK if I go get it?"

She nodded slowly. "I'm fine. Go get your phone and bring me a pair of clean leggings. The doctor's number is on the refrigerator."

He took one last inquisitive look at her to make sure she was alright before sprinting to the kitchen. His phone was on the table. He grabbed it and dialed the doctor's office only to get an answering service and a very adamant woman who wasn't moved at all by his frantic demands for a doctor. "They are going to call us back," he said as he reentered the bathroom.

"Pants," she reminded him.

"Oh yeah." He ducked back into the bedroom and grabbed the first thing his fingers found in her drawer. He walked back and handed them to her.

She frowned and handed the glittery fabric right back to him. "Try again."

He let out an exasperated sigh and returned to the bedroom. For his second attempt, he dumped the entire contents of the dresser drawer out onto the floor. He grabbed a pair of gray pants and held them around the bathroom door before wasting his footsteps. "These?"

"Those are fine," she replied. "I also need some panties."

He rifled through another drawer and found a pair of pink thongs that he hadn't seen in a long, long time. He carried both of them to her and presented them proudly. She dangled the thong from her index finger. "Are you serious?" she asked. "Help me up. I'll do it myself."

"No, I can do this!" he argued.

"Apparently not. Help me up," she repeated.

He helped her to her feet and out of the shower. The wet spot on her pants was definitely spreading. He thought his heart was going to beat out of his chest.

She threw the thongs across the room and draped the gray pants over her shoulder. She kept one hand securely under her stomach. "I feel like this baby is going to fall out onto the floor."

Marcus almost cried. "Please dear God no!"

She stopped shuffling and turned to face him. She grabbed both sides of his face. "I need you to keep it together. I am not even having bad contractions yet. This is going to get a lot worse before it gets better. I don't need you pussing out on me now."

"But you are having contractions?" he asked.

She nodded. "Have been on and off all day."

"All day?!" His voice cracked like he had just hit puberty.

She gave him a warning look. "Marcus."

He snapped his lips closed. "Sorry."

When they reached the mess of clothes he had made on the floor she put her hand on her hip and glared at him. He just gave her an awkward half-smile and shrugged his shoulders. She pulled open her panty drawer and retrieved a pair of underwear he was pretty sure would fit him and her at the same time if necessary. She also pulled out his New England Patriots sweatshirt, that he had been looking for all winter. She carried the ensemble back to the bed.

"Can you get me a hand towel?" she asked as she leaned against the mattress. "That's the one that's between the size of a washcloth and a—"

He cut her off. "I know what it is!"

He saw her chuckle out of the corner of his eye as she shimmied out of her black pants. His phone buzzed in his pocket. "Hello?" he answered quickly.

"This is Dr. Heerman," a woman said on the other end.

He carried a hand towel back to the bedroom and handed it to Journey. "Hi, this is Marcus Garrett. My wife is leaking and is having contractions, and she feels like the baby might fall out on the floor—"

"Give me the damn phone," Journey insisted as she shoved the folded hand towel between her thighs.

Marcus passed her his cell phone and helped her pull on her ridiculously oversized underwear. He listened intently to her end of the conversation. "Sorry about that," she said. "My husband is losing his mind." Marcus helped his wife stuff the towel into the panties as best as he could. Journey continued talking to the doctor, and she carefully stepped into the clean pair of pants. "I've been having contractions very sporadically all day and didn't pay them too much attention until now.

They aren't very bad at all, but now I'm pretty sure that my water has broken… Uh, huh. OK, we will come on to the hospital now. Yes. Thank you. I will tell him." She laughed and ended the call. "The doctor said to tell you, 'slow deep breaths, just like we practiced,'" she teased.

"Shut up," he whimpered.

He pulled the stretchy pants up over her butt, the towel, and the offensively large panties. As he rose from the floor, she grabbed him again by the face and pulled him up to meet her. She smiled and pressed her lips to his. "Are you ready to be a daddy, Mr. Garrett?"

. . .

Genesis Evelyn Garrett was born at 6:13 AM on the morning after Valentine's Day. Marcus chose the name Evelyn for his late grandmother, and Journey picked Genesis to symbolize the beginning of their new family. "Genna" was a plump eight pound baby that screamed for the first two hours she was born. Marcus equated that to her not being a morning person, just like her momma.

13

Hand Guns and Diaper Bags

JOURNEY WAS surprised the day that Marcus decided to catapult their family into the 21st century by bringing home their first desktop computer. He had always been so adamant about not having one at home because he used one so much at work. She really didn't care if they had one or not. If she needed the Internet, she would go to her mom's house or Kara's apartment. She eyed him suspiciously as he lay under the desk in the office connecting all of the wires. "How much money did you spend on that thing?" she asked.

"I had to get it for work," he said. "I need to be able to check the office bulletins."

"Whatever." She folded her arms across her chest and leaned against the doorframe. "You just want to look up naked women online."

He laughed out loud. "Do you think I have a death wish?" He slid out from under the desk and pressed the power button on the computer before standing up.

Genna cried out from her playpen in the living room. Journey walked into the room and found her little girl sitting up, playing with her feet. "Ba, ba, ba, ba, ba, ba," she babbled.

"Genna!" Journey cooed.

The bald baby girl dressed in pink looked up with her daddy's big crystal blue eyes. "Mum, mum, mum, mum." Journey thought her heart might melt into a puddle. Genna lifted her tiny arms up, and Journey scooped her up into her arms and kissed her little face.

"Who is Mommy's sweet baby girl? Did you have a good nap?" She kissed Genna again before carrying her back to the office. Marcus was seated in front of the screen. She walked over and wedged her way into his lap.

He laughed and kissed his wife. "Dad's beautiful girls," he said, rubbing Journey's back.

Journey draped her arm around his shoulders. "I'm going to change her diaper and go over to my mom's for a while."

"How is your mom?" he asked.

Journey's mother had undergone gallbladder surgery that week. "She's OK. Still in a lot of pain, but she's getting better. Genna and I are going to go to the grocery store for her and then maybe cook dinner for her and Dad. Do you want to go or are you going to stay here and play with your new toy?"

He gave her a guilty look.

She laughed and kissed his forehead. She bounced Genna on her knee. "Daddy's already neglecting us because of the Internet. It's just you and me, kid."

Marcus laughed and kissed Genna's little fingers. "I'll come over there for dinner. Just call me when it's almost ready."

She began to stand up, but he pulled her back down by her shirt and gave her a long, slow kiss. "I love you."

"Love you too, Daddy." She gave him a quick peck on the tip of his nose.

Journey packed what seemed like a month's worth of essentials into the diaper bag, changed Genna's wet diaper, and buckled the baby into her car seat. It was still summertime, so she quickly changed into cut off jean shorts, a sleeveless shirt, and her favorite pair of blue flip-flops. She checked her reflection in the mirror and silently thanked God that she had finally shed her baby weight. She pulled her hair up in a messy knot on the top of her head.

Genna was kicking her feet in her chair and shaking her plastic baby car keys. Journey lifted the car seat, which was getting heavier every day, and hooked her arm through the handle. "Are you ready to go see Nana?"

"Na na na na na na na," Genna repeated over and over again.

"Marcus, we are leaving. Call me later," she called as she carried the baby and half of the nursery down the hallway.

"Hey, I'm going to create an email address for you. What do you think about 'mrsmarcusgarrett-leavemywomanalone@yahoo.com?" he called from the office.

Journey paused to pick up her keys in the kitchen and laughed. "Whatever you think is best, babe."

"Love you!" he yelled. "Tell your mom I asked about her."

"I will. Love you too!"

Journey missed the days when she could shop for groceries alone without stressing about germs, questionable strangers, and poopy diaper emergencies. She hoped to make her trip in and out of FoodMart as quick as possible. About half way through the short list of essential items that her mother had given her over the phone, she turned down the drink aisle and froze in her tracks.

Brian Drake was lifting a case of cheap beer out of the cooler.

Journey shuffled a few steps backward, but before she

could get around the corner he looked up and saw her. Her breath hung in her chest as she turned her cart around slowly. Out of the corner of her eye, Brian moved in her direction. She let go of the cart and reached for Genna's car seat to make her exit without the items she had picked out, but a hand landed firmly on her shoulder.

Her heart was pounding so loud she could barely think.

"Journey, right?" Brian asked.

She slowly turned to meet his nearly black eyes. They were lined with creases which made him look older than his thirty-something years. His black hair was buzzed close to his scalp, and a faded green tattoo snaked up the side of his neck. His pants were at least two sizes too big, and his white shirt hung strangely around his waistband. She suspected he was carrying a gun.

"Sure you are," he said. "You were my brother's girlfriend. You were the one who put him in prison." He laughed, but neither of them were amused.

Journey swallowed hard. "What do you want?"

He held up his hands in defense. "Oh, I just wanted to say hello. It's been a really, really long time. How long has it been since you were screwing my brother... and then *screwed my brother?*"

Journey didn't answer, and as she moved toward the door, he stepped to block her path. He stepped closer to Genna's car seat. "Oh, is this your baby?" He reached out and let her clasp her tiny hand around his finger. He laughed again. "Look at that! She likes me!" He leaned toward her. "Do you want to come home with me sometime, pretty baby?"

Journey jerked the car seat away from his tattooed hand. "Get away from me," she hissed. "My husband's a cop."

He laughed. "Oh, that's right! The hero of Emerson that put my brother away! Where is he?" he asked, looking around.

Brian's voice and his eyes turned dark. "Oh, he's not here. *Is he?*"

"Get away from me!" Her raised voice drew the eyes of other patrons.

He raised his hands and slowly backed away from her chuckling softly.

She took advantage of the distance and darted toward the exit. She didn't stop running till she reached her car and unlocked it. She snapped Genna's car seat into its base before getting in the driver's seat and slamming the door closed. The loud noise made Genna start crying. Journey hit the door's lock button and dropped her forehead against the steering wheel.

When she raised her head, Brian was standing on the sidewalk about ten feet away leering at her. His menacing scowl radiated hatred. She quickly jammed the keys into the ignition and put the car in reverse. He continued staring at her until she couldn't see him anymore.

Genna was screaming.

Journey tried to soothe her daughter, but she was almost in hysterics herself. Rather than driving to her parents' house, she went directly back home. She kept checking in the rearview mirror, certain that she was being followed. She wasn't. As soon as she got the car into the garage and pulled Genna out of the backseat, she ran into the house.

Marcus came out of the office laughing. "What did you forget?"

The terror on her face was evident to her husband. He quickly stopped laughing and rushed to take the car seat from her. Her hands were trembling. He put Genna down on the table and began unfastening her safety restraints. "What's the matter?" he asked with wide eyes.

She sank into the chair at the table as Marcus pulled the

baby out of her seat and cuddled her to him. In his arms, Genna began to calm down.

"I just ran into Brian Drake at FoodMart." She rested her elbows on the table and dropped her head into her hands.

His mouth fell open. "Are you serious?" He sat down beside her. "Are you sure it was him?"

"Oh yeah."

"Did he talk to you?"

Journey nodded. "Yes. He knew exactly who I was and who you were. He knew it was me that put Steven in jail and you that locked him up."

"Did he threaten you?" Marcus asked.

She gave a noncommittal shrug. "Not exactly, but he scared the hell out of me. He kept talking about Steven and what you and I did and then he started talking to Genna." Journey shuddered.

"Come here," he said and pulled her against him. He kissed the side of her head, and she immediately began to relax. "Are you OK?"

She nodded and pulled back to wipe her eyes. She didn't even realize she was crying. "Yeah, I'm fine. Just really freaked out. He watched me from across the parking lot until I got onto the highway. He's just so evil."

"Can you take her?" Marcus asked, handing her the baby. "He's got a warrant out on him for a drug charge. I'm going to call in and have someone go look for him."

She nodded and took Genna into her arms. Genna reached up and put a hand on Journey's face. Marcus rose from the table and went back to the office. Journey pulled out her cell phone and called her mother to explain why she would be late, or not coming at all. By the time she ended the call, Marcus had returned.

He knelt down in front of her and cupped her jaw in his

strong hand. "Don't worry," he said. "I'm never going to let anything happen to you. I can promise you that."

. . .

After Marcus confirmed that the grocery store was clear of anyone from the Drake family, he strapped on his Glock 22 . 40 caliber and escorted his wife and daughter to the grocery store and her parents' house. Recently, he had a growing suspicion that Emerson's biggest drug dealer was back in town, and Journey's encounter with him confirmed it.

Brian Drake was being investigated by the DEA for heroin trafficking. There had been two overdose deaths in their small town so far that summer. Being that Emerson was between Atlanta and the coast, the federal government was anxious to find out the connection. Now that Brian had personally confronted his wife, Marcus was anxious as well.

Marcus knew better than to underestimate Brian, and he took all of the precautions he could through the police department. As soon as Marcus had made the initial phone call into the station, several groups of officers immediately began to search. A few, including Curtis, went to work on their day off. He also increased patrols near their home and planned to alert their closest neighbors to be aware of any suspicious activity. Everyone in his department immediately made capturing Brian Drake a top priority.

Once Marcus and Journey got home after dinner at her parents', and he did a thorough sweep around their house to ensure it was safe, he led Journey to their bedroom. He took Genna, who was sleeping peacefully in her arms, and laid her in the center of their king sized bed. He positioned pillows around her to keep her from rolling.

"Come with me," he said and pulled open the door to their huge master closet. He had designed the closet to be able to house his gun collection. He opened the first of two safes and searched for a moment before locating the Taurus Millennium G2 he had purchased for Journey when they got married.

She backed up a couple of steps. "Oh no," she said, shaking her head.

He removed the clip, locked the slide to the rear, and checked the chamber and magazine well. "I don't care what you say, Journey. You're going to start carrying this for a while."

She let out an exasperated puff. "And where am I supposed to carry it, Marcus? In the diaper bag between the formula and the butt rash cream?"

He scowled. "You can carry it taped to your forehead for all I care, but you are going to keep it with you at all times till we lock him up."

"You know how much I hate this." She carefully took the small handgun and kept it pointed safely away from them.

He folded his arms across his chest. "Tell me. Would you have been quite the disaster today if you had known you could blow his head off if it were absolutely necessary?"

She didn't answer.

Journey could outshoot some of the guys on the police force, and she had agreed, at his insistence, to get her concealed carry permit when he bought her the gun. However, much to his dismay, her gun stayed locked in the safe if they weren't behind the house shooting at targets.

He slipped his hand behind her neck and pulled her in for a soft kiss. He rested his forehead against hers. "Do it for me?" he asked, stroking the soft skin of her neck with his thumb.

She nodded, and he pulled back to examine her eyes. She was wearing a green top, which always brought out green in her golden eyes. Perhaps it was because Marcus was from a broken home, or maybe it was because he had spent so many years trying not to fall in love with her, but he actually ached with love for his wife. Her unfortunate rendezvous that day probably scared him more than it even scared her.

He kissed her again and cradled her face with both hands. Her nails pressed into his right side as he slid his hand down her arm and took the gun from her. He rested it on top of the safe before pressing into her body again. Her hands pushed his shirt up over his stomach, and her nails scraped down his bare skin causing him to shudder. He grasped her ponytail and released the band from her hair, letting it fall down around her shoulders. He ran his fingers through it and pulled her to his lips again.

And then there was a soft cry from the bedroom.

He groaned, and she covered his mouth. "Shhhh…" She silently laughed. "Maybe she will go back to sleep."

He squeezed her hipbones and waited before he got himself any more worked up than he already was. Sure enough, loud cries erupted from their bed. He closed his eyes and let out a slow, deep breath. "Damn," he growled.

"Nature's birth control," Journey laughed as he followed her out of the closet.

He leaned in the doorway to watch his wife crawl onto the bed and scoop up his baby girl into her arms. She kissed Genna's face. "What are you crying about?" she cooed at her.

He smiled as their daughter nuzzled into her mama's chest. "Want me to get a bottle?" he asked after a moment.

"Please," she replied. "And her jammies from the diaper bag."

The diaper bag was at the bedroom door. He retrieved the pajamas and the bottle of water and powdered formula dispenser. As Journey changed Genna into a pair of purple pajamas, he mixed up her bedtime bottle. "Want me to feed her?" he asked.

"You can if you want to," she said.

He held out his arms, and Journey placed the baby in his care. He kicked off his shoes and sat back against the pillows. Journey stretched out next to him as he offered Genna the bottle. Genna's sleepy eyes were fixed on his as she opened her mouth. He smiled, and Journey rested her head against his bicep. She was playing with Genna's finger, and Marcus noticed her fingernails were painted black. He smiled.

"I'll carry the gun," she said after a little while.

He nodded. "Thank you," he said quietly. "We can get some shooting practice in tomorrow before I go into work."

"I wonder if they make diaper bags with built-in holsters," she said.

He shrugged. "I don't know. I wouldn't be surprised. Honestly, I would rather you carry it on your body for at least a little while. We could get you a concealed waistband holster."

She sat up a little and looked at him. "Or a thigh holster or one of those new bra ones," she suggested.

He pressed his eyes closed and groaned a little. "Please don't talk about that right now. I'm having a hard enough time as it is, if you know what I mean."

She giggled and pushed herself up. "While you feed her, I'm going to get my pajamas on."

He looked at her seriously. "Either you wait until she falls asleep and I put her in her room, or you go change in the damn bathroom with the door closed." He laughed. "I mean it woman."

She laughed also and looked at him for a moment. Finally, she leaned over and kissed his lips. "I think I'll wait."

14

GHOSTS

MARCUS PICKED out the plot of land where he built his house for a few very specific reasons. At the top of the list was that it was outside of city limits. That meant lower taxes and less restrictions on what he could do on his private property. One of those benefits included not having to worry about strict firearm discharge laws. He could hunt and target shoot on his own property without interference from the city. Their secluded, wooded property line backed up to absolutely nothing, so Marcus built his own portable shooting range out of plywood and two-by-fours.

As promised, the next morning Marcus set up the targets in the backyard for some shooting practice. Twenty-five yards away, he set up a folding table and prepared the pistols and two spare magazines for each. He set out an extra box of ammunition as well; he knew how competitive practice shooting with his wife would probably become.

When Journey laid Genna down for a nap in her crib, she

came outside with a ball cap and sunglasses on. She carried the baby monitor in her hand. When she reached Marcus, he took the monitor and clipped it to his utility belt. Watching him, Journey doubled over laughing.

"What?" he asked.

She giggled and kissed him. "Nothing, baby. You're just such a good daddy." She pulled out her cell phone and took a picture of him, still snickering. "That's the funniest thing I've ever seen."

"Shut up," he said and stuck up his middle finger.

She laughed and tucked the phone back into her pocket. He watched as she picked up a pair of ear protectors and slipped them on before picking up her handgun. She was wearing jeans and a white halter top. As she slipped a magazine into the well and chambered a round, it was all he could do to not grab her. Watching her handle a firearm was one of the sexiest things he had ever seen.

Her triceps flexed as she raised the gun, aimed, and pulled the trigger. The target board shook with fury as she emptied her clip. She dropped the empty magazine out, checked the chamber, and placed the Taurus back onto the table. She held up her empty hands. "Your turn." She smiled, daring him to compete.

He laughed and put on his hearing protection. He picked up his Glock and chambered a bullet. "Are you ready to lose that grin?" he asked before firing one continuous round after another.

She was clapping when he removed his ear protectors. He checked his pistol before laying it down beside hers. "Not bad, Officer Garrett."

"Detective Garrett," he corrected her.

She bowed to him dramatically. "Excuse me, Detective."

He charged toward her like a linebacker and grabbed her

around the thighs. He tossed her over his shoulder and smacked her on the butt. She kicked and screamed as he carried her across the yard to the targets. He surveyed the impact spots from their bullets before setting her down. "Maybe someday, you'll be able to shoot like a pro, but you're not there yet," he teased, showing her how the majority of his shots hit the two inner circles center of his target.

She examined both targets before placing a finger near a stray bullet hole on the plywood. "And is this a pro's shot right here?" she asked, pulling her sunglasses down to the tip of her nose and flashing her eyes up at him.

"That's yours," he insisted.

She jerked up straight, letting her ponytail fly back into place. She pointed at him. "Lies!" she shouted.

He laughed, knowing he had missed the target altogether on at least one of his shots. He shrugged his shoulders. "I didn't want you to feel too bad about yourself."

She kicked him in the shin, and he winced.

"Wanna go again?" he asked.

She repositioned her sunglasses. "Heck yeah, I do!"

An hour later, they were out of ammo, and it was time for him to go into work. She helped him clean up the yard before he went inside to get dressed. As he was changing clothes, she walked in carrying Genna in her arms. "Look who woke up just in time to tell Daddy to have a good day at work." She bounced the baby on her hip.

He finished strapping on his tactical belt before reaching out and tickling Genna's hand. "Hey, sweet girl."

"Da, da, da, da," she sputtered.

He loved that sound.

He leaned over and kissed her and then kissed his wife. "Come with me. I want to show you something."

She followed him to the refrigerator in the kitchen. He

tapped the list that he had hung up with a magnet just above the ice dispenser. "This is the schedule of the patrol officers that will be coming through here. These are the officers' names and their cell phone numbers. If you have any problems, or see anything weird, call them directly. Don't waste time trying to call dispatch."

She nodded. "Thanks for doing that, honey. It makes me feel better."

He reached for her hand. "I can take the night off if you want me to. I can get someone to pick up my shift."

She squeezed his fingers. "No, don't do that. We'll be OK. I know you'll come running if we have any problems. I want you to go in and find that jerk."

He nodded. "Well, if you change your mind, just call me. Making sure you feel safe is the most important thing to me."

She kissed his lips. "I know."

"What are you going to do tonight?" he asked while he opened the refrigerator to pull out some leftovers to take for dinner.

She retrieved his lunchbox from the pantry. "Kara is going to come over for dinner. We'll probably watch some movies or something."

"Good. I'll feel better if you're not here alone," he said.

Outside, a car's horn sounded in the driveway. "I'll bet that's her now."

. . .

Kara walked into the house without knocking. "Hello, hello!" she called from the foyer.

"In the kitchen," Journey answered as she helped Marcus pack his meal for dinner.

Kara came in wearing a navy velour sweat suit and tennis shoes. "There's my favorite godchild!" She took Genna from Journey and kissed her face.

"Godchild?" Marcus asked, catching Journey's eye. "Are we Catholic now?"

Journey just laughed and shook her head. She pulled some frozen ground beef out of the freezer and placed it in the stainless steel sink. "How does baked spaghetti sound for dinner?" she asked Kara.

"Perfect," Kara replied. She danced around the dining room table and sang to the baby.

Marcus leaned over and kissed Journey on the lips. "I've gotta go. I love you."

"Love you, too. Be careful," she said.

He pointed at Kara. "You, try not to corrupt my family while I'm gone."

Kara laughed. "Corrupt your family? You're married to Journey, and you're worried about me?"

Journey threw a dish towel at her. "Hey!"

Marcus laughed. "You know she has a point."

"You go to work!" Journey barked at him.

"I'll be off at ten," he called from the doorway.

When he was gone, Kara pulled out a seat at the breakfast table. "OK, what happened yesterday?"

Journey retrieved two Diet Cokes from the refrigerator and sat down. She told Kara the whole story about seeing Brian Drake the day before.

"Are you going to press charges?" Kara asked.

Genna shoved her fist into her mouth and drooled onto Kara's lap. Journey got up and handed Kara a paper towel. "No. He didn't actually threaten me. Marcus is looking for him though. He has a warrant out on him." She peeled a banana and smashed it up in a bowl.

"I'll bet Marcus was furious," Kara said.

Journey carried the bowl and the spoon back to the table. "Oh yeah, he was," she answered, offering Genna a spoonful of bananas.

"Wasn't Steven eligible for parole a while back?" Kara asked.

Journey nodded. "Yeah, but Marcus heard it was denied because he assaulted a deputy."

Kara looked surprised. "Assaulted a deputy?"

"I was kinda shocked too, but Marcus said it was pretty common. Like, probably some kind of initiation thing for getting in with white supremacists in order to get protection in prison."

Kara thought for a moment. "But wasn't he only sentenced for four years? Shouldn't he be getting out soon?"

The thought alone made Journey shudder. "I'm not sure, but it seems like you might be right."

Kara thought for a moment. "Would he serve four years from when he was arrested or from when he was sentenced?"

"I'm pretty sure that all the time he spent in jail would count toward his time served," Journey said.

"He was convicted in June of 2000, right?" Kara asked.

Journey nodded and did the math in her head. She swallowed hard. "That means he should be out already."

Kara frowned. "That's not good. Are you worried about it?"

Journey pondered the question for a long moment. "Well, I'm sure he's not out or I would've already heard about it. I'm not thrilled about him being released, but I don't think I'm exactly worried either. I mean, I don't think he would try and come after me. Hopefully after spending four years in prison, the last thing he would want to do is risk going back, right?"

Kara shrugged and pushed her hair back off her shoulder. "That is the point of prison, I guess. She didn't sound convinced.

"Besides, even if he did want to hurt me, Marcus would

kill him," Journey added.

Kara nodded. "And Marcus will certainly keep an eye on him when he gets out and will make sure he doesn't put a toe out of line."

Genna sputtered bananas at Journey. "You little stinker." She laughed and wiped the baby's mouth and then the front of her shirt.

"So, what else is new with you?" Kara asked.

Journey rolled her eyes. "Marcus brought home a new toy yesterday."

Kara laughed. "A new assault rifle?"

"Close," Journey said. "A computer. He signed us up for Internet service and everything. I may never see him again."

Kara laughed loudly. "Look at you finally catching up with the rest of the universe! I'm so proud of you both!".

Journey rolled her eyes. "Shut up."

"You're going to start text messaging soon. I can feel it."

"Whatever," Journey said.

"Where is the computer? I want to see what he got," she said.

"It's in the office. I'm going to go change Genna's outfit if you want to go figure out how to turn it on."

Kara rose from the table and cuddled the baby to her chest. "No way. I wanna change her. You go and boot it up."

Journey laughed. "OK. She probably needs a new diaper too."

Kara held Genna up in the air. "Aunt Kara can handle it. Isn't that right, baby girl?"

"Don't give her cigarettes and alcohol while I'm not watching," Journey teased.

Kara chuckled as she started up the steps. "I'll save my bad influences on your daughter till she's at least sixteen."

"You'd better not let her Daddy hear you ever say that,"

Journey said.

She walked into the office and flipped the light on. After a few seconds of searching, she located the power button on the computer and pressed it. Melodic bells played as it booted up. A picture of the New England Patriot's logo came up on the screen and small icons hovered over it. There was a button that said 'Mail', and she clicked on it. There were two inboxes: one for 'det.garrett' and one for 'journey.garrett.' She clicked on her name. There were no new messages, but Marcus had added a few contacts for her, like her mom and her sister.

She opened a new message to Elena and began to type. *Hey sister. Just thought I would let you know that I actually have email at home now, and this is my address. Maybe I can even figure out how to send you some new pictures of Genna. Love you, Journey.*

She clicked on the Internet Explorer button, and the Yahoo homepage opened up. Without knowing what else to look at, she clicked on the search field and typed in *Brian Drake Emerson GA* and clicked 'Search.' Other than one obituary for a deceased aunt of Brian and Steven's, there were no legitimate results.

She put her own name in and clicked the search button again. A link to West Emerson High School came up on the top of the list. She clicked on the link and found where Marcus had signed the guestbook of an alumni page for their high school and named her as his wife. His email address was listed under his name. She signed the guest book as well and added her email address.

Kara appeared in the doorway with Genna in a yellow dress with a big bow on her bald head. Journey laughed. "Is she going to a ball?"

Kara danced the baby around the room. "Maybe," she said. "A girl always needs to look and feel her best."

"Did you tape that bow to her head?"

"Yeah, I had to. This child is never going to grow any hair," Kara replied.

Journey nodded. "She gets that from me. Mom said I was bald until I turned two."

"I'll just have to buy her a wig," Kara cooed as she joined Journey at the desk. She pulled up the extra chair and sat down. "What are you looking at?"

"Did you know our high school has a page for alumni?" Journey asked.

"Oh no," she answered. "Why would I want to go looking for that? I live here, and I don't want to reconnect with anybody. Most of the people from high school I wish I had never known to begin with." Kara shifted in her seat and motioned back to the computer. "Have you looked to see if David is on the list?"

Journey shook her head and clicked the 'x' button to close the page. "No, I haven't, and I'm not going to. Someone once gave me some good advice and told me that I should forget about him and I have."

Kara laughed. "Sure you have."

Journey just shrugged. "David's a ghost. I just try my best to not let him haunt me these days."

. . .

Marcus was home by ten-thirty that night. Journey put Genna down after Kara had left around nine, and she was reading in bed when he walked into their bedroom. "Hey, honey," she said.

He groaned and dropped his duffel bag on the floor. "Hey, babe," he replied.

His eyes were heavy, and his shoulders were slumped. "Rough day?" she asked.

He nodded. "Just frustrating and exhausting."

Her hopes deflated a little. "So, I guess you didn't find Brian Drake?"

He shook his head as he unbuttoned his shirt. "Not even a trace of him," he said. "It's like the guy vanished."

"I swear I'm not crazy." She sat up in bed and closed her book. "I really did see him yesterday."

He nodded his head as he pulled his uniform shirt off and draped it over the chair in the corner of the room. "I know that. He's just good at hiding. How was your night with Kara?"

Journey was a little distracted as he removed his body armor. "Huh? Oh, it was good. We watched *Notting Hill* and played on your computer."

"*Our* computer," he corrected her. "How is Genna?"

"Spoiled. Kara held her all night and gave her chocolate pudding."

He laughed and stripped down to his boxer briefs. "That's funny. If she's anything like you, I'm sure she loved it."

Journey rolled her eyes as he disappeared into the bathroom to brush his teeth. When he returned, he stretched out beside her. "So, what are you going to do now?" she asked.

"Pass out," he answered.

"About Brian," she said.

He put one arm behind his head and reached for the remote control. "Keep looking. I talked a lot with the DEA today, and they are probably going to launch a full scale manhunt for him soon. I would really like to be the one to nail him."

"What on earth would the DEA want with a small town punk like Brian?" she asked.

He shook his head. "He's not as much of a small town punk as he wants everyone to believe," he said. "They think that he's muling and dealing heroin and coke out of shipments from Mexico that are coming in around Savannah. They want to catch him and find his supplier."

She was surprised. "Really? He doesn't strike me as that smart."

Marcus smirked. "I wouldn't go so far as to call him smart, but he's resourceful, well connected, and obviously has invisibility powers. I think we've busted down almost every door in Emerson in the past twenty four hours."

Journey's mind shifted. "When does Steven get out of prison?"

Marcus thought for a moment. "I looked it up not long ago, and I think he gets out sometime in December. He had about six months added to his sentence when he assaulted that deputy. Remind me and I'll look it up when I'm at the station." He rolled his face toward her. "Why? Does it worry you?"

She shrugged and placed her book on the nightstand. "I dunno. Worried isn't exactly the right word, but I'm not looking forward to it." Her mind flashed back to the image of Steven lunging toward her at the jail. "I think he would've broken my neck or bashed my face in if the cops hadn't restrained him that day when he was arrested."

Marcus reached out and pulled her under the covers beside him. "Come here," he said.

Journey rested her face against the smooth skin of his chest and traced her finger across the tattooed tribal lines that swirled over his heart and down onto his side. He pressed a kiss into her hair and draped his arm across her back. "Steven won't be a problem when he gets out," he said.

"How do you know?"

He closed his icy blue eyes. "Because if he comes near you, I will kill him."

15
Now?

A MONTH went by with no sign of Brian Drake or any new leads on his whereabouts. It seemed to frustrate Marcus more and more each day, but Journey was starting to relax since he hadn't resurfaced in her life either. She still carried her gun but only because she had promised Marcus that she would.

Unfortunately, Journey had started a mental countdown till the day that Steven would get out of prison. Marcus had confirmed that he would be released the day before Christmas Eve. Journey couldn't help but shake the feeling that her past was coming home with him as well. The town of Emerson seemed to have forgiven and forgotten her involvement in one of the most publicized tragedies in the town's history, but she knew it was only due to her three year hiatus and the fact that she married Marcus, the closest thing Emerson had to a superhero. Steven's release felt like an old dusty book of scary stories that was coming off the shelf because the final chapter had yet to be read.

She had 117 days to enjoy till doomsday.

Genna was growing faster than Journey could buy her clothes. She was crawling all over the house, and every day Journey had to baby-proof some new part of their home. Marcus had nearly wet his pants trying to figure out how to raise the toilet seat on more than one occasion. With all of Genna's changes, it was really nice to have the computer and the Internet at home. She was able to regularly send pictures to Elena and a few other friends and family members who lived far away.

Journey had also discovered the joys of online shopping. As a mother who had to tote around the majority of the contents of her nursery to go anywhere, Amazon and EBay became very addicting. Marcus's birthday was coming up in early October, and she had been scouring online auctions for a new pair of his favorite tactical boots. Journey had finally found a pair in his size and engaged herself in a bidding war to win them.

Early one morning, while Marcus was still at work after being on third shift, she went to the office and booted up the computer before Genna started screaming from her crib. While the computer started, she retrieved her babbling baby from the nursery, changed her diaper, and carried her to her high chair in the kitchen.

"Does my girl want Cheerios this morning?" she asked as she slid the high chair table into place. She kissed Genna's head and dumped a handful of Cheerios onto her tray. Journey fixed Genna a bottle and made herself a cup of coffee.

"Ba ba ba ba ba ba," Genna sputtered.

Journey handed her the bottle, which she put straight into her mouth. "You sit tight. Mommy will be right back."

She carried her coffee back to the office and saw that she had three emails waiting in her inbox. The first was from

Elena, responding to bath time pictures of the baby, the second was an update that she had been outbid on EBay, and the third one was from an email address she didn't recognize. She clicked it open.

Hey Stranger, I found your email address on the West Emerson webpage and couldn't help but drop you a line. I understand if you don't write me back, but I really hope you do. I would love to hear all about your life now… married to Marcus? Is that right? I would love to catch up. - David.

Journey froze.

She stared at the screen for what felt like an eternity. She checked the email address for any sign of confirmation. It stated clearly, dbritton1979. She sat back so hard in her chair that it tipped over backward.

"Damn it!" she yelled and scrambled to her feet.

She left the chair on the floor and backed into the wall. In the kitchen she heard the familiar thump of a plastic baby bottle hit the tile floor. Thankful for the distraction she ran from the room like she was fleeing an assailant.

Mushy Cheerios peeked out between Genna's fat fingers as she pounded her fists on her table. "Mam, mam, mam," she repeated smacking her gums.

Journey unfastened her seatbelt and lifted the baby into her arms. She carried her toward the kitchen window and looked out upon the steamy morning dew in the back field.

Her mind raced in circles. *David Britton? Now? Seriously? Should I write him back? Should I talk to Marcus before I do anything? Hell, what is Marcus going to say? David? Seriously?*

Genna tried to shove a soggy bit of cereal into Journey's gaping mouth. She couldn't help but laugh. "You stop that." She squeezed Genna's belly, making her giggle.

She carried Genna back to the office and read the message again. Her emotions were bouncing all over the spectrum. She was happy. She was excited. She felt guilty about feeling excited. She was painfully heartbroken. But most of all, she was angry.

"It's been five years!" she finally shouted at the computer. Genna flinched and cried out in her arms. "Shhhh..." She bounced her on her hip while stroking her bald head.

She continued her rant internally as she paced the room. *It's been five years, and now he shows up when I'm happy and in love and have a new baby! Are you freaking kidding me?!*

Journey shut off the monitor and carried Genna back upstairs to the nursery. She changed her clothes, packed the diaper bag, and went to her room to get ready to go and visit the one person who could tell her exactly what she needed to do.

. . .

Her mother was seated at the kitchen table paying bills when Journey hauled the car seat and the diaper bag into the house. Curiously, she peered up over the top of her glasses. "Well, hello," she said.

Journey rested the car seat on her father's chair at the head of the table and dropped the diaper bag onto the floor. "Hey," she replied.

Carol slipped off her glasses, folded them closed, and laid them on the table. "I wasn't expecting to see you today." Carol was still in her nightgown; she hadn't expected to see anyone.

Genna was still asleep so Journey didn't disturb her. "Yeah, I know. I hope I'm not barging in on a busy day."

Carol shook her head and stood up. "Not at all. Do you want some coffee? The pot is fresh."

"That would be great." Journey sank into the chair across from her mother's.

Carol brought a cup and set it down in front of Journey before putting away her bills and checkbook and sitting back down. "So, to what do I owe the pleasure of your company today?"

Journey took a long, slow gulp of her coffee. After several thoughtful moments, she finally met her mother's inquisitive gaze. "I had a bit of an interesting morning."

"Really?"

Journey nodded and took another sip. "Yeah. I got an email from David Britton."

Carol's eyes widened with surprise. "That *is* interesting," she agreed. "How did he find you?"

"Our school's alumni website," Journey answered.

Carol nodded. "Well, what did he have to say?"

Journey shrugged her shoulders. "Not much. He just said he wants to catch up and hear about my life."

"Does he know you married Marcus?"

"Yeah," Journey said. "He wanted to hear about that too."

Carol tried unsuccessfully to suppress a chuckle. "I'll bet he does."

Journey ran both hands through her hair. "I don't know what to do."

Carol shifted in her chair. "Have you talked to Marcus about it?"

"No. He's at work. And I'm not exactly too sure how he will take it," Journey said. "He knows how much history is there."

Carol leaned forward on her elbows. "Exactly what kind of history *is* there?" Her eyes were wide as though she expected to receive a long lost puzzle piece.

Journey sat back in her chair. "I don't know. I mean, nothing really."

Carol raised a skeptical eyebrow. "If it were nothing, you

wouldn't be sitting at my table at eight o'clock on a Saturday morning."

Journey sighed. "Just a lot of feelings I guess. Nothing ever happened with us. We kind of had a couple of awkward days when he came home from boot camp, but we got into a fight and never spoke to each other again."

"A fight about Steven?"

Journey nodded. "Mostly about my life in general, but yeah. He absolutely hated Steven. He wasn't very supportive of the decisions I was making or the direction that my life was headed."

Her mom was quiet for a second. "That boy really loved you, Journey."

Journey felt her chest tighten, and it seemed the air suddenly became very thin. "I know."

"Did you love him?"

Journey shot her mother a knowing glare. Carol simply nodded her head slowly. After a few beats of silence she spoke again. "You have to talk to your husband about it. And I recommend talking to Marcus before you do anything at all with that email."

Journey felt her face involuntarily twist downward into a frown.

"You made a commitment to forsake all others, remember?"

"Mom, if I didn't know that I wouldn't be here talking to you about it."

Carol reached over and patted her daughter's hand. "I'm proud of you for that, sweetheart."

Journey slumped over the table and buried her eyes in her folded arms. "Why now?" she mumbled.

She felt her mother's hand come to rest on the back of her head. "I don't know, Journey. But I believe everything, even this, happens for a reason."

. . .

Marcus was at the computer, staring at Journey's inbox, when he saw her car come down the driveway. The house was silent, save for the quiet tick of the clock on the wall and the gears grinding in his head. He realized he hadn't moved, or looked away from the computer screen, in eight full minutes. He wasn't exactly sure how he felt about the fact that David had contacted his wife. He also wasn't sure how he felt about knowing she had received the email, knocked her chair over, and then left in a hurry. The coffee pot had been left on, the house alarm wasn't set, and she had completely forgotten to close the garage door behind her. It was obvious how much the message had affected her.

He got up from the desk and went to the garage to help her with the baby. When he opened the door, she was already lifting Genna's seat out of the car. She jumped when she saw him. "You scared me!"

He crossed the garage and took the heavy car seat from her. "I'm sorry," he said. "Where have you been?"

"My mom's," she replied. "Sorry I didn't let you know I was going out. I didn't even think about it."

Marcus nodded and walked into the house with Journey trailing behind him. Genna was asleep, so he carefully rested the car seat on the breakfast table. "How's mom?" he asked.

"She's good. She said to give you her love, and she wants us to come to dinner Sunday," she answered as she put a half-empty baby bottle in the refrigerator. When she closed the door, she slowly turned around. "Marcus, we need to talk."

He felt a chill. He nodded. "Yeah, I know."

"You saw the email?"

"Yeah," he said. "You didn't reply."

She shook her head and walked around the kitchen bar.

She lifted herself up on the countertop in front of him. "No. I knew we should probably talk about it first."

That made him relax a little. He put his hands on her thighs. "I appreciate that."

She covered his hands with her own. "What do you think I should do?"

He had pondered that question for almost the last half hour. He took a deep breath and let it out slowly.

"Are you mad?" she asked.

He shook his head and met her worried eyes. "No, I'm not mad at all." He really wasn't angry with her, or even with David. He laughed. "I'm not happy about it either."

She smiled.

After another few moments of reflection, he squeezed her thighs gently. "I love you. And, I trust you," he said. "Dave was a really big part of your life for a very long time. I know you still think about him, and I know you have a lot of regrets about how you left things." He noticed the surprise in her face. He traced his thumb across her lips. "But I also know you love me and you respect me."

She nodded. "I do, Marcus."

He smiled. "Can I tell you something that I've never told you?"

She raised an eyebrow.

"Dave is kind of the reason that you and I got together," he said.

She laughed. "What?"

"Before he left again after boot camp, he showed up at my house. He told me that you guys had a big fight and that he had to walk away for a while. He made me promise to take care of you." He smiled up at her. "I hope I've done a good job of it."

His wife wrapped her arms around his neck and pulled

him close. She kissed his neck and pulled away laughing. There were tears in her eyes. "You've saved my ass more times than I can count!"

He laughed. "Yeah, maybe once or twice." He leaned forward and pressed his lips to hers. "I think you should write him back."

"Really?"

He nodded. "Yeah. I'm serious. He was my best friend too, you know? I would kind of like to know where the hell he's been for the last five years." Marcus paused. "And Dave's a good guy. He won't cross any lines."

Her shoulders relaxed. "OK," she agreed, running her hands over his chest. When her fingers touched the buttons of his shirt, her lips spread into a thin smile. She freed one button and then another. She pulled him close and let her lips brush against his as she spoke. "But not right now."

. . .

After dinner that evening, Journey settled into the chair in front of the computer. She pulled up the email from David again. She felt better about the whole thing after discussing it with Marcus. His confidence, understanding, and love for her never ceased to be surprising. She read David's words again before clicking on the 'Reply' button.

David,

I got your email this morning, and to be honest, I've been in so much shock that it has taken me all day to try and respond. I have so many questions and so much I would love to tell you. How on earth are you? Where have you been? I tried for years to find you after you left, mostly to tell you I'm sorry for the way I acted. I was a horrible friend, and I will always regret how I treated you and disregarded our friendship. I hope you can forgive me.

Yes, I married Marcus! We got married about a year ago, and we have a little girl that is eight months old. Her name is Genesis, but we call her Genna. She's bald and chunky and the cutest baby you've ever seen. I will attach a picture for you to see. Marcus is now a detective at the police department. I wouldn't be surprised if he didn't wind up as the Police Chief. Everyone here loves him so much.

Marcus really saved me when my life spun out of control. To make a long story very short, Steven was put in prison for manslaughter, and I went to rehab in Tennessee near Elena. I started in college in Tennessee and maybe someday I will finish. Haha. Having a baby and becoming a wife sort of put that on hold for a while. Anyway, life is great, and we are really happy. Marcus said to be sure to tell you hello from him.

How is your life? I wrote letters to your parents' old address hoping they would be forwarded to wherever they moved, but they were always returned back to me with no forwarding address. I always wonder where you are and, mostly, how you are. I'm really glad you found me again, and I hope to hear from you soon. If you're ever in Georgia, I hope you visit.

-Journey

Journey pressed send on the email and let out a sigh of relief. Before turning off the computer, she logged onto EBay and checked on the tactical boots for Marcus. The auction was over, and she had lost.

16

The Hard Drive

DAVID WAS sitting on the back patio of his three bedroom duplex in Lacey, Washington, chain smoking and reading the email from Journey for the millionth time since he had received it almost two weeks before. He wished more than anything that he had never attempted to make contact with her. He had successfully restrained himself from contacting her all the times before: when he first left Emerson with immense guilt for walking away from her; when he graduated from Army Ranger school, and she was the person he wanted to share it with the most; and even when his mother sent her engagement announcement to him while he was deployed to Afghanistan. He had always known that if he ever opened the door to her again that nothing but the gut-wrenching frustration in the pit of his stomach would be the result.

Yep. I should never have sent that email.

So much had changed in the five years he had been gone from Emerson. David was a member of one of the most elite military fighting forces in the world. He had been deployed to Iraq twice during Operation Iraqi Freedom and had been to Afghanistan four different times. After his third deployment, he accomplished one of his professional dreams when he completed Army SOTIC, Sniper School. During combat, he had received many commendations and awards including the Army Commendation Medal and a Bronze Star.

Personally, his life was pretty great as well. After being stationed in Tacoma, Washington he was out at a bar one night with some friends and encountered a bachelorette party. One of the girls was a beautiful, young schoolteacher who had recently graduated from the University of Washington. He began dating Allie Johnson and had proposed to her after returning home from Afghanistan the year before. They were married in a small ceremony on the beach, and they moved to Lacey, a few miles away from Ft. Lewis.

The one thing that hadn't changed in five years was his regret for how he had left things with Journey. It had taken two years and then nine long hours in a foxhole in Iraq before he finally figured out exactly why their relationship had crumbled so dramatically. Journey had practically been a privileged orphan as long as he had known her. All she had wanted was for someone to make her their priority, and David had done just the opposite. He should have just been honest with her… about everything.

No matter how hard he tried to move on and leave her in the past, she was never absent from his thoughts. He had hauled her memory all over the world like a cumbersome piece of broken luggage. No one knew, though his mother suspected, that he proposed to Allie only after hearing that Journey had married Marcus. He loved the life he had built, and he loved his wife, but he could never shake the feeling that everything he had accomplished had only pushed him farther and farther from the place he had always wanted to be.

As he stared at his laptop screen contemplating a response to her email, he wondered what he could honestly say to her. He wanted to be happy for her, but he couldn't feel it. He wanted to ask about the details of what had happened after he left, but the thought of it made him sick. He wanted to ask about Marcus, but he couldn't help but be a little angry with him. He wanted to ask about her daughter, but it made him sad that Genna wasn't his own. He realized how selfish and unreasonable his emotions were. And he knew, beyond the shadow of a doubt, that everything that had happened was his own fault.

"Hey babe, you want some lunch?" a voice called from the house. "I'm about to make myself a sandwich with some of that deli roast beef you like."

He turned and saw Allie leaning her head out of the sliding glass door. She was wearing one of his Dallas Cowboys long-sleeved t-shirts, and her dark brown hair was in a long braid of her shoulder. He closed his laptop. "Absolutely," he said and rose from his seat. "I'll come help."

He followed her into the kitchen. "What are you so wrapped up with out there?" she asked as she pulled the refrigerator door open.

Her question spawned a twinge of inner panic inside of him, but David was always truthful almost to a fault. "Do you remember me telling you about my friend Journey, from high school?"

She placed the package of shaved roast beef on the counter. "The crazy girl with the short blond hair?"

He chuckled a little and opened the loaf of bread. "Yeah, that's her, though her hair was more multi-colored than it was blond."

"What about her?" Allie asked.

David started preparing a sandwich. "I got an email from her a couple of weeks ago."

Allie handed him the mayonnaise jar. "Really?" she asked. "How did she find you?"

David swallowed. "She didn't. I found her."

His wife looked up with surprise. "You did?"

He nodded, but didn't meet her eyes. "Yeah, she had a post on our school's website. I sent her a message a while ago."

Allie slowly turned back to her sandwich. "Hmm."

He forced a laugh to lighten the mood. "She actually married my best friend, Marcus. I'm pretty sure I told you about him. We played football together. They have a baby girl now."

That information seemed to relax his wife a little. "Oh, well that's good. Have you been talking to her a lot?"

He shook his head. "I haven't written her back yet."

She raised her eyebrows. "And you got her message a couple of weeks ago?"

David shrugged. "It's kind of hard to write a letter to your past, you know? A lot has changed since I lived in Georgia."

She smiled at him and winked her eye. "I hope some of it was for the better?"

He leaned over and kissed her. "Absolutely."

When they finished making their lunch, they carried it to the table and sat down. Allie opened her diet soda. "Do you think you will ever go back to Emerson?"

He took a bite of his food and pondered the question. "I don't know. I mean, we really need to go visit my parents, and they don't live far from there. It might be fun to show you around my old stomping grounds." He knew he wasn't answering the question the way she intended.

"To live," she added.

"Not as long as I'm in the Army. I mean, even if I get

stationed back at Ft. Benning, that's a few hours away," he said. "Maybe we should go to Georgia for Christmas this year."

His statement surprised him as much as it surprised her.

She was silent for a moment. "Maybe," she said, signaling the end of the conversation.

They finished their lunch in silence. David didn't know why he had suggested going to Georgia for Christmas, but he knew he meant it. Whether or not his subconscious was trying to reopen a door or finally find closure, he wasn't sure. Whatever it was, he couldn't help but feel excited about the prospect of going home. He would have to find a way to convince Allie to leave her family for the first time in her life at Christmas, but he was determined to do it. Except for an unexpected deployment, nothing would keep him from Emerson that year.

. . .

Journey,

I'm sorry it has taken me so long to get back with you. I would like to lie and say it's because I've been busy, but that's not true. I haven't really known what to say to you. You asking for my forgiveness is just crazy. There is nothing to forgive. I feel so terrible for the way that I walked out on you when you needed me the most. I was the horrible friend. Not you. I hope you can forgive me for that. God knows, I can't forgive myself. There were so many times that I wanted to come back, but I couldn't do it. I just pushed forward and focused on my career. But don't think that I didn't care. I never stopped caring.

I kept up on what was going on in your life every now and then. My parents moved out of Emerson but not far. They are in Jackson, and Mom has always kept up with Emerson news. She told me about Steven going to jail. They hadn't yet moved when he was arrested, so I figured if you wanted to talk to me about it then you would reach out. When you didn't, I decided you didn't want to, so I never tried. I'm sorry about that too.

I'm glad that Marcus took care of you and that you're happy. Genna is beautiful. She looks just like you—bald head and everything. Tell Marcus that I said hello and congratulations. He's really done well with his life.

I'm still in the Army. I've been a Ranger for four years now. I'm overseas and off the grid a lot, so that is why you were never able to find me. I just got promoted to Staff Sergeant last month, and I'm stationed in Tacoma, Washington. The weather here sucks, but this is my final duty station, so I will be here awhile.

Last year, I married a girl named Allie. She's really great, and I think you would like her. She's a schoolteacher at the elementary school on the base. We don't have any kids yet, but she talks about it a lot. We do have a dog. He's a black lab named Jack. I got him at the animal shelter when I first settled in Tacoma.

I'm thinking about visiting my parents for Christmas this year. I haven't been back to Georgia for Christmas since 2002 between deployments. I'm usually gone for at least six months out of the year, but since I just got back a few weeks ago, and we don't have anything on the books until January, I should be in the U.S. for Christmas. If we do visit, I hope we can all plan dinner or something together. I would love to see you and Marcus and meet your daughter.

Take care and write back if you can,
Dave

The thought of seeing David again made Journey's heart pound nearly out of her chest. She was excited and terrified at the same time. It was her greatest desire and her worst nightmare all wrapped into one. However, for that moment she allowed herself to just be excited. She planned to leave the email open for Marcus to read it when he got home, but she immediately hit 'reply'.

David,

You're a Ranger? That's awesome… and badass. Good for you! I always knew you would do great things in life. Please be careful though. I'm sure it's really dangerous. Thank you for your service. I hope that doesn't come off as cliché.

Congratulations on getting married. I'm sure that Allie is wonderful. I hope I get to meet her someday. Please send me a picture. You've always had taste in exceptionally beautiful girls, and I'm sure she is no different. I do hope that you both come for the holidays. It would be wonderful to see you again and meet your wife.

As for you and me, I'm not sure what you think you need to apologize for. You were only trying to help me, and you were one of the few people that would really stand up to me and confront my behavior. I should've listened. I was a complete idiot and a jerk to you. I'm not sure where my head was at back then. It clearly wasn't functioning properly. I made so many bad choices that it baffles me now in hindsight. Thank God that I got out of it before something really horrible happened to me. I know I don't deserve the life I have now, and I am very thankful for it. I've even mended things with my family. And who would've thought I would end up married to a cop? Haha.

Hope to hear from you again soon.

Love,
Journey

Journey sent the email and finished writing another message to Elena. Before she shut the computer down, a new message came through.

I always thought you would've married me.

· · ·

David knew it was wrong, but he hit send before he could think better of it. He had no right to finally tell her how he had always felt about her—not now—not now that she was married to his best friend. He deleted the email from his sent file for fear of Allie being hurt by it, and he wrote Journey again.

I'm sorry. I had no right to say that. I guess I'm just a little nostalgic today, and my emotions got the better of me. Please forgive me.

He sent the message and waited for a response. He lit another cigarette and stared out at the setting sun. It would already be dark in Emerson. He wondered what she was doing.

A moment later, another message was downloaded. He clicked it open.

David,

No worries. I understand. I would be lying if I said I hadn't ever thought the same. But we've both made different choices, and there is no going back. I'm just glad to have you back in my life in some way... even if it is just as a pen pal across the country.

J.

· · ·

Journey felt guilty about deleting the last couple of messages between her and David, but there really was no sense in worrying Marcus or making him angry for nothing. She hoped that David would take her cue and drop the whole line of conversation. A few moments later it became evident that he had dropped it.

Being a Ranger is exciting, but it isn't like it is in the movies. It's really hard and pretty dangerous at times. The best part of the job is that no two days are ever the same. I like that a lot. The biggest downside is being gone so much. Half of my adult life will pretty much be spent in combat boots. I guess I wouldn't have it any other way though.

Attached is a picture of me and Allie from our wedding last year. I don't think we've had time to have any other pictures made together. How sad is that? Our wedding was simple. Our parents came and a couple of friends, but that was it. Mom saved me the picture of you and Marcus from your wedding announcement. You guys looked great. I still can't get over you with long hair.

I will let you know about what we decide to do for the holidays. I'm pretty sure we can work it out to come. I'll just have to talk to Allie about it. Speaking of Allie… I'm meeting her for dinner in a half an hour, so I have to run. We'll talk more soon. If you text, my number is 243-555-0908. That might be easier than email since I move around so much.

David

Much like the computer, text messaging was another form of communication that Journey was in no hurry to utilize. Her newest cell phone was capable of texting, but she rarely ever used it except to ask Marcus to pick something up on his way home from work. David just might change all that.

Journey clicked the picture file open, and after a few seconds of loading, she was looking at David for the first time in five years. He looked, as usual, like a Ken doll with a crewcut. He wore a gray suit and a bright blue tie. His wife was equally as beautiful. She wore a simple white sundress and carried a small bouquet of pink flowers. She was fair skinned with long brown hair and a bright smile. Her hand was on his chest, and her hair was blowing in the breeze. They looked happy.

She was genuinely glad he was happy, but her happiness contained a familiar twinge of sadness. It was hard for her not to let her mind run wild with what would have been if she were the smiling girl next to him in the picture. She closed the email and sat back in her seat. Genna was pulling on the hem of her track pants.

She looked down at the baby and smiled. She lifted her into her arms. It was hard to wish her life had turned out any other way when she considered her family. She kissed Genna's messy cheek and tickled her tummy. "I say we take a bath and get our jammies on before Daddy gets home, baby girl."

"Ba ba ba ba ba," Genna babbled while trying to shove a fistful of Journey's ponytail into her mouth.

She shut down the computer, determined to leave David's memory locked up the hard drive if even for just the night.

17

Zero Hope

MARCUS HAD to work on his birthday that year, but it didn't matter to him. The chief had given him excellent news twice in one day. The first was that he was being considered for a promotion, and the second was that the DEA had finally launched a full-scale manhunt for Brian Drake. They had confirmed evidence that he was directly involved with moving drugs in from the coast, through Emerson, and into Atlanta. It was one of the best birthdays Marcus had ever had.

Brian Drake had never been high on Marcus's radar before, but since he had directly threatened Journey, Marcus had become a bit obsessed with finding him. Now that Brian's capture could also really boost Marcus's career, he was exceptionally motivated. However, his involvement in the manhunt would have to wait until Monday. It was his birthday, and his wife had a thing about birthdays.

As he was leaving the police station, his cell phone buzzed in his pocket. He pulled it out to read the text message on the screen.

Happy birthday, man. Hope it's a good one.

It was from David. They had spoken sporadically since David had resurfaced the month before. It made him feel better that Dave was including him in the conversation, rather than just chatting up his wife every few days. He knew Dave was a good guy, but Marcus had his pride—and a detailed knowledge about how in love David had once been with Journey. He trusted his old friend but only so far.

Marcus got into his car and drove the six miles to his house. When he pulled in, he found numerous cars in the driveway. He parked on the grass, and a small crowd gathered on his porch waving furiously. He laughed and parked in his yard.

"Happy birthday!" everyone cheered in unison when he got out.

Journey was standing in the front holding Genna. His in-laws, who were more like parents to him, were next to her. Kara and Justin were there, as well as Curtis and several other friends from the police department. He laughed and shook his head all the way to the porch. Journey came down and met him with a kiss and a beer. She had always loved birthdays more than anyone else he knew.

"Happy birthday," she repeated.

He accepted the beer and kissed her again. "Thank you."

He reached out for Genna, who was stretching her arms toward him. "Dada, dada, dada," she repeated over and over. He kissed her head and climbed the steps.

"Thanks everyone," he said, holding his beer in the air.

One by one, he greeted all of his friends and family. Journey was looking proud and accomplished knowing that she had surprised him. When they finally got inside, he grabbed her waist. "Didn't you tell me the party was tomorrow? On Sunday because I had to go in and work on that case today?"

She laughed. "Yes. I wanted it to be a surprise."

"I'm only turning twenty-five. That isn't some big milestone, you know?" he asked with a grin.

She shook her head. "Not true. You can finally rent a car."

He laughed and pulled her close to him. "You're crazy."

"And you love me," she said, kissing the tip of his nose. "How was work?"

"Fantastic," he replied. "You're gonna go nuts when you hear about it."

"Well, tell me!" she insisted.

He shook his head and stepped away from her toward his father-in-law. "Poppie, can you hold your granddaughter for a moment?"

Randall nodded. "Of course I can," he said, taking Genna from him.

Marcus turned toward the stereo and turned up the volume. *Smooth* by Rob Thomas and Santana was playing. He reached for his wife. "I'll tell you, but not till you dance with me."

"Now who's crazy?" She laughed as he spun her around in front of their guests.

He pulled her close and put his hands on her hips. "Now, I know this is kind of hard for you, but move with the music."

She playfully punched him in the shoulder. "You can't dance either, Marcus Garrett."

"Baby, my grandfather was from Morelia, Mexico." He turned her around again. "Dancing is in my blood!"

Her face was beaming as he twirled her around the room. When the song ended, he dipped her far back toward the floor and kissed her. Everyone in the room clapped. His conservative mother-in-law even cheered. Truth be told,

Marcus had no idea how to dance, but apparently he could fake it with the best of them. Journey couldn't stop giggling.

"I love you, my wife."

She draped her arms around his neck. "I love you too," she said. "Now, tell me what I'm going to go nuts over."

Marcus's smile widened. "Chief Branson pulled me into his office today and said they are considering giving me a promotion. It looks like you may be married to a Detective Sergeant soon."

Her mouth fell open, and she clapped her hands together. "Are you serious? That's awesome!" She hopped up and down in his arms. "Congratulations, honey!"

"Don't get all excited yet. It's just in the 'talking' phase at this point," he said. "But Chief seemed really positive about it."

Journey's dad had overheard everything. "That's really wonderful, Marcus." He reached out and shook Marcus's hand. "Congratulations, son."

"Thanks, Dad."

Curtis joined their group. "What's all the cheering out here about?" he asked.

Journey was still hanging off Marcus's shoulders. "My man's movin' up again!"

Curtis bumped Marcus in the shoulder with the bottom of his beer bottle. "Are you serious? You're getting promoted again? Tell me. Whose ass are you kissing?"

Marcus shook his head. "It's not definite yet. And don't say anything to the other guys."

Curtis reached out to shake his hand. "Congrats man. You really do deserve it."

Marcus felt really proud. Few people advanced through the ranks the way he had already. He loved being a police officer, but he also knew that he had gotten very lucky early in his career. "Typically they do big promotions at the beginning of the year," he said. "So it might be as soon as January or February."

Journey kissed his cheek. "That's really awesome, babe."

He smiled at her. "Thanks."

By the time the party ended, Genna was starting to get fussy, as she usually did late in the evenings.

Marcus kissed her tiny fingers as he bounced her on his lap. "Why don't you go get Genna ready for bed, and I will start cleaning up?" he asked.

Journey nodded and took Genna from his arms. She pointed at him. "No sneaking and eating more cake while I'm not looking, sergeant."

He feigned offense. "You calling me fat, woman?"

"I don't want to be married to a chunky detective!" she called as she went up the stairs.

He laughed and pulled a trash bag out from under the kitchen sink and began bagging up the trash. A very short while later, Journey reappeared in the kitchen with the baby monitor in her hand. "That was fast," he said.

"She was falling asleep as I changed her diaper," she said, laughing. She carried the cake from the table to the kitchen counter.

"All partied out. Reminds me of someone else I used to know," he said, swatting at her backside with the dish towel.

She dodged away from him. "You hush your mouth," she said.

"I got other news at work today, too," he told her.

She stopped and looked over at him. "What is that?"

"The DEA is going after Brian Drake," he said.

Her eyes widened. "Really?"

He nodded. "Yep," he said, tying the garbage bag closed and carrying it toward the garage door. "They busted a couple of members of the Aryan Brotherhood in Atlanta for possession of a large amount of cocaine and heroin. One of them fingered Drake as part of the transport. I don't know a lot of the details yet, but apparently they have enough evidence against him now to charge him with trafficking."

Journey shuddered. "The Aryan Brotherhood? I've seen specials on television about them. That's scary."

Marcus nodded. "Yeah, they are no joke."

"Are they here in Emerson?" she asked.

He shook his head. "We've got plenty of racists around here, but none are gang related that we know of."

"That's really strange," she said. "Do they know where he is?"

He shook his head. "I don't think anyone knows where he is. But they will put together a task force and go after him."

"Do you think he's here in town?" she added.

Marcus registered the look of sincere concern on her face. "I don't think he's anywhere near here," he assured her. "We haven't stopped looking for him just because his trail went cold. I promise, babe."

"I know," she said. "He just really creeps me out."

"We will catch him," he said confidently. "Are you still carrying your gun?"

She nodded but frowned as she covered the cake with its plastic dome lid. "Yeah. And I wish you would lock him up so I can put it back in the safe permanently where it belongs."

He shrugged his shoulders. "You should really carry it regardless of whether Drake is in prison or out of it."

"Speaking of Drakes and prison, any updates about Steven?" she asked. "He's supposed to get out in eighty-five days."

He raised his eyebrows. "You're counting?"

"Yes," she said.

He leaned against the counter and shook his head. He held a hand out toward her. "Come here," he said.

She stepped into his arms. He pushed her bangs away from her golden eyes and studied her face carefully. She was genuinely worried. "Do you really think for one second that I would let anything bad on this earth ever happen to you?"

She dropped her head. "No."

He put his hand under her chin and lifted her face back up. "Journey, look at me," he insisted. Her eyes finally met his. "I would rain down fire on heaven for you if I had to. Nothing is going to get past me."

She put her arms around his neck and hugged him tightly. "I love you," she whispered.

He closed his eyes. "I love you, too."

. . .

Journey woke up early the next morning and rolled over toward Marcus. He was lying on his back, still asleep. She stared at him, contemplating how she wanted to wake him up. She hadn't lied. They were celebrating his birthday that day, and she had plans.

"Whatever it is you're thinking about doing, knock it off," he said without moving or opening his eyes.

She shoved his arm. "I thought you were asleep."

"I was. But you're staring at me contemplating evil things, and it woke me up," he said, still not looking at her.

She cozied up next to his warm body. "How do you know I wasn't contemplating nice things?"

He laughed. "Because you are incapable of nice things before ten in the morning." He opened one eye, just to be sure.

"That's not..." She stopped herself when he turned his full gaze on her with a warning in eyes. "OK, that's not always completely true."

He closed his eyes again. "Yes it is. So, wake me up at ten. It's my birthday and my day off."

"Your birthday was yesterday," she reminded him.

"Same thing," he insisted. "We celebrate your birthday for like a month. I can have an extra day to sleep in."

She nudged him again. "Not today, you can't."

He groaned. "Woman, sometimes I don't know why I agreed to marry you."

Her mouth fell open. "You *agreed* to marry *me*?"

He was straining not to laugh or open his eyes again. She poked him hard in the ribs, which he absolutely hated. It worked. He scrambled away so fast that he nearly fell off the bed. Exasperated, he rolled over and looked at her. His face was inches from hers. "What do you want?"

She smiled and admired how blue his eyes were in stark contrast to his black hair and tan face. "You never told me your great-grandfather was Hispanic."

"Did you really wake me up to have a talk about my family tree?" he asked, propping his head up with his arm.

She scooted closer to him in the bed. "No. We have to get up and get moving."

He groaned and pulled the pillow over his face. "No…"

She pulled the pillow away from him and leaned over him. "Yes."

He rolled, tackling her onto her side of the bed. "I don't want to," he said, pinning her hands against the pillows above her head.

"We have to have Genna to my mom's by nine," she said.

He raised a curious eyebrow. "Why?"

She couldn't keep a secret any longer. "Because I have two tickets to the Atlanta-New England game today and kickoff is at one o'clock."

His mouth fell open. "Are you serious?"

She laughed.

He sat up and grasped her sides. "If you're lying to me, I'm going to tickle you until you wet the bed."

She squirmed. "I'm not lying! The tickets are in my nightstand! Don't tickle me."

He leaned over and opened her drawer. He pulled out an envelope and then inspected the tickets inside. "Holy crap. These are really good seats."

She laughed again. "I know. It's a good thing you're getting promoted. You'll be receiving a hefty credit card bill to pay off soon."

She stared up at him. Knowing he loved football almost as much as he loved her and Genna, she wondered momentarily if he was going to cry.

"You're the best wife ever."

She smiled. "I know."

Within an hour they had dropped off the baby at her parents' house and were on the interstate toward Atlanta. She grinned over at him from the passenger's seat. "So, you were really surprised? You really didn't know?"

He nodded. "I really didn't know. How would I?"

"You could be like me and check the transaction history on the…" her voice trailed off when Marcus's eyes shot toward her and she realized what she was telling him. She felt her cheeks flush, and she covered her mouth with her hands.

"Do you check the credit card statements when I buy you gifts?" he questioned.

She dropped her face into her hands. "No," she said and her voice cracked.

He gasped. "You're a horrible liar! That's absolutely terrible!"

She grabbed for his arm, smiling wildly. "Please don't be mad at me."

He laughed. "Oh, I'm not mad. I just know to pay cash from now on!"

She put her feet up on the dashboard, though she knew it drove Marcus crazy. Metallica came on the radio, and she turned up the volume.

"Have you heard from Dave recently?" he asked.

She smiled knowing Metallica had similar memories for Marcus as well. "Not in a few days," she answered truthfully.

"He sent me a happy birthday text yesterday," he said.

She nodded. "That's nice of him. You text David?" she asked surprised. "You don't even text message me."

He gave her a smirk. "You wouldn't answer if I did."

She just laughed.

"Do you know if he's still planning on coming home for the holidays?" he asked.

Journey didn't know for sure. "He hasn't mentioned it in a while, but he seemed pretty sure of it the last time I heard from him."

"He's a Ranger. His off time could probably change really suddenly," he pointed out.

She nodded. "True. But he said he wasn't scheduled to be deployed until after Christmas. He said it was pretty certain that he would be in the U.S. because they were putting together a mission for January."

"He told you all that?"

"Yeah. Why?"

Marcus shrugged his shoulders. "You just seem to know a lot of information, that's all. What do you guys talk about?"

"Everything," she said. "Well, almost everything."

Marcus went quiet. She noticed he was staring at the road, lost in thought. She finally leaned forward a little and looked at him directly. "Does it bother you that I talk to him?"

Marcus gave a half-laugh, almost as if to say *'duh'*.

After another moment he looked over at her with serious concern. "Should I be worried?" he asked.

She had asked herself, a few times since getting back into contact with David, how she would feel if it were Marcus who had rekindled a relationship with a girl he had once been so close to. She knew he was being a much more understanding and tolerant spouse than she could ever be. However, she had resolved to not let things get inappropriate with David again and to keep the conversation limited.

She answered confidently. "No. I love you, Marcus. And I wouldn't cheat on you with anyone. Not even David." She thought for a moment. "And if you're even a little bit uncomfortable, I won't talk to him anymore. I'll cut it off."

He reached for her hand and drew it to his lips and kissed her palm. "No, I don't want you to do that. I trust you." He looked over at her. "Just be careful. I like David, but he's still a guy. And he's a guy that was in love with you for a really long time. I think he would have a hard time not being tempted if he ever had an inkling of hope."

She squeezed his hand and smiled at him. "I promise to emit zero hope."

He laughed. "I know." After the song ended, he spoke again. "Why didn't you and David get together when we were younger?"

She had asked that question for years. She sighed. "I don't know. He never asked."

Marcus laughed. "I know."

It was Journey's turn for questions. "If it was so obvious how he felt, why do you think he never made a move?"

Journey could tell Marcus was turning the question over in his mind. Finally, he looked at her. "I think you scared the crap out of him."

She laughed. "What?"

He nodded. "Hell, you still scare me sometimes."

She playfully slapped his arm. "Shut up."

"I'm serious. Did you know that some of us from the football team would wait in the cafeteria for you to come in every morning?" he asked.

She rolled her eyes. "Whatever."

"I'm serious!" he insisted. "It started after you began riding to school with Dave in the morning. We would wait for the two of you to come in just to see what you were wearing."

She let out an exasperated sigh. "You did not."

"It's true! We used to place bets on what you would be wearing each day and what color your hair would be. Some days you would be in pink fuzzy pajama pants and the next you would be wearing a leather miniskirt. On Monday your hair would be fire engine red and on Tuesday it would be purple." He laughed. "Ask Dave if you don't believe me."

She peered at him. He nodded with persistence.

"I think Dave was scared to death because you were so unpredictable."

She frowned. "But you say you love me because I'm unpredictable."

He nodded. "Well yeah. That's one of many things I love about you. I'm sure Dave was attracted to that too, but consider all his other girlfriends, like that freaking Rebecca girl. Really, could you be any more of a complete opposite to her? He was used to girls like Rebecca. You scared the hell out of all of us."

She laughed and punched him again. A lot of what he said seemed to fit with David's personality. David liked rules, training, and being in charge. She probably did scare him back in high school. She never thought that it would come from a conversation with Marcus, but she was glad to finally have what seemed like the missing piece of the puzzle from her history with David.

She almost wanted to call her mother and tell her the good news.

18

CRASH AND BURN

DEAR JOURNEY,

Hey girl… Guess who just bought two plane tickets to Georgia? Yep. This guy. We will be flying into Atlanta the day before Christmas Eve and then leaving the day after Christmas. We have to come back here to be with my in-laws for New Year's. That was the deal I brokered with my wife to be able to come. I wish we could stay longer, but anytime is better than nothing. I'm so excited that I can't stand it. December 23rd can't get here fast enough.

You know what we should do—or what you should do, anyway? You should throw one of your epic parties for Christmas. I haven't been to a party in ages. I'm not sure if I still even remember how to party. Haha. I would love to see our old group again. It's really been too long. Talk to Marcus and let me know what you think. I will help buy food or beer or whatever you need. If that won't work with your plans, maybe Allie and I can just take you guys out to dinner somewhere. Ha... maybe even Lottie's Diner if it's still open. I'm pretty sure I still owe you a meal from there. Just kidding. Please don't beat me up when you see me!

I hope you all have a great Thanksgiving. I'm a little jealous if you will be eating at your mom's and having her crazy-amazing sweet potato casserole. I've eaten the best food from all over the world, and I swear that's the best stuff on the planet. We will be at Allie's parents' house in Seattle. You should pray for me. Haha. Her dad seems to think that because I was raised in the South and I'm in the Army that I'm some sort of uncivilized redneck. Maybe it's the way I talk. Who knows?

I've got to go clock some hours on the range today, so I have to run. It seems as though I've been neglecting my duties a little since I found you again. Look at you already being a bad influence on me. (wink) Give me a shout later if you get a chance. I will be back online later this evening.

I hope you have a great day,
Dave

Allie walked by David's office just as he clicked the 'send' button. She paused at the door and then let out a frustrated sigh. "Boy, you didn't even wait until daybreak to talk to her today," she said with a smirk.

He leaned back in his chair and rolled his eyes up toward the popcorn ceiling. "For the millionth time, I don't talk to her all that much, and when I do, I tell you about it. I'm not sure why you're so defensive all the time. She's on the other side of the world, and I'm not lying to you. You can check my computer anytime you want."

She walked on down the hallway. "Whatever you say, David."

He got up and followed after her. "Allie, wait," he said,

jogging to catch up with her.

She stopped just inside their bedroom door. She turned back to look at him. Her eyes were wet with tears. "What?"

"We're just friends—" he began.

She held up her hand to silence him. "Please don't talk to me like I'm stupid and naive. Don't look me in the eye and tell me that you're not in love with her because we both know that's a lie."

Her blunt honesty stunned him.

She folded her arms slowly over her chest and cast her gaze at the carpet. "You've changed since she came back. You're more peaceful. You sleep better at night, and you smile as soon as you wake up." She reached up to wipe her face with the back of her hand. "You've never done that before." She was shaking her head back and forth. "I always thought it was the stress of your job and how much it weighed on your mind that kept you so closed off from me. But it's been her all along."

David was frozen to the floor and certainly lacked any kind of coherent response. She brought her sad eyes up to meet his after a long silence. He had to say something. He held out his hands, palms up, in surrender. "I'm sorry," was all he could mutter.

She turned away and closed the door on him, leaving him shut out in the hallway.

. . .

Journey nearly fell off her chair when she found out that David had actually bought plane tickets. It was really happening. She would finally see him again. She tried to suppress her excitement when she told Marcus about it over dinner that evening, but there was no denying how thrilled she was. Marcus loved the idea of throwing a Christmas Eve party and inviting all of their friends. Journey always worried that Marcus was secretly unhappy that David was back in the picture, but the closer it got to Christmas the more excited Marcus seemed.

Journey had written David back immediately after receiving his email, but days passed without any more messages from him. She sent another email simply asking if he was OK and didn't receive a response to it either. Momentarily, she thought about calling or text messaging him, but she knew David well enough to know that if he wasn't answering, he had a good reason. He could be 'off the grid' again with his unit for all she knew.

She and Kara got started on planning a Christmas party the day after Thanksgiving when they finished their Black Friday shopping spree. Marcus had stayed home with the baby so they could have some girl's time out of the house together without an infant in tow.

Journey was writing out a guest list over lunch. "So, I've got twenty-two people I'm pretty sure will come. Can you think of any more?"

Kara shook her head. "I don't think so."

Journey thought for a moment. "You know, I remember when I would come home from Tennessee that it was so hard to pack in all the people I wanted to visit in one weekend. Can you think of anyone else that David might want to see while he's in town?"

Kara tapped her finger over her pink lips. "Rebecca Ashburn?"

Journey launched a french fry at her head. "Shut your mouth!"

Kara tossed her head back laughing. "Bad joke, I know," she said and took a bite of her sandwich. She washed it down with a sip of her drink. "So, Journey, on a scale of one to ten, how excited are you about him coming back?"

Journey sucked in a breath through a clenched smile. "Oh,

about a twelve or thirteen."

Kara laughed and pushed her hair back off her shoulders. "Does Marcus know that?"

"Marcus thinks I'm about a seven on the excitement scale," she said, picking up her drink.

Kara's face became a little more serious. She leaned forward and lowered her voice a bit. "Are you going to be OK seeing him again?"

Journey nodded. "Yeah. I've thought a lot about it. I've tried really hard to get over all of those 'what if' feelings, you know?"

Kara pulled her straw out of her cup and pointed it across the table at her. "You just used the word *tried* though. You didn't say you were actually over having those feelings."

Journey shrugged. "I don't know if you can ever completely get over that sort of thing with anyone. But, I choose Marcus. I made a commitment to him, and I do love being with him. I don't want to mess that up. I honestly mean that."

Kara nodded. "I know you do. I also think you're kidding yourself if you don't believe that you're going to be on emotional overload when you see Dave again for the first time."

Even the thought of it made Journey's stomach flutter. "I'm just hoping it's going to be the start of a new chapter for us. We are both married. We have lives on opposite sides of the country. Those are the thoughts that I hope will keep me grounded."

"Just make me a promise," Kara said.

"What promise?"

Kara looked at her very seriously. "Don't be alone with him. You and he both need some accountability around at all times."

Journey nodded toward her. She wholeheartedly agreed. "You are going to be the designated chaperone in the absence of either of our spouses."

Kara stretched her hand across the table and Journey shook it. "Deal."

. . .

David looked at the phone in his hand, dialed the phone number, hesitated, and placed it on the patio table again. He lit another cigarette and looked up at the dim, cloudy sky. The sun was setting off of the Washington coast, but he couldn't see it through the haze. He blew out a long puff of smoke and picked up the phone again. He quickly dialed the number and pressed send before he talk himself out of it once more.

As the phone rang, he prayed to hear a voicemail recording.

"Hello?" came a curious, small voice on the other end of the line.

His heart was in his throat. "Journey?"

"David?"

He laughed softly, trying desperately not to break out in a sobbing mess at just the sound of his name on her lips. "Yeah, it's me," he answered. "I'm sorry for calling so late. I know it's like almost ten there. I hope I didn't wake anyone up."

"Are you kidding? I'm so glad to hear your voice," she said, her voice trembling. "And no, you didn't wake anyone up at all. Genna's asleep upstairs, and Marcus is out with his partner."

His head was spinning because she was actually on the other end of the line. He had wanted to call her so many times before, but she didn't think it was a wise idea. He knew she had been right. Nothing about their reunion had ever been a good idea.

"Are you OK?" she asked, bringing his attention back to

the conversation. "I've been really worried about you."

He sucked in a quick breath, fighting for control over his emotions. "I know. I'm sorry. I didn't mean to worry you."

"It's fine. I'm just glad that you're alright," she said. "I didn't know if you were dead or in the desert fighting the Taliban somewhere or what."

"No, nothing like that."

She sighed. "Well, thank God."

He paused and tried to collect his thoughts. He rubbed his eyes with his free hand. "I know you asked me not to call, but I really needed to talk to you and not by email."

"OK," she said hesitantly on the other end of the line.

He took a long drag on his cigarette and breathed it out slowly. "Allie doesn't want us to come to Georgia for Christmas." When Journey offered only stale silence, he continued. "She said that I can go without her, but if I do… she won't be here when I come back home."

Still, there was only silence.

"Journey?" he finally asked into the void.

He heard a stifled sniffle over the line, and his heart shattered.

"Yeah, I'm sorry. I'm here." She coughed to obviously cover her quavering voice. "You really don't have to explain. I completely understand, David."

"I don't," he whispered, dropping his face into his hand. "I don't understand how we always end up here."

"I don't either," she agreed.

His voice was trembling so much he could hardly control it. "I love you too much to make you the other woman in my life. I made a commitment to her, Journey."

She was quick to respond. "Of course you did. You wouldn't be my David if you did anything other than honor your wife's wishes."

"I'm so sorry. I've let you down, *again*," he said.

"David, this is probably the best thing for all of us. I don't know how honorable I would be facing you in person. I don't even trust myself enough to text message you," she laughed through evident tears.

He laughed too, but it was painful. "God, don't tell me that." A single tear erupted from his eye, and he quickly brushed it away with his sleeve. "I love you so much," he whispered, gripping his cell phone so hard he feared it might break.

After a brief pause she said, "I love you, too, David."

And with those words the line went dead.

David wasn't sure how long he spent on his back patio, but when he finally collected himself enough to go inside, there were stars peeking through the fading clouds. The sun had completely disappeared. He went into the still house and locked all the doors to the outside. He fed the dog and filled his water bowl. He checked his gun safe to ensure it was locked and adjusted the thermostat in the living room.

When he couldn't busy himself with anything else that wasn't completely ridiculous, he walked down the hall toward his bedroom. Allie was lying in the bed reading a book by the light of her bedside lamp. He didn't make eye contact with her but went straight to the bathroom and took an extra-long time to brush his teeth. He stripped down to his boxer briefs, dropped his clothes in the laundry basket, then sat on the edge of the bathtub for no reason at all. Finally, he got up and carried his cell phone back to their bedroom.

Allie slowly closed her book and looked up at him expectantly.

"It's done," he said. He walked around to his side of the bed and stared at it, unwilling to lie down beside her. He grabbed his pillow and yanked his phone charger from the wall before turning toward the door. "I'm going to sleep in the guest bed tonight. I need to be alone for a while."

"David, I—" she began.

He pointed an angry finger to silence her. "No," he snapped. "I did this *for you*, and that's all you get for tonight."

His words stung her; it was obvious from the way her expression seemed to melt from her face. But, in that moment, he didn't care.

He closed their bedroom door behind him a little harder than he probably should have and went to the spare room. As he sat down on the double bed, a holdover from his single life in on-base housing, he contemplated calling Journey back, begging her forgiveness, and getting on the first plane to Georgia. However, he knew that would only cause more damage to everyone involved. He had to consider her daughter and the vows that she had given to Marcus. And while he didn't like Allie very much at the moment, she was still his wife that he loved.

From every angle that David examined the whole situation, he was bound by his honor and his integrity to stay in Washington.... even if his heart was in Emerson.

. . .

Journey was thankful for Marcus's absence that night. She never wanted him to see her crying over David again. She hadn't thought it was possible for David to break her heart any more than he already had in the past eight years, but she was dead wrong. It was like her personal phoenix burning to ashes all over again.

Much like the first time that the relationship came crashing down on top of her, this too was her own fault. She had no right to get her hopes set so high on the thought of entertaining another man in her life—no matter who it was. It wasn't fair to Marcus or Genna. It wasn't even fair to herself.

Once again, she deserved the miserable, cold bed which she had made.

She agonized over how to explain David's sudden change of plans to Marcus and Kara, as well as the other friends she had gushed to in the past week. With Marcus and Kara she knew she had to opt for the truth, or at least a close version of it, since she would have to explain David's unexpected disappearance from their lives once again. She also knew Marcus occasionally talked to David, and she didn't want to be caught in a lie to her husband.

Explaining it to Marcus was going to be the most difficult part. She knew she would never be able to look her husband in the eye and tell him the exact reason for David's abrupt change of plans. She couldn't imagine his reaction to telling him that David was still in love with her and that he couldn't make Journey 'the other woman' in his life. However, Marcus knew them both too well to buy a cheap version of the story. She prayed that he would just accept the worries of a jealous, disconnected wife and let it go, but she knew she obviously wasn't that lucky. Fortunately, even if she had to tell Marcus the entire truth, she wouldn't have to worry about the repercussions for long. David would completely vaporize from existence once more.

It was over… *again*.

Somehow though, despite that they had finally laid their feelings for each other bare, exchanged 'I love you's', and even implied a final goodbye, she felt that the connection between them still wasn't broken. She thought that maybe as long as they both were breathing it never would be completely over. And in that too, she hoped she was wrong.

19

Christmas Eve Party

JOURNEY HADN'T been the same since David called and said he was no longer coming to visit for the holidays. Marcus hadn't missed the marked disappointment she was so desperately trying to hide. He tried not to dwell on it since he had, after all, given his blessing on David's return to their lives. But he would be lying to himself if he tried to believe for one second that the power that David still possessed over his wife didn't bother him. Truth be told, if David would have been in the state of Georgia when she told him, with tears in her eyes, that David still loved her, he might have run the man over with his patrol car and then shot him for good measure. He had told David as much over the phone the next day.

Rationally, Marcus reasoned that he had enough to keep him busy without worrying about a conversation that he had been expecting to come for almost a decade. It was done, so he decided to let it go. Besides, David was half a world away, and he knew he would probably have to cheat to beat David in a fight.

The week before Christmas, Brian Drake's trail reappeared through Emerson, and U.S. Marshals had moved in from Atlanta to apprehend him on behalf of the DEA. Drake was slick though, and he evaded them at every turn. He was able to scatter to the shadows like a cockroach when a spotlight lit up. Marcus was hell-bent on finding him. He was determined to make headlines again and secure his future with the department.

With the pressure of the Drake case looming over him and the strain of the pending holidays, it was all he could do to not fall into a coma when he returned home late each night. Two days before Christmas, when he got home, he found his wife lying on the bed with a glass of wine in her hand and her handgun in its holster on the nightstand. He glanced curiously around the bedroom before dropping his bag near the closet and pulling off his jacket.

"Hi honey," he said cautiously. "Whatcha doin'?"

She flipped the channel on the television with the remote control. "Just waiting on you to get home," she answered. "How was work?"

"Busy," he said. "What's up with the gun?"

She took a sip from her glass. "Don't you remember what today is?"

He thought for a moment. "Christmas Eve, *Eve*?" he asked.

"Steven's release day," she reminded him.

He paused as he was unbuttoning his shirt. "Oh yes. How could I forget?" He stripped off his shirt and took his gun out of its holster. He cleared the chamber and placed it on top of the dresser. "Are you still worried about that?"

She reached over and tapped the Taurus with her fingertips. "Not a bit," she answered.

He eyed her carefully. He couldn't remember the last time she had given him anything more than a fake half-smile. "I'm sorry I haven't been here all day. Did you go out at all?"

She nodded. "I picked up the food for the party tomorrow night, but I still have some prep work to do in the morning."

"I forgot all about the party," he admitted as he sat down on the bed to untie his shoes.

"Do you have to work?" she asked.

He shook his head. "No. Not unless I get called in. I have a couple of cars sitting on Barbara Drake's house to see if her son shows up for the holidays, but if nothing happens, I'll stay home. I have off for the next few days."

She nodded. "Good." After a moment, she spoke again. "I've been doing a lot of thinking today."

He couldn't help but be a little worried about that statement from her. There was no telling what her brain had been mulling over all day. "Go on," he said. He kicked off his shoes and stretched across the bed so he could rest his head on her stomach.

"I think I know how Brian Drake got linked up with the Aryan Brotherhood," she said.

Those words got his attention. He rolled over and looked at her. "I would love to know that answer."

"Steven," she said.

He raised his eyebrows hoping she would elaborate.

"You told me that Steven assaulted that deputy in prison to probably get protection from a white supremacist group," she reminded him. "He's involved."

Marcus was shocked that he hadn't yet considered that. "Makes a lot of sense," he said.

She turned her eyes toward him. "You follow Steven, and you'll find his brother."

He rolled onto his back and stared at the ceiling fan.

"Damn Journey, maybe you should be the detective. I had decided to watch the family but didn't put the Aryan thing together till you just mentioned it." He laughed. "I'm impressed."

"I want you to catch that bastard, Marcus," she said with an icy chill in her voice.

He grasped her hand and kissed it. "I will. I promise." He rested her hand on his chest and let out a slow breath. "How has Genna been today?"

"She pulled up on the coffee table," she said almost smiling.

He laughed. "Really? Did you video it?"

"No," she answered and turned her attention back to the television.

He groaned. "Baby, I need you to cheer up. It's Christmas."

She placed her hand on his head. "I'm sorry, honey. It's just been a rough day."

"No more from David, I assume?" he asked as he twisted a button on her pajama shirt.

She just shook her head.

"I love you," he said with his best pouty face.

She gave him a phony smile. "I love you, too."

He had an idea. He pushed himself up and offered her his hand. "Come with me."

She groaned.

"Come on," he insisted, stretching his hand further in her direction.

She finally placed her hand in his, and he pulled her off the bed. He took her glass of wine, finished what was left of it, and placed it on the nightstand beside her gun. He led her into the living room where the Christmas tree was still glowing. The scent of fresh pine was almost overwhelming.

He searched for a moment until he found the box he was looking for. He picked it up and offered it to her. "Here, I want you to open this early. I was going to wait till Christmas morning, but I think you need a little Christmas spirit tonight."

She raised an eyebrow. "What is it?"

He rolled his eyes. "You have to open it, silly."

She took the small, rectangular box from him. He led her to the sofa and pulled her down onto his lap. Carefully, she peeled away the wrapping. She removed the lid from the box and pulled out the blank, white envelope inside. She turned it over in her hand before raising the flap and sliding out a piece of paper. He carefully watched her eyes as she read, and to his delight, her face brightened.

She laughed for the first time in weeks and covered her face with the paperwork. "Mexico? Are you kidding me?"

He reached up and pulled her long hair back behind her shoulder. "I remember this irrational young girl who always liked to run away when she was upset. I figured this time we could run away together for a little while."

She giggled and melted into his arms. "Why are you so good to me?"

He rubbed her back and kissed a spot of bare skin on her neck. "Because you're mine and I can."

"When are we going?" she asked, looking back at the travel papers.

"In February. I already took the time off of work and arranged for Nana and Poppie to keep Genna for the week," he said.

She wrapped her arms around his neck and pressed her lips to his. "I promise I won't be sad anymore."

He pointed at her seriously. "I'm going to hold you to that," he said. "No more moping around, feeling sorry for yourself, and being worried that a convict is going to burst down our door."

"No more," she agreed, nodding her head.

He tangled his fingers in her hair and kissed her deeply. They hadn't kissed that way in far too long. Her nails scratched across his shoulders, making his entire body tingle. He hooked an arm under her legs and secured the other behind her back. Lifting her in his arms, he carefully stood. He kissed her all the way to their bedroom and kicked the door closed when he carried her inside.

. . .

Kara was the first of the guests to arrive at the party that evening. She had promised to come early to help Journey get things set up, but Journey was almost finished by the time she got there. It had been Kara's idea for the party to be semi-formal dress and though Journey had bucked the idea in the beginning, she was glad for it when Kara sashayed into the kitchen. She looked spectacular in a fitted red satin party dress that was cut low on the top and cut short on the bottom.

"Wow," Marcus said, looking up from where he was mixing bourbon into the eggnog.

Kara did a model's turn in the kitchen. "Thank you!"

Journey shook her head and sighed. "Once again, I feel underdressed next to you." She was wearing the short navy dress she had worn to the last police banquet.

Marcus leaned over and nibbled on Journey's bare shoulder. "Personally, I think you're *overdressed*," he said.

"Oh, get a room," Kara teased. "Why are you letting Marcus mix the booze? Do you want this to be a party or not?" she asked, taking the bottle from him and turning it completely vertical over the punch bowl.

"Hey!" Marcus shouted.

She shooed him away with a well-manicured hand. "I've

got this. Why don't you go get dressed?"

He looked down at his jeans and white button-up. "I am dressed," he said.

She looked him up and down and frowned. "Go get dressed again."

Journey covered her mouth so she didn't burst out laughing. Marcus looked at her with his mouth hanging open and then pointed at Kara. "She's mean." He looked down at his clothes, then back at Journey. "Do you think I should change?"

Journey pressed her lips together.

Kara pushed him toward the hallway. "That's a yes," she said. "Go."

Journey laughed, and he swatted her on the butt as he passed by.

Journey stepped over beside Kara and looked up at her. She laughed at their height difference. "You're like 'Attack of the 50ft Tall Woman'," she said, glancing down at Kara's huge red heels.

"You just need to put some shoes on. That's a cute dress," she said.

"Not as great as yours. That thing is spectacular."

Kara dunked her finger into the eggnog and licked it. "You don't think it's too much?"

Journey shook her head. "Not at all. You look gorgeous. Where's Justin?"

Kara groaned. "At his stupid shop. Some guy's wife bought him a bike, and Justin has been working day and night to get the thing done in time for Christmas."

Journey's eyes widened. "Is he coming tonight?"

Kara rolled her eyes. "If he doesn't, I'll kill him." She looked around the room. "Where's Genna?"

Journey nodded toward the steps. "Upstairs asleep. I'm

hoping she's down for the night, but being that it's so early I kind of doubt it."

Kara grinned mischievously. "I want to go wake her up."

Journey pointed at her. "Do you have a death wish?"

Kara poured two glasses of eggnog and handed one to Journey. She held it up for a toast. "Merry Christmas, chick."

Journey smiled and clinked her glass. "Merry Christmas."

Half of the party guests had shown up by the time Marcus finally came back down the hallway. He was wearing the same suit he had worn at their wedding.

Journey laughed. "What have you been doing in there?"

He straightened his jacket. "I came out once, but Kara intercepted me in the hallway. She told me no and sent me back in." He looked down at the suit. "I finally put this thing on since she's the one who picked it out for our wedding."

Journey hooked her arm around his neck and kissed him. "You look smokin' hot, babe," she said.

He smiled and slipped his arms around her waist. "Maybe I should wear it every day then," he suggested.

"Journey, your sister is here!" Kara called from the front door.

She grabbed Marcus's hand and pulled him through the living room. The party was on the wrap-around porch outside. Marcus had decorated the porch in the front and the large deck in the back with white Christmas lights. He had put out big kerosene heaters, even though the evening was pretty mild.

Elena was walking up the front steps in a black dress with her hair shorter than Journey had ever seen it. More impressive than her new hairstyle, was the man who was holding her hand. He was tall with long brown hair and a salt-and-pepper goatee. He was wearing boot cut jeans, a Rolling Stones t-shirt, and a blazer. Journey had only heard about her sister's new boyfriend over email and in phone calls, but she liked him immediately.

"You made it!" she cheered, embracing her sister. "Merry Christmas!"

"Merry Christmas," Elena said. "The house looks great!"

"You look great! I love your short hair!"

Elena laughed. "I look like the high school version of you!"

"Nah, it would have to be blue or pink," Marcus teased, stepping forward to give Elena a hug.

"Merry Christmas, brother," she said.

She pulled away and turned to her boyfriend. She put her hand on his shoulder. "Derek, this is my little sister, Journey, and her husband, Marcus. This is Derek Gilmour."

Marcus and Derek shook hands. "Nice to meet you, Derek," Marcus said.

"Hey, hey, hey," Kara sang as she danced toward them.

Elena cheered. "Kara, I haven't seen you since the wedding! You look amazing!"

Kara had to bend down to hug her. "Your hair is awesome!" Kara exclaimed.

Marcus nudged Journey in the side and nodded to Derek's pants. "Why does he get to wear jeans?" he whispered.

Journey giggled and elbowed her husband in the stomach. Inside, the house phone was ringing. Marcus moved in the direction of the door, but Journey grabbed his arm. "I'll get it, babe," she said, smiling a little too wide.

He cut his eyes at her. "Why?"

She shook her head and kissed his cheek. "Hey, Kara!" she called. "I need you in the house!"

Kara followed Journey back inside. The phone stopped ringing. Journey looked up at her. "Out in the garage, in the extra refrigerator, are a bunch of champagne bottles. Can you grab them and bring them in for me?"

Kara cocked an eyebrow. "Since when do you drink

champagne?" she asked.

Journey shook her head. "I don't, but other people might."

"Alright," Kara said, walking toward the garage door.

Once she was gone, Journey walked over to the stereo that played through the speakers outside on the deck. She put in a homemade CD and pressed play.

"Are you freaking kidding me?" she heard Kara yell in the garage.

Journey cringed and laughed as she ran to the front door. "Marcus!" she whispered as loud as she could.

He looked over. "Yeah, babe?"

She pointed back toward the driveway where she saw Justin's truck pulling in the drive. "Go help him!" she said as loud as she dared.

"What?" He asked over the music. "I can't hear you!"

She pointed again. "Go help him!'

He looked toward the driveway, and when he started, obediently, down the stairs, Journey went to the garage just as Kara stepped back into the kitchen shaking her head furiously. "What the hell happened out there?" she yelled at Journey. "I can't get to that stupid fridge. There's too much crap in the way. Make Marcus get it."

Journey shook her head and grabbed Kara's hand. She pulled her back toward the garage. "Come on. I'll help you. I sent Marcus to put a sign down by the road."

Kara groaned as they walked back to the garage.

Between them and the champagne was a maze of boxes, tool chests, hunting gear, bicycles, and Marcus's motorcycle. Kara put her hand on her hip. "How did you even get it over there?" she asked.

"Marcus crammed all this stuff in here today when I told him to clean up the house for the party. I guess he didn't realize I would need to get to the fridge," Journey explained.

She started moving boxes out of the way and slowly cleared the path across the two-car garage.

"Well that's freaking stupid," Kara grumbled as she pushed a rolling tool chest toward the wall.

Ten minutes later the girls finally reached the refrigerator. "Your husband is a moron," Kara said as she yanked the refrigerator door open.

Journey sighed. "I know."

Kara passed two bottles to Journey, then loaded the other three into her arms before kicking the door closed with her heel. Journey led the way back into the house. "Where do you want these?" Kara asked.

"Just put them on the bar for now," Journey answered.

Journey placed her bottles on the counter and quickly shuffled out onto the deck. Kara's parents, Jann and Rod, were there. So were Justin's parents and his older sister, Leanne. They were all standing in a line on the grass, each holding a blown up photo of Justin and Kara together from Christmases past. Marcus was at the end of the line holding two photos. Journey rushed down the steps and took one from him. Justin was nervously tugging at his suit.

She winked up at him and smiled. "You look great."

A bead of sweat trickled down the side of his face.

Kara's heels clunked across the hardwood floor inside. "Hey, Journey, where do you keep the…" Her words trailed off as she stepped onto the deck. Everyone was silent. Kara laughed and covered her mouth with her hands.

Justin's face was a hodgepodge of different shades of red. "Sorry I'm a little late, babe," he said.

Kara put a hand on her hip as she looked at the photographs. "What is this?"

Justin looked down the line and everyone turned their photos around. Each person held a different letter and spelled out "MARRY ME". Justin held up a question mark in one hand and a ring box in the other.

Tears spilled out of Kara's eyes as she laughed. Journey nudged Justin with her elbow. "Get up there and ask her," she said.

He handed her his question mark, and he took the steps two at a time to where Kara stood crying. He got down on one knee, held out the ring, and said, "Kara, will you marry me?"

Kara giggled and nodded her head. Everyone cheered.

Marcus slipped his arm around Journey's waist, and when she looked up at him, she saw tears in his eyes. She rested her head against his chest. "You planned this?" he asked, looking down at her.

She nodded. "Yeah. We've been talking about it for weeks, and I snuck out this morning to nail down the details."

After they kissed and Justin put the diamond on her finger, Kara pointed down the steps at Journey. "You tricked me, you little tramp!"

Journey laughed and held up her hands in defense. "Just a little friendly meddling my dear." She pointed toward the house. "Now you know why I bought champagne!"

20

LIGHTS OUT

JOURNEY AND Marcus spent Christmas day at home with Genna and celebrated with her family on the day after Christmas. Before dinner, they opened gifts in the living room in front of the Christmas tree, as the roast finished cooking in the oven. Genna was sitting in the middle of the living room floor in a mess of torn wrapping paper and mangled bows. Marcus was videotaping her with the video camera Journey had given him for Christmas the day before. "I think she likes the wrapping more than she likes the gifts," he observed.

Carol laughed and crawled toward her granddaughter. "Babies usually do," she said.

Journey smiled up at Marcus when she realized he had turned the camera on her. She waved him away. "Turn that thing off," she whined.

He stepped closer and zoomed in on her face. "Come on, Mama. Say *hello* to the camera," he said.

She put her hand in front of the lens and giggled.

"Let me see that thing," Randall said, extending his hand.

Marcus paused the recording and handed it over to where her dad sat on the sofa. Then he plopped down next to Journey on the floor. "It's the latest model," Marcus told him. "I've been wanting one for a while."

Elena was sitting on the loveseat with Derek. Journey really liked him a lot. He was a studio drummer in Nashville. "Journey, what did Marcus give you?" she asked.

Journey and Marcus exchanged smiles, and he put his arm around her. "He's taking me to Cozumel, Mexico in a couple of months," she replied.

"How romantic," her mother said. "Randall, why don't you take me anywhere romantic?"

"I bought you a lake house, my dear," her dad replied, not looking away from the camera which he was studying.

She laughed, balled up a piece of wrapping paper, and threw it at his head. "I don't remember ever asking for a lake house, smarty-pants!"

"You have a lake house?" Derek asked.

Carol shook her head and pointed at her husband. "Randall has a lake house."

"You know," Elena began. "We should do Christmas there next year. We've not done that since I still lived here. It's really beautiful in the winter."

Carol nodded in agreement. "That would be lovely."

"We could go hunting," Marcus agreed.

Journey laughed. "No firearms on Christmas."

"Why not?" her dad asked. "Your mother bought me a Browning .30-06 hunting rifle for Christmas."

"Sweet," Marcus said, nodding his head. "You should've brought it over. I would have set up the targets."

"Maybe tomorrow?" Randall suggested.

Marcus grimaced. "I've got to work tomorrow. This is

going to be a crazy week. Maybe this weekend though."

Randall gave him a thumbs up. "Absolutely."

"Dad, what did you buy for Mom?" Elena asked.

Carol tilted her head back to show off her new shiny necklace. "It's a *diamond*," she said dramatically.

They all laughed, and Journey leaned forward to take a closer look. "It's really pretty," she said.

"Speaking of diamonds," Elena said. "Justin's proposal the other night was so sweet."

Journey smiled and nodded her head. "Yeah. He did a really good job. She was shocked."

Carol sat up a little. "Justin and Kara are engaged?"

Journey nodded. "He proposed at our Christmas party the other night."

Carol's bottom lip poked out. "Oh, that's so sweet. Why didn't you call and tell me?"

Elena laughed. "Mom, why are you surprised? She didn't tell us when *she* got engaged, remember?"

Marcus laughed. "We didn't tell anybody for a long time. I was too afraid Journey would change her mind."

Journey cut her eyes at him, and he kissed her nose. "Marcus didn't actually propose," she interjected. "He sort of burped out syllables for around a half an hour. 'Uh, do you, ummm… think you might wanna, uh, maybe uh… you know we're having a baby, and uh…'"

He pinched her sides, making her squirm. "You said 'yes' didn't you?"

She playfully rolled her eyes. "It was a miracle."

He nodded. "I'll agree with that."

She put her arms around his neck and leaned her head against his.

"This has been a wonderful Christmas," her father stated.

"Here, here!" Derek agreed, raising his glass of sweet tea.

Marcus's cell phone buzzed in his pocket. Journey shifted so he could retrieve it. He glanced at the number and said, "Excuse me. I've got to take this."

She slid off his lap and stretched out toward Genna. "Mama," Genna said, slapping a bow on Journey's forehead.

"I'm gonna get you," she teased, pinching the fat on Genna's inner thigh making her roll over laughing.

Marcus disappeared to the bedroom, and a few minutes later, he called to Journey. She excused herself and walked out of the living room. When she reached their room, he had his shirt off, and he was strapping on his body armor. She was surprised. "What are you doing?"

"You were right," he said, securing a strap of velcro around his waist.

"About what?"

He checked his Glock and secured it in his waistband holster. "After our conversation the other day, I talked to the task force lead guy. They had the prison send over all of the records of Steven's visitors and phone calls while he was locked up. Brian stopped all contact with him about two years ago. Since then, a man named Travis Morgan has visited Steven once a month like clockwork. Guess who Morgan is affiliated with?"

"The Aryan Brotherhood," she answered.

"Guess where he's from?"

"Atlanta?" she asked.

He shook his head. "He's originally from a small town just outside of Savannah." Marcus buttoned up his shirt. "And guess where he lives now?"

Journey's stomach tightened. "Here in Emerson."

Marcus nodded as he draped his badge, which was attached to a long silver chain, around his neck. "As of two years ago," he said. "Morgan has a lease on an apartment in

East Emerson, right off the interstate."

She gasped. "That's where Brian is."

Marcus nodded his head again and shrugged into his leather jacket. "We think so. A couple of the Marshals have been sitting on the building for the past two days and have seen Steven's Chevelle coming and going from the residence. They have enough probable cause that Brian is inside to move in today."

Journey covered her mouth with her hand. "Why do you have to go? You're not a Marshal," she said. "Isn't this their job?"

He nodded. "Yes, but it's my job too, honey. They need local support, and I'm the one who has been working on this case all year. Besides, if I make this bust, that promotion is mine."

She smiled. "That promotion is yours regardless and you know it."

He kissed her. "I also want the personal satisfaction of putting him away."

She nodded. "I know. Just please be careful."

He cupped her face in his hands and looked carefully into her eyes. "We are going to have a whole team. I promise you; I will be careful."

She nodded as he drew her in for a long kiss. She put her arms around his neck and kissed him just below his ear. "Slap those cuffs on him extra tight for me."

He pulled back and smiled before returning to the hurried task of packing his tactical bag.

He apologized to her family for skipping out on dinner and kissed Journey again at the door. She hugged him tight. "Good luck," she said, kissing his neck. "I love you."

He traced his thumb along her bottom lip. "I love you, too," he said with a wink.

. . .

The police station, which normally would be run by a skeleton crew on the day after Christmas, was pulsing with activity when Marcus pulled his new black SUV into the parking lot. His partner, Curtis, pulled in right behind him.

When he got out of his car, Curtis slapped the hood. "Today is the day, man. I feel it!" he exclaimed.

Marcus laughed. "God, I'm so ready for this to be done." He pulled his heavy bag from the backseat.

Members of the Southeast Regional Fugitive Task Force were already at work when they got inside. A U.S. Marshal slapped Marcus on the back. "Good work, Detective," he said.

Marcus dropped his bag on the floor and walked toward the conference room where several others were gathered and ready to go. "What have we got?"

The leader of the group, who Marcus knew only as Jones, pointed to the map spread on the conference table. "We already have two of your unmarked units here and here," he said, pointing to each end of the street where the apartment building entrance was. "We have another surveillance van, two of our guys, in the parking lot. They haven't seen any movement inside since the black Chevelle pulled in at 0900 hours." He paused and pointed at a burly Marshal who stood a head taller than everyone else. "Campbell is going to be in the lead. He will kick the door in, if necessary. Garrett, you'll be with me since you know these guys better than anyone else. If Drake is in the house, once we get a positive ID, Diaz and White will make the arrest. Everyone else will be crowd control and security. There is only one way in and out of that apartment, but we will have guns in the front and in the back."

Marcus nodded. His heart raced with adrenaline. "Let's do this," he said, clapping his hands together.

Forty-five minutes later, he was riding shotgun in a black

SUV with Jones and Campbell. It was just after 6:30 PM, and it was already dark outside. Marcus recognized Steven's black Chevelle when they pulled into the parking lot. "That's his brother's car," he said, pointing.

They parked, unloaded their arsenal, and Marcus checked his Glock. The team of six headed slowly up the stairs to the second floor. Marcus followed, third in line. When they reached the door to apartment 17B, everyone behind Marcus fanned out with their weapons pointed at the door.

Jones rapped on the door with his fist. When there was no answer, Jones pounded on the door again. "Police, U.S. Marshals. Open the door!"

Someone's radio transmitter went off. "A light went out inside," a distant voice told them.

"Open the door or we are going to take it down!" Jones shouted.

A second later, the door opened just a crack, and Campbell pushed his way inside. Marcus and Jones trained their sights on Steven. "Put your hands up!" Campbell shouted.

Steven obeyed.

"Step slowly out of the apartment! Is anyone else inside?" Campbell asked.

Marcus scanned the dimly lit room. He saw empty pizza boxes on an old table, some shabby furniture, and plenty of beer bottles but no other signs of life.

Steven stepped cautiously out into the breezeway. "There's no one else here!" he shouted.

Campbell and Marcus pushed forward inside as two officers cautiously moved to secure Steven into handcuffs.

Suddenly, the lights inside the apartment flickered out, cloaking the room in a sinister darkness. The whole scene unfolded into slow motion chaos.

Steven hurdled over the two-story hand railing.

Shots rang out from down the hallway, and the distinct sound of a door flying off its hinges and slamming into a wall echoed throughout the room. Flashes of light sporadically lit the room as Marcus and Campbell returned gunfire.

A bullet burned through Marcus's thigh, dropping him to his knees. He kept firing. A flashlight flicked on in time for him to see Brian Drake leering down the barrel of an AR-15.

Another bullet slammed into Marcus knocking him backwards, and the light flickered out.

. . .

Journey wasn't able to eat the dinner that had been slow roasting in the oven since earlier that day. The house smelled like Southern home cooking and Christmas, but she didn't have an appetite. She checked her cell phone again. It had been nearly two hours, and she still hadn't heard from Marcus. Her stomach was in knots.

Her mother placed her hand on top of Journey's. "You really should try and eat something. It's delicious."

Journey sighed. "I'm sorry. I'm just worried. I wish I knew what was happening."

Suddenly, an idea came to her. She jumped up from the table and ran down the hall to their bedroom. She flipped on the light in the closet and opened one of Marcus's safes. After digging around for a moment, her fingers found his spare police scanner in the back. Marcus had made her promise, on more than one occasion, that she would never try to use his radios, but she didn't care. She clicked it on, but the battery was dead. She carried it to the bedroom and placed it on the charger. After a few seconds, she tried again and it came to life.

The familiar shrill beep from dispatch rang out over the line. "All units, 10-3 clear the line for emergency transmission." The shrill beep came again. "All lines cleared," a female voice said. After a couple of beats of silence the voice returned. "All available units, 10-39 immediate backup to 1747 West Copeland Avenue. Shots fired. Repeat. All available units, 10-39. 1747 West Copeland Avenue. Shots fired."

Journey's stomach lurched. "Dad!"

A moment later, Randall crossed the bedroom. "What is it?"

She sank down onto Marcus's side of the bed.

Other voices came through. "Unit 622 en route." A moment later, "Unit 34 en route." And again, "Unit 138 en route."

Another breathless voice came over. "Suspect, possibly injured on foot heading westbound through the woods behind West Copeland toward the interstate. White male, black jeans, white t-shirt, dark brown hair in a ponytail. Repeat. Suspect heading westbound on foot from West Copeland Avenue. Considered armed. Two officers currently in pursuit."

Her whole family gathered in the room. Elena was bouncing Genna in her arms.

"This is unit 832. One suspect inside confirmed dead at entryway. Gunshot wound to the head. Another suspect unaccounted for." There was so much commotion on his end of the radio that it was hard to decipher his message, but Journey recognized Curtis's frantic voice. "This is unit 832. 10-00. Two officers down inside. Second suspect confirmed dead. Repeat. Two officers down. 10-52. We need Medic!"

The dispatcher came through again. "Medic en route. Officers down. Repeat. 10-00. Officers Down." There was a brief, loaded pause. "Unit 832, Can you confirm is it Emerson PD? Is it our officers?"

"One confirmed EPD. 10-45 Critical condition."

Journey doubled over and dropped her face into her hands. Her father knelt and put his strong arms around her.

"10-00. Repeat. Officer down."

Journey worked herself free from her father's grasp. "Where are my keys?"

Randall stood to block her path. "Sweetheart, no."

She pointed at him. "I'm going! You can come along or you can just get out of my way, but I'm going!"

He reached into his pocket for his keys. "I'll drive."

Five minutes later, she was strapped into the passenger's seat of his sedan with a firm grasp on the police scanner. Randall spun up gravel from her driveway as he peeled out onto the main road. Her legs and hands trembled uncontrollably. The ride was a blur, and the noise from the scanner was a flurry of confusion.

"Dad, you have to go faster."

The drive to West Copeland would normally take twenty minutes; they made it in ten. Her dad put the car in park behind a spectacle of fully lit emergency vehicles. Journey was out of the passenger's side door before her father could stop her. She had pushed her way nearly through to the front of the line of frantic officers and EMTs before a pair of strong arms intercepted her. She didn't recognize the man who held her in place as he yelled to get her attention, nor did she hear what he was saying.

"Let me through!" she screamed, pounding his bulletproof chest with her fists.

Her eyes fell on Curtis a few feet away. When he realized who she was, he crossed the gap in a matter of steps. "Journey!" he shouted. The man holding her released her to Curtis who pushed her back a few steps.

"No!" she screamed.

"Journey!" He shook her shoulders. "Look at me!"

EMTs were clearing the staircase to the second floor. Everyone was shouting.

"Look at me!" he repeated, forcing her face in front of his.

His chocolate brown eyes were terrified.

She knew.

"No!" she bellowed again, so blind with tears that everything was a blur of red and yellow lights. Her knees buckled, and if it weren't for Curtis's firm grasp around her, she would've melted into a puddle on the concrete.

"He's alive, but they've got to get him to the hospital," he said. "You have to listen to me. Look at me."

She blinked and saw the stretcher coming down the stairs. She recognized the worn-out tactical boots that she had never gotten around to replacing.

"Curtis, please," she begged.

Knowing he wasn't going to be able to hold her for long, he ushered her through the crowd. She pushed everyone away that moved toward her. When she broke through the police tape, she lunged toward her husband as they carried him to the ambulance. His eyes were closed, and his mouth was open. They had stripped off his vest. Blood was everywhere and splattered across his perfect face. She grasped for him, and the emergency workers paused long enough for her to touch his cold chest.

"Marcus!"

"Get her out of here!" someone angrily demanded.

Curtis clotheslined her with his arm as she tried to follow the stretcher. "Stop!" he shouted, digging his fingers into both of her arms. "You can't go! We'll follow." He shook her again. "Journey! We will follow him."

The ambulance was rolling before they even slammed the doors closed. Journey watched a paramedic straddle Marcus's legs holding a firm compression on his thigh with all of his body strength. Curtis practically dragged Journey to his SUV and buckled her inside. Her father got into the backseat behind her and put his reassuring hands on her shoulders.

Curtis got in, started the engine, and quickly shut his radio transmitter off. Curtis answered questions for her father the whole 4.3 miles to Emerson Regional Hospital, but she didn't hear a word that they said.

In her lap, her palms were face up and coated with Marcus's blood.

21

SLEEP

AT 9:22 PM, Journey stumbled out of the front door of the Emerson hospital. Several police cruisers and news vans were parked in the front. Expectant officers and reporters were gathered in small huddles, but she staggered past them through the parking lot. Somewhere behind her, she heard the sound of her name, but she didn't look back. When she reached the end of the lot, she sank down into the grass beside a newly planted tree that still had stakes tied to its base for support.

Her cell phone was in her hand.

She brought up a blank text message, searched for David's name, and typed out words she knew she could never say out loud.

Marcus is dead.

Her thumb left a bloody print on the send key.

She stared at the phone for a moment, then hurled it as far as she could into the woods. Her body slumped onto the cold, wet earth as painful sobs erupted from deep inside her.

After some time, Elena stretched out beside her. Without a word, Elena pulled her winter coat open and gathered her sister under its protection from the cold.

. . .

David paced the room for ten minutes trying to call Journey's cell phone to no avail. When he couldn't get an answer on Marcus's phone either, he called his parents. His mother sounded grave when she answered the phone.

"I was just about to call you," she said.

David sank down at his kitchen table. "Is it true?"

"Marcus was shot and killed tonight in a shootout in East Emerson," she confirmed. "That's all I know."

His face dropped into the palm of his hand. "I'm on my way," he said and disconnected the call.

He rose from the table and went to his bedroom. He was cramming clothes and toiletries into a duffel bag when Allie got home after seeing a movie with her friends. When she came in, she halted in the doorway with surprise.

She dropped her purse at the door. "What are you doing?"

He didn't pause to look at her. "Going to Georgia. My friend Marcus was killed tonight."

She said nothing. He pulled his suit out of their bedroom closet, and as he stuffed a pair of dress shoes into the bag, she stepped forward. "You're not going to Georgia," she protested.

Anger nearly boiled over inside of him, and he turned his fierce gaze on her. "I don't think I asked for your permission."

She looked taken back but indignant. She opened her mouth. "David, I won't—"

He cut her off. "You *won't* say another word about it," he said. "I'm sorry if you don't like it, but if you don't understand why I have to go, then maybe you *shouldn't* be here when I get back."

She stumbled back against the wall as he brushed past her. He wanted to feel like a jerk, but he didn't. There was no time for remorse or apologies.

. . .

The next couple of days were a foggy mix of disjointed events. People came and went from Journey's house, bringing food and flowers and insufficient words of condolence. Journey spent most of her time confined to her bedroom, hugging Marcus's pillow, just to be comforted by his fading scent imprinted in the fabric.

In the chaos that ensued during the invasion of the apartment on West Copeland, Brian Drake had shot her husband twice: once in the shoulder and once in the thigh, shattering his femur and sending shards of bone into his femoral artery. He had bled to death before the ambulance reached the hospital.

Brian had also been shot multiple times. Marcus had succeeded in crippling him with a bullet into his ribcage before Billy Campbell, another officer injured in the shootout, delivered a fatal blow to Brian's skull. The other shooter, Travis Morgan, also died at the scene. Steven, however, escaped over the balcony into the woods. He was still considered armed and dangerous.

After two days of being at home, surrounded by everything to do with Marcus, she asked her parents if she and Genna could stay with them for a while. Without hesitation, they helped her pack some essentials, and they drove her and the baby back to their house. She left most of the funeral arrangements to her mother and to the police department, but she did ask that the service be held at Marcus's grandmother's church. He would've wanted that.

Journey was buried under a mound of covers in the comfort of her childhood bed, when she heard a gentle knock at the door. She didn't answer. The door creaked slightly and warm light spilled into her dark room.

"Journey?" she heard a deep voice say.

She pressed her eyes closed. "David," she whispered.

Slowly, he walked into her field of vision and knelt down beside her bed. His fingers gently trailed down her face. She grasped his hand and held it tightly over her eyes as the sobs came again. The edge of the bed sank down under his weight, as he gathered her into his arms and held her head against his shoulder. He stroked her hair as she heaved against his chest.

"I'm so sorry," he cried with her.

She curled her fingers into his shirt and wept uncontrollably for what felt like an eternity. He cradled and rocked her in his arms until her wailing subsided. When she could finally speak again, she stayed nestled under his chin and asked, "What are you doing here?"

He pressed a kiss into her hair. "I came as soon as I got your message. I've been trying to find you for days. This is my third visit here because I didn't know where you had moved."

"What about your wife?"

"Oh, she didn't come," he said, shaking his head.

"Was she mad?"

He chuckled softly. "Yeah."

She pulled back and looked at him. His hair was a mess, and he had a perfect three-day-old, five o'clock shadow. Aside from a few lines around his eyes, he hadn't changed a bit. She looked into his eyes. "You shouldn't be here."

He digested the sentence for a moment before finally tracing the outline of her face with his fingertips. "Journey, I should never have left in the first place."

She dropped her head and sighed.

After a moment, he nudged her with his shoulder. "Come on. Get up. Your mother tells me you haven't eaten in almost three days."

She groaned, but he wouldn't allow her to fall back onto the mattress. "Up, I said," he repeated, tugging on her arm. He pulled her legs around to the side of the bed and hoisted her up onto her feet.

He took in the full sight of her. "Whoa." His eyes were wide. "You need a hairbrush. That mess is scary."

She covered her head with her arms and walked to the dresser. She picked up her brush and yanked it through the tangles in her hair. Finally, she turned back toward him. "Better?" she asked.

He tilted his head to the side. "Not really." He laughed and took her hand. "But it will have to do. Come on."

Downstairs, in the living room, everyone looked very surprised to see her. Kara and her mother were there, along with her own parents and Elena and Derek. "Well, I'm glad to see someone got you out of the bed," Elena said smiling.

Journey pushed her hair away from her face. She looked around the room. "Where's Genna?" she asked.

"She's asleep in her pack and play in our room," her mother replied. "How about some dinner?"

Journey nodded and walked toward the kitchen. She stopped to hug Kara's mother, Jann. David sat down at the table next to her.

"David, can I fix you a plate?" her mother asked from the stove.

He shook his head. "No ma'am. I already ate with my parents."

"Are you sure? I made your favorite," she said.

His eyes lit up. "Sweet potatoes?"

She laughed. "Yes, sir."

He smiled. "Maybe I'll have a little bit."

Journey laughed for the first time in days. Her mother put a plate full of ham, sweet potatoes, green beans, and two rolls on the table in front of her. Journey felt overwhelmed. "You know I can't eat all this."

Carol squeezed her shoulder. "Try."

David ate the bowl of sweet potatoes that her mother made for him and then ate half of Journey's as well. Kara, Jann, and Elena joined them, and when he started talking about his deployments with the Rangers, Journey's dad came and sat down also. Journey found it a relief to hear about anything other than the shooting, the funeral, or even about how wonderful Marcus was.

"I think the baby is awake," Derek said, coming from the guest bathroom down the hallway.

Carol wiped her hands on the dish towel. "Thank you, Derek."

Journey pushed her chair back. "No, Mom. I want to go get her," Journey said, turning toward the hallway. She walked down to her parents' master bedroom and quietly pushed the door open.

Genna was on her back with her hands grabbing onto her feet. She was babbling away as usual. "Mama!" Genna yelped when she saw her.

Journey smiled, reached down, and lifted her out. Journey hadn't held her daughter in days. She kissed the top of her little head as more tears filled her eyes. "Ma ma ma ma ma," Genna continued while trying to stuff her fingers into Journey's mouth.

"I've missed you," Journey said, wiping her eyes on the back of her sweatshirt sleeve. She hugged Genna until she squirmed.

When she carried her back to the kitchen, David stood

when she entered. He laughed. "She looks just like you," he said and laughed. "You know, back in high school when you didn't have any hair!"

Journey smiled and stopped in front of him. "This is Genna," she said.

He reached out to take her. "Hi Genna." He dangled her awkwardly out in front of him. "I'm your Uncle Dave."

Carol put her arm around Journey's shoulders.

"She's not a football, David," Kara said. "You look like you're ready to spiral her across the room."

He laughed and pulled the baby close to him, balancing her against his shoulder. She played with his beard and giggled when he rubbed his scruffy chin against her cheek. "How old is she now?" he asked.

"Ten months," Journey answered. "She will be one in February."

David smiled at her as he bounced Genna in his arms. "You did good."

"Thanks," she replied.

Kara and her mother stood up from the table. She walked over and pulled Journey into a tight hug. She was able to rest her chin on the top of Journey's head. "It's getting late, and I've got to drive Mom home, so we are going to take off. I'm glad to see you out of bed," she said.

Journey looked up at her. "Thanks for being here."

Kara winked at her. "I'll be back tomorrow."

Jann hugged Journey goodbye as well. She looked just like Kara, only a foot shorter with more wrinkles and dark auburn hair.

Journey patted her on the back. "Thanks for stopping by, Jann."

Jann gave her a sad smile. "I'm so sorry for your loss, sweetie." She squeezed Journey's hands. "When is the funeral?"

Journey's mouth fell open. "I have no idea." She looked around for her mother. "Mom, when's the funeral?"

Carol stepped toward them. "Visitation is on Thursday evening from four to seven, and the funeral is Friday afternoon at three. Both will be held at First Presbyterian. There will be a processional after the funeral to the Oakdale Cemetery for a graveside service."

"A processional?" Journey asked confused.

Carol nodded. "The department told me that it's pretty standard for fallen police officers. There will be police officers there from all over the place."

Journey forced a smile. "That's nice." She felt tears in her eyes again. She didn't think it was possible for a human being to cry as much as she had that week. "Excuse me. You guys be careful," she said, walking out of the kitchen and to the back door.

She stepped out on the back deck taking deep breaths and focusing on the mountains instead of the twisting pain in her chest. She wiped her eyes again when she heard the door open behind her. "You still smoke?" David asked, holding out a pack of cigarettes.

She sighed with a little bit of relief. "I do today," she said, accepting one. He lit it for her, and she sat down on top of the wooden picnic table.

David sat down next to her, stretching his legs out over the seat. Journey hugged her knees to her chest and took a long drag. "I don't know how to do this, David," she said, blowing the smoke out slowly.

He looked up at the night sky. "Nobody does, kid," he said. "No one is meant to go through anything like this."

She shivered, and he took his coat off and wrapped it around her shoulders. "Thanks," she said.

"No prob," he replied.

After another beat of silence, she shook her head. "This is my fault."

He put his feet up on the bench and leaned his elbows on his knees. "You know that's not true," he said.

She looked at him. "Do I?" she asked. "Marcus was hell-bent on finding Brian Drake because he threatened me. Hell, the only reason we knew any of the Drakes is because of me."

He frowned. "Journey, Marcus was hell-bent on catching a criminal because he was a good cop. And Brian Drake was trouble long before and long after you had anything to do with the situation. It has nothing to do with you."

She wasn't convinced, but she didn't argue.

David leaned slightly toward her. "You saved Marcus," he said.

She laughed with sarcasm. "Shut up, David."

"Journey, he was a freaking orphan before he married you. He had his old grandparents until they died and that was all besides a few distant relatives that he had by marriage. I mean, how many family members of Marcus's have you ever actually met?" He motioned back to the house. "You gave him a family. And I didn't need to be around for the past few years to know that your family took him in like their own." He shifted. "And Genna… I can only imagine how much he loved being a dad."

She closed her eyes and briefly recalled the sight of Marcus with the baby monitor strapped to his utility belt. She smiled through her tears and sighed. "I miss him so much," she cried.

He put his arm around her shoulders and rested his head against hers. "I know." He looked down at her. "Wanna hear something funny?"

"Please," she begged.

He laughed. "Marcus called and cussed me out about a month ago."

She whirled around and looked at him. "What?"

He nodded. "Yep. It was the day after I called you and said I wasn't coming." He held up his hand in the shape of a phone, pressed it to his ear, and began to mimic Marcus's voice. "David Britton, you've been a dumbass for as long as I've known you, but this is a new low even for you! If you ever make my wife shed one more mother-fucking-tear over your sorry ass again, I will hunt you down, run you over with my car, and put a bullet into your thick, stupid skull!"

She covered her mouth and laughed. "He did not."

He held his hands up. "True story."

She chuckled again. "That does sound like him."

He laughed. "I was glad I was across the country that day."

She smiled. It felt good to laugh. She looked over at him. "He loved you," she said.

He raised his eyebrows, nodded his head, and laughed again. "And hated me at the same time. He told me that too."

"That's for sure." She relaxed a little and stared out over the moonlit horizon. "He took care of me, just like you asked him to."

He paused. "He told you about that, huh?"

"Yeah, he did."

He leaned into her shoulder. "Between you and me, Marcus took it too damn far. I never told him he could marry you."

She sighed. "But he did. And we were really, really happy."

He squeezed her hand gently. "I'm glad."

She turned her body to face him. "David, you have to go home and fix things with Allie."

He started to object, but she held up her hand to silence him.

"No, let me say this," she insisted. "I'm sure that in some alternate universe you and I have a fairytale, but it's not in this one. You're not the guy who walks out on his commitments, and no matter how much of a rebel I can be sometimes, I care too much about you to let you ruin your marriage without saying something. You and I would never work—not in a million years—if you were to walk out on your wife. We would always have that hanging over us. And I love you too much to live that way, even if it means we could be together."

She took his hand and looked carefully into his pained eyes. "I spent so many years regretting that you and I never had a chance; I don't want to ever spend a minute regretting that we *did*."

They were both silent for a long time. "I know you're right," he said. "I don't like it, but I know you are."

"So, you'll go home?"

He nodded. "After the funeral."

22

10-7

JOURNEY WOKE up on Friday morning with her eyes nearly swollen shut. The four hour visitation the night before had been emotionally brutal and utterly exhausting. Journey was amazed at the outpouring of visitors from their community and well beyond the city of Emerson. She spent hours listening to countless stories of how Marcus had impacted people's lives inside and outside of his police work.

The most heart-wrenching visit had been from the family of Julie and Marci Kennedy, whom Journey hadn't seen since Steven's trial. Mrs. Kennedy had wept openly in Journey's arms and had thanked her profusely and, in Journey's opinion, unnecessarily for her and Marcus's involvement in finding peace and justice for their family. The couple had moved out of the state of Georgia in an attempt to start their lives again without the overwhelming memories that Emerson held for them on every corner. Journey was quickly beginning to understand their decision. She sincerely appreciated that they had traveled so far, and had reopened so many painful memories, just to convey their condolences.

As Journey sat wrapped in a towel after her shower, she lacked the energy or the desire to get ready for what would surely be one of the most excruciating days of her life. It felt as though she were being tasked with dressing herself for the guillotine. It was the last day of the year, but it felt like the last day of her life.

"Knock, knock," Kara said, poking her head around Journey's bedroom door.

Journey looked up as she walked inside carrying a garment bag. "Hey there," she offered.

As usual, Kara looked beautiful in a simple black, knee-length dress and cardigan sweater. Carefully, she laid the hanging bag across the bed and knelt down in front of Journey. She pushed Journey's wet hair back off of her face and lightly kissed her forehead. "I came to do all the work, so you can be pretty without lifting a finger."

Journey closed her eyes, willing herself to not begin crying again already. "Thank you," she whispered.

Kara took her hand. "Come on. Let's go commandeer your mother's big bathroom."

An hour later, Journey's hair was dried and flat-ironed down her back. Her makeup was simple and waterproof. Kara had brought her a black sweater dress, borrowed from her cousin, which had short sleeves, simple rhinestones at the neckline, and a belt around the middle. She had also bought for her a pair of dressy boots with a low heel. Journey felt comfortable—and miserable.

The police department had rented a black town car to pick her up and drive her to the funeral, which was convenient because she had left her car in the church parking lot after the visitation the night before.

Her parents and the baby rode with her to downtown Emerson. She was overwhelmed at the sight of cars parked along the street for a stretch of at least a mile in each direction of the church.

Once inside, the only available seats were those reserved for family. The church, which had at least a capacity of a thousand, was beyond standing room only. The vestibule and the courtyard out front were full of people who couldn't even get inside. Kara, Justin, and David were in the pew behind Journey and her family. David silently squeezed her shoulder when she sat down.

Among the crowd, were more police officers than Journey had ever seen in her life combined. Each wore their full dress uniforms, fitted and polished brilliantly. Judging from the different styles and colors, she decided that there had to be at least fifty or more different departments represented. An entire section of the church was devoted to the entire Emerson police force. Curtis Martin, Marcus's brother on the force since the day he received his badge, was seated on the front row opposite of the aisle from Journey. When she caught his eye, she motioned him over.

He stood to attention and then gracefully closed the area between them. He knelt and cried as he embraced her. "You look beautiful," he whispered.

"Thank you," she answered. She pulled back and looked into his tearful eyes. "Will you sit with me?"

His lower lip trembled.

"You're family," she said, scooting across the pew to make room for him.

He sucked in a brave, deep breath and sat down beside her.

The church was covered in flowers. Beneath the altar, surrounded by a fragrant spray, was the large, dark walnut casket draped with the American flag. At Journey's insistence, it was closed. His formal, peaked police cap, was perched on the lid. On either side stood an officer, in full dress, standing at attention. Marcus's police headshot, framed in expensive mahogany wood, was perched on a four foot high stand.

Journey couldn't look at his face.

The police chaplain, who had also performed their wedding, gave a poignant, heartfelt message about loyalty, duty, and the ultimate sacrifice. He noted Marcus's achievements but praised his integrity, heart, and magnetic personality. He prayed a thoughtful prayer of encouragement for Journey and Genna and then reminded her that the police force would always be her family. After he spoke, to Journey's surprise, Lt. Governor Richard Weidman, offered a brief statement and conveyed his condolences to Journey on behalf of himself and the entire state of Georgia. When he finished, Randall Durant rose from his seat, walked up to the microphone, and shook the Lt. Governor's hand.

Slowly, her father turned to face the enormous crowd. From his jacket, he pulled a small sheet of paper and laid it on the pulpit. Journey reached for her mother's arm. His hands were visibly shaking, and he took a long and labored breath before he spoke.

"Detective Marcus Gabriel Garrett, has been rightfully recognized and commended here today as an exceptional police officer, a diligent detective, an honorable man, and a faithful friend. It is my wish, and that of my wife, to specifically recognize the man Marcus Garrett was without his badge.

"Marcus became a member of my family long before he married my youngest daughter." Randall paused to dab his handkerchief at his eyes. "He loved and supported my little girl in times when a father's love just wasn't enough. He rescued her, cherished her, and restored our family during a time when we were lost and broken. He was an exceptional husband and father, and I will be forever in his debt for making our family complete.

"On behalf of my family, Marcus's wife Journey, and baby Genna, thank you all for your continued love, support, and prayers through this dark season. I believe that our sovereign God orchestrates everything in His perfect timing, and while I will never understand why my son left us so soon, your presence here today is evidence of the wonderful legacy he leaves behind. Thank you."

Journey was weeping by the time he finished. She stood and embraced her daddy as he left the platform of the sanctuary. "I love you," he whispered before kissing her cheek and taking his seat. When he sat down, he pulled Genna from Carol's arms and held her against his chest.

Bagpipes played "Amazing Grace" as Curtis and five other officers from the Emerson Police Department gathered in formation at the front of the church. Police Chief Gerald Branson called them all to attention, and they saluted the casket. Slowly, they lifted it from its base and carried it down the aisle.

The ride to the cemetery was as overwhelming as the service. The fire department draped the largest American flag that Journey had ever seen over the highway. The processional of a countless number of cars was lead through the town by thirty uniformed police officers on motorcycles. It seemed as though the entire state of Georgia had shown up to line the streets with flags and banners. Officers and members of the military saluted, citizens stood reverent with their hands over their hearts, and small children waved flags as they passed by.

When they gathered at the graveside, the chaplain read from The Message version of the Bible, Ecclesiastes 3:1-12. "Everything that happens in this world happens at the time

God chooses. He sets the time for birth and the time for death, the time for planting and the time for pulling up, the time for killing and the time for healing, the time for tearing down and the time for building. He sets the time for sorrow and the time for joy, the time for mourning and the time for dancing… He sets the time for love and the time for hate, the time for war and the time for peace… I know the heavy burdens that God has laid on us. He has set the right time for everything. He has given us a desire to know the future but never gives us the satisfaction of fully understanding what He does. So I realized that all we can do is be happy and do the best we can while we are still alive."

When he closed his Bible, he offered a prayer, and then Taps was played on a lone trumpet behind them. Two officers carefully folded the American flag and placed it, along with Marcus's cap, in Journey's lap. The crowd was silent as the entire police force of the city of Emerson stood at attention and saluted.

All of their radios went off in unison with the same voice of the female dispatcher who had taken the calls the night Marcus was killed.

"Emerson to No. 347," she called out.

And then again.

"Emerson to No. 347."

And then a third time.

"Emerson to Detective Marcus Garrett."

Then finally…

"Detective Marcus Garrett is 10-7, off duty. Gone, but never forgotten."

23

SMOKING GUNS

THE POLICE department, the Presbyterian church, and Journey's parents' church all coordinated a meal in the fellowship hall at First Presbyterian after the conclusion of the services. David, Kara, and Justin stayed for dinner at Journey's insistence. David desperately wished there was something he could do to ease the pain of the horrific day she was having. However, since he didn't have a magic wand to wave it all away, he watched her closely all evening for the slightest hint of someway he could help.

Near the end of the dinner, her parents came to the table where she sat next to him with Genna on her lap. "We are going to let the car take us home. Are you ready to go?" her mother asked.

Journey let out a slow sigh. "I am ready to go, but would you mind taking Genna with you? I think I'm going to drive myself home because I could really use some alone time," she said. "My car is still here."

Carol exchanged a worried glance with her husband.

David leaned forward. "I can follow her home and make sure she's alright," he offered.

That seemed to relax her mother, and Journey smiled gratefully at him. "Whatever you need," Randall said, reaching out for Genna.

Journey kissed her daughter on the cheek before passing the baby to her father. Carol hoisted the diaper bag onto her shoulder. She hugged Journey. "Be careful. We'll see you at the house."

Journey nodded. "I'll be close behind you."

When they had gone, she rested her head against David's shoulder. "Thank you. I don't think I can stand one more car ride with awkward silence and nothing good to talk about."

He squeezed her hand. "Whatever I can do," he said.

Kara slapped her hand on the table. "I say we go get drunk!" she exclaimed, making Journey smile genuinely for the first time all day.

Justin laughed and nodded his head. "It is New Year's Eve. I agree."

David nodded to the ring on Kara's hand. "After seven years, how did you finally get him to propose?" he asked.

Kara pointed at Journey. "I'm pretty sure she forced him to ask me."

Journey sipped her glass of watered-down sweet tea. "I did no such thing. I just helped coordinate the details. Besides, I believe that you have done your fair share of interfering in my love life over the years."

Kara smiled at Justin. "I'm not complaining."

Justin kissed her. "I'm not either."

Journey groaned. "Enough of that," she whined. She looked at David. "I'm ready to go home and chill out."

He nodded and stood up. He helped her to her feet as

Kara and Justin came around the table. Kara hugged her. "I love you," she said. "You did good today."

Journey was surprised that 'barely surviving' was a praiseworthy feat. "Uh, thanks."

Justin hugged her as well. "If you need anything at all, you have my number."

Journey looked at him with sincere appreciation. "Thank you."

David helped her slide into her coat, and he waited as she said her goodbyes to the others who were still in the dining hall. Finally, he offered her his arm, and she linked hers through it. "Let's go home," he said.

She sighed. "Please."

He walked her outside to her car. "I'll be right behind you."

"Could you do me another favor?" she asked.

He looked at her intently. "Anything."

She laughed. "Beer sounds really good. Wanna stop and get us a six pack and bring it to the house?"

He laughed. "Absolutely!" He hesitated for a second. "Are you sure you're OK to drive? I promised to look after you."

She nodded. "Yeah, I'm fine. I promise."

"OK," he said. "I'll stop and catch up with you. What kind of beer do you want?"

"Surprise me," she said.

He smiled and opened her car door. "Will do."

David pulled his dad's truck out of the parking lot behind Journey and followed her almost all the way to her house until they reached Norm's Gas Mart, the gas station where they had spent a lot of time tailgating in high school. When he pulled into the parking lot, he saw that Norm, himself, was working that evening. He laughed and got out of the truck, leaving it running near the door. He walked inside and Norm smiled.

"David Britton, I haven't seen you in a month of Sundays!" The old man laughed and stepped around from behind the counter.

They embraced, and David slapped him on the back. "I can't believe you still run this place, you old coot. How have you been?"

He nodded. "I'm good. Arthritic and tired, but good." He squeezed David's shoulder. "Your mother says you're a big war hero now? An Army Ranger, I hear?"

David registered movement in the corner of his eye. He turned and saw a hooded figure open his truck door and climb inside. "What the…" His shout trailed off as he rushed toward the door, and the truck pulled away from the curb.

His brain set off warning bells of recognition when the thief turned to look for oncoming traffic. It was Steven Drake. "Damn it!" David shouted. He whirled around back toward Norm. "Norm, I need your keys. Please!"

Norm's mouth fell open. "David, we need to call the police!"

"Norm please," David begged. "Call the police, but I need to borrow your car!" He yanked out his wallet. "Here… you can hold my wallet till I bring it back, and you can have all the cash inside."

Norm looked confused but finally shook his head. "That's not necessary," he said, shuffling to the back room. He returned as fast as his arthritic hips could carry him. "Here, take my car. I'll call the police. Just be careful."

"I owe you, big time." David took the keys and darted out to the parking lot.

Steven had several minutes of a head start on him if he was heading to where David knew he was. He realized Steven must have been following them, and had decided to steal David's truck and leave his own when he was presented with the opportunity. Steven was going after Journey, and she had no idea it was him driving David's truck.

He tried to call her cell phone but remembered she had chucked it into the woods the night Marcus had died. He couldn't recall her parents number so he dialed 911 instead. He knew he would still beat the police by at least twenty minutes.

. . .

Journey parked in her parents' driveway and rested her head against the steering wheel for a moment before finding her purse and getting out of the car. She clicked the lock button on her key fob and headed toward the front door. Headlights turned down the driveway, and she laughed a little out loud. "That was fast," she said, shaking her head.

She paused to wait for David to park and join her. He wrenched open the squeaky truck door, forgetting to turn off the headlights. She laughed in the direction of his silhouette as he slammed the door. "You forgot the lights!" she called to him as he approached.

She hadn't remembered that he was wearing jeans.

It was too late to run when she saw Steven's face. She darted toward the door and pulled on the handle, but it was locked. Before she could knock, fumble for a key, or even scream he was on top of her with his hand clamped over her mouth.

"Hello again," he snarled in her ear.

He reeked of cigarettes and whiskey.

She struggled against him, but he had a firm grasp on her right arm that she had so badly injured in her car accident less than two years before. When she winced with pain, he dug his fingers into her old scars even harder.

"Let me tell you how this is going to go. If you scream, your parents are going to come running. Maybe they will even have that new baby girl of yours. I will blow their fucking heads off as soon as they open the door. Do you understand?"

She feverishly nodded her agreement. He slowly removed his hand from her mouth and retrieved a gun from his waistband. He pressed it to her temple. "We are going to get into your car, and you're going to drive until I tell you to stop."

"You'll never get away with this," she said.

He laughed. "With the widow of the hero with me? Yeah… I will." His voice was so even and controlled that it sent chills through her.

Just then, a small red compact sedan screamed into the driveway catching both of them by surprise. It screeched to a stop, angled in behind her car, and the front door flew open. It was David. Before Steven could react, David had his gun aimed from behind the car door, straight at them.

"Drop the gun, Steven!" he warned.

Steven laughed. "Look who it is… the guy who's always been in my way."

"Let her go!" David demanded.

"Are you fucking kidding me? She's my ticket out of here." Steven shouted. "You'd better think carefully about what you're doing, Britton. I don't have anything else to lose. And I promise you, Dave, I'll put a bullet through her ear if you don't move that car by the time I count to three."

"You so much as make her whimper, and you won't have a chance to remember how to pull the trigger," David threatened.

Steven pressed the barrel hard against her skull. "You won't do it. You won't risk missing me and killing her."

"I'm a sniper. I don't miss."

"I suggest you aim steady then," Steven growled, ushering her forward a step. "One!" he challenged David. When David didn't move, Steven forced another step.

What are you waiting for! Journey screamed in her head.

"Two!" Steven hissed.

David's arms flinched, catching Steven's attention.

"*Three,*" a cool voice came from behind them.

Steven turned in surprise as a bullet exploded from her father's rifle. Steven flew backwards at least two feet, toppling Journey to the ground with him. She clawed to get away and scrambled across the grass.

Her father's new Browning .30-06 was still smoking. Steven was struggling for breath. The blast had blown right through his chest, but no one moved to help him.

David kicked Steven's gun across the yard before he practically dove on top of Journey. She was shaking uncontrollably in his arms. Her hands were, once again, covered with blood. As she watched Steven desperately fighting to live, the disturbing truth occurred to her that for the second time in a week she was watching the life literally drain out of a man who had loved her.

"Are you OK?" David asked, ripping her jacket open and checking her for wounds.

She tried to slow her breathing. "Yeah, I'm OK." She grasped his forearms in hopes of steadying her trembling body.

Her father knelt down beside her. "Are you sure?" he asked, placing the rifle on the ground.

"I'm sure." Her teeth were chattering when she looked up at her dad. "Good shot."

Steven sputtered out blood and gurgled as he tried to cough. They all looked over to where he was bleeding onto the grass. Her father stood up and walked over toward him. He took a knee beside Steven's convulsing body and leaned over him. "I warned you to never come around my house again."

. . .

Steven Drake died on the front lawn before the paramedics or the police even arrived. Curtis had been among the first of the officers to respond. He called the coroner when he couldn't find Steven's pulse. Journey sat wrapped in David's coat on the front porch swing with Elena while her father and David relayed the events of the nightmare to the police.

David crossed the yard and joined them on the porch. He looked like he had aged a decade since the funeral. He pointed back to the swarm of emergency responders. "Your dad has to go down to the police station to make a formal statement, but I don't think it will take too long." He looked at Elena. "I've got to take Norm's car back to the gas station. Do you think your boyfriend could follow me and bring me back?"

Elena nodded. "Yeah, absolutely," she said and went into the house.

David sat down and put his arm around Journey's shoulders. "How are you?"

She sighed. "I think my brain is still trying to catch up."

"I know what you mean." He was drawing circles on her arm with his finger. "Your dad asked me to hang out here for a while because he doesn't know how long they are going to keep him at the station. I hope that's OK."

She nodded. "Is Dad in trouble?"

He shook his head. "No. It's just a formality whenever anyone is shot and killed."

"OK," she said. "Why didn't you shoot Steven?"

"I saw your dad had a clear shot behind him. If he hadn't been there, I would've put him down before he got you to the car. I just didn't want to take the chance if I didn't have to."

She cut her eyes over at him. "You're a sniper?"

He grinned and looked away. "Yeah. Don't tell anybody."

"That's badass."

He hugged her, and she rested her head against his

shoulder. Derek came onto the porch holding his keys. "Are you ready to go now?" he asked.

David nodded his head. "Yeah." He looked down at Journey. "Why don't you go get your pajamas on and start settling down. If I crash here, do you think you can take me to the airport in the morning?"

Her stomach tightened, but she nodded. "Of course."

"I'll be back in a little bit."

"Hurry." She sighed as he stood up.

He studied her for a moment, then leaned down and pressed a kiss into her hair. "I promise."

When David was gone, Journey's mother came outside and handed her a cup of steaming hot tea. "Here. This will help settle your nerves," she said.

"I hope it has Valium in it," Journey said, accepting the cup.

Carol settled in the swing beside her and gently rested her head against Journey's. "Are you alright?" she asked.

Journey stared out into the spectacle of flashing lights in the driveway. "Do you think I've finally gotten all that I deserve? That maybe, now, all of this hell is over with?"

Her mother pulled back with surprise. "All that you deserve?" she asked.

Journey motioned to where they were zipping up the body bag on the lawn. "I can't shake the feeling that this is somehow the back end of 'what goes around, comes around.' I mean, no matter what you say to try and make me feel better, my mistakes set all of this into motion years ago."

Carol grasped her daughter's hand. "Journey, look at me."

Journey's gaze slowly turned to her mother.

Carol's eyes were tired but brimming with a wide range of emotions. "You listen to me very carefully," she began. "We've all made terrible choices and mistakes in our lifetimes that we can't undo or take back. But, Journey, it's time for you to forgive yourself and let that part of your past go. Your mistakes do not define who you are as a person. They define who you *are not.*"

Journey curled into her mother and wept against her shoulder. "I love you, Mom."

Carol kissed her cheek. "I love you more than you will ever know."

. . .

Steven Drake no longer being a threat was the one and only thing that made David feel remotely better when Journey and her parents walked him to the terminal at the airport.

"I wish you didn't have to leave," Carol told him with tears in her eyes at the entrance to the security checkpoint.

He dropped his carryon bag on the floor. "You and me both," he agreed. Emotion was pooling in the pit of his stomach. He hugged Journey's mother and kissed her cheek. "Save me some sweet potatoes at Thanksgiving," he said with a wink.

She blushed.

Randall Durant extended his hand, and David welcomed it. Instead of just shaking it, her father pulled him into a tight embrace. "You are welcome with us anytime, David. I hope we will see you again soon."

David smiled as he felt her father's hand squeeze his shoulder. He released him and nodded. "You'll see me again."

David's eyes fell on Journey.

Randall cleared his throat. "Journ, we'll meet you in the lobby. David, Happy New Year," he said.

David smiled. "Happy New Year."

As Randall ushered Carol back to the entrance, David turned back to Journey. He carefully tried to memorize everything about her: her boot cut blue jeans over a pair of clunky black boots; her fitted Pink Floyd t-shirt and Army-green jacket; her long, blond hair and purple fingernails. She was the exact same girl he had fallen for in Geometry class, just a little more grown up and with a lot more hair.

"Come here," he said, taking her hand and pulling her close.

After a long moment, that could never be long enough, she pulled away. "When do you leave for Afghanistan?"

He thought for a moment. "Next Thursday," he answered.

"Please be safe."

He cupped her face in his hands and wiped away her tears with his thumbs. "Always," he said.

She took a deep breath and swiped her sleeve across her face. "You have to go before I never let you leave."

He wanted to kiss her.

As if reading his mind, she looked down and took his left hand. She pulled it up and examined his wedding ring in the fluorescent light. "Tell Allie that I asked her to forgive you for coming here, but that I'm not sorry that you did."

David broke and cried in front of her. She pulled him close and held him in her arms. "I don't want to leave you."

She pulled his hand up and kissed his knuckles. A silver ring sparkled on her thumb. He realized that she meant for him to see it. "And you never will," she said with a smile.

He pulled her head to his chest again and lingered as he pressed his lips against her hair. She still used coconut shampoo. "I love you more than life itself," he whispered.

"I love you, too," she said.

24

THE BLUE BRIDESMAID

ALLIE HAD met David at the airport when he arrived home on New Year's Day, and he was able to smooth things over with her in the week before he left with his unit for Afghanistan. She seemed genuinely concerned about his best friend back in Georgia which had, for him, been a step in the right direction. He had called Journey from the plane when it landed and once again before he left the country. She seemed to be doing OK, all things considered. She was thinking of selling her house and moving to the lake. She gave off the impression that she wasn't going to wallow in misery forever, and for that he was grateful. He hadn't been able to communicate with her, or anyone else, while he was gone.

"So, do you think you're going to re-enlist?" David's commanding officer, Kody Vickers, asked as they packed up after their last session of debriefing back on the base in Washington.

David had pondered that question during every down

moment of their six-month mission. He had signed up for six years, and it was nearing the time for him to reevaluate his future. He shrugged his shoulders and zipped his bag closed. "I haven't made up my mind yet. I've got to talk it over with my wife before I decide."

Vickers nodded his head. "Yeah." He nudged David with his elbow. "Gotta ask the General."

David's deployments didn't get the pomp and circumstance of regular units. His homecoming was quiet and unannounced, which he appreciated after spending months on end wandering the mountains of Afghanistan and trying not to get shot. His uneventful arrival also allowed for him to be husband-of-the-year and surprise his wife whenever he returned. She wasn't expecting him for another week, and he hadn't told her any different. On his drive home, he picked up flowers at the supermarket, along with a six-pack and steaks for the grill. It was summertime, and all he wanted was a hug and kiss, a hot uninterrupted shower, and a beer.

Instead, there was an unfamiliar truck parked in his spot when he pulled into his driveway.

He knew what was coming before he even walked into his house, but it didn't lessen the shock of another man asleep in bed with his wife. The irony of the sight disturbed him even more than the reality of it. It was true that he had made a lot of mistakes in his relationship with Allie, but none that warranted this.

Rather than wake the blissful couple, David dropped the flowers in the bedroom doorway and backed slowly out of the house. He slammed the front door hard enough to take it off its hinges and got into his truck. He pulled out of the driveway as the front curtains shifted, and Allie peeked outside.

For three days, he dodged Allie's phone calls and ignored her text messages. Vickers let him move into his guest room while he decided what he was going to do. He wasn't overly surprised that Allie figured out where he was staying, but he was absolutely shocked that she had the guts to show up at Vickers' doorstep.

"Hey," she said timidly when he finally opened the door. She had a stack of mail in her arms.

He just folded his arms across his chest.

"Can I come in?" she asked.

"No," he replied, void of emotion.

"I'm sorry everything happened the way it did." She looked down at the bundle in her arms rather than into his eyes. "I wanted to talk to you when you got back. I wasn't expecting you to show up early."

He smirked. "Clearly."

She brought her eyes up to meet his. "I filed for divorce last month," she said.

Her words rolled over him like a tank. "You did what?"

She sighed and shifted on her feet. "David, I really admire your determination to honor your commitment, I do. But I don't want to be with someone who wants to be with someone else. You're too honorable to call this what it is and do what needs to be done, so I did it."

He realized his mouth was hanging open.

She reached out and handed him a business card. "This is my lawyer. I can either have you served or you can go to her office and sign the paperwork. I don't want anything from you, so there shouldn't be anything to fight about. I don't see any reason for you to get a lawyer or anything. I've already opened my own checking account and had my direct deposit changed. All of your money is accounted for. I've just been splitting the rent on the house between us."

He ran his fingers through his hair. "This is what you want?"

She nodded. "Yes. And we both know it's what you really want too."

He looked at her carefully. "Allie, I never cheated on you."

She nodded. "I know. I believe that you never broke our marriage vows. I just don't think you should have ever said them to me to begin with."

Her words stung, but he couldn't deny their validity.

Before she turned to leave, she offered him the stack of mail. "Don't just throw this stuff on a table somewhere; there's a letter from Emerson in there."

And then she was gone.

. . .

Journey realized very quickly that the only way to recover from the tragic death of a spouse was to just keep on living. Once she was able to do more than simply will herself out of bed each morning, she made it a goal to do one thing—anything—each day to keep moving forward. She started small, like making her bed each morning. Then after a few days she got out and went grocery shopping. After that, she went to the movies with Kara. Before she knew it, she had moved back home and had begun the long process of packing up her old life. Things would never feel the same in that house without Marcus, and it was too painful waking up there each morning with nothing but his memory.

The house sold in six weeks, and she used the money to purchase the lake house from her parents. Her mother reasoned that they didn't need it, but her father wasn't willing to let it go too far from his possession. It turned out to be a win-win situation for everyone. Some of her best memories in life had happened there—happy memories, albeit rebellious ones. It seemed like the best place to start a new life without packing up and running away. Looking back, she found it amusing that running away had only led her so definitively back home again.

At the end of February, she went to Cozumel, Mexico with Kara. Marcus would have wanted her to. It was there that Kara asked her if they could have the wedding at the lake, and Journey couldn't offer the use of her new home fast enough. It was beyond time to make some new and joyful memories. She hadn't been that happy since Christmas.

She hadn't heard from David since he had gotten back from Afghanistan, other than a short email telling her he was home and very busy. He promised he would be in touch when life slowed down a bit. He asked her to pray for him, which she did every single day.

Kara's wedding came at the end of summer. After five months of being treated like Kara's paper doll, Journey was exhausted. For months, she had been forced into more satin dresses and ridiculous high heels than she could count. Journey was convinced that the only reason Kara had chosen her for her maid of honor was for the sheer enjoyment of torturing her. It was like high school prom all over again. However, on the morning of the wedding, even Journey thought she looked pretty spectacular standing in front of the full length mirror in her bedroom.

Her dress was short and sleeveless and molded to her body like she had been dipped into it. The waist was gathered at the side with a simple rhinestone cluster. The fabric was, what Kara referred to as, 'atomic turquoise'. Translated, it was a summery blue with a hint of shimmer to it.

Journey's hair was even more beautiful than the dress. Kara had curled it, loosely braided several pieces, and then tied it all up behind her head. She secured a cream colored flower in the side and left a few wispy pieces around her face. Journey, however, insisted on the final touch of adding one defined streak of 'atomic turquoise' hair dye.

As much as she loved how she looked, her shoes, however, were absolutely absurd. They were open toe sandals with a 5 ¼ inch heel, a one inch platform, and blue, cream, and navy swirls. Journey worried that she would break something or hurt someone by the reception.

"Well?" she heard Kara ask from behind her.

She turned around to see her best friend glide into the room in a white satin, trumpet style gown with a sweetheart neckline and embroidery and beading all the way down the side.

Journey covered her mouth with her hands and gasped.

Jann, Kara's mother, stepped toward Journey. "Doesn't she look like an angel?"

Journey fanned her eyes so as not to ruin her makeup with tears. "Yes, a really, really freaking tall angel!"

Kara proudly lifted her dress to show off a pair of bright blue heels that made Journey's sandals look conservative.

Journey doubled over laughing. When she regained her composure, she walked over and embraced her best friend. "I'm so happy for you," she said. "And for Justin."

"You're like my sister," Kara said. "I love you so much."

"I love you, too," Journey sniffed.

Kara pulled back and playfully pushed Journey's shoulder while dabbing at her eyes with a tissue. "Now, knock it off, hooker. You're gonna ruin my mascara."

The string quartet began playing outside. "Where's Genna?" Journey asked.

"Your mom has her. She's ready," Kara answered.

Journey picked up her bouquet of flowers and walked to the living room behind Kara. She looked around for her mother but didn't see her in the house or on the lawn. All of the guests were seated in white chairs facing the water and Justin, the minister, and Justin's brother were all waiting under a flowered arbor. She still couldn't spot the flower girl anywhere.

"Are you sure mom knows it's time? I can't find her," Journey said, adjusting the top of her dress.

Kara nodded. "I'm positive. My uncle and your mom were getting her settled into the wagon. Relax. You're more nervous than me."

Journey laughed.

Kara nudged her forward. "It's your turn."

Journey straightened upright and then carefully navigated her way out of the French doors onto her porch. Slowly, she placed one foot gently down in front of the other while going down the steps to the lawn. She prayed the whole time that she wouldn't face-plant into the grass. Justin winked at her when, by some miracle, she made it to the front of the crowd without incident. She blew out a sigh of relief and then began looking for the wagon that Kara's uncle was going to pull Genna down the aisle in.

She saw heads turn in the direction of the side of the house. She turned to look but caught both of her parents looking at her with wide, expectant eyes. Her mother had a curious smile. The wagon came into view, and when they started down the aisle at the back row, Journey's breath hung in her chest.

David was pulling the wagon.

He laughed when she finally realized it was him, and her mouth fell open. Journey looked over at Justin who was smiling at her. Her mother was already crying, and her dad was just nodding his head proudly. When David reached the front, he pulled the wagon toward her and stopped. "Surprise," he whispered, leaning over to give her a soft kiss on the cheek.

He lifted Genna out of the wagon and sat down in the seat on the front row that was supposed to have been reserved for her mother to hold the baby. Journey looked at him again, trying not to burst into tears in front of Kara's family and friends. David winked at her and smiled. She realized he was wearing the same light gray suit and cream colored tie as Justin and his brother.

The minister asked everyone to stand as Kara's father escorted her down the aisle. After exchanging a first glance with the groom, Kara flashed a smile at Journey. "You'll never beat me at meddling," she whispered just loud enough for Journey to hear.

. . .

When the ceremony ended, Journey followed Kara and Justin back to the house. She wanted to tell them 'congratulations,' but "what did you do?" came out instead.

Kara turned toward her and laughed. "Don't make me smack you in the head again. Get your ass out there."

Journey turned back toward the door and laid her flowers on the sofa. David was waiting at the bottom of the steps, with his hands stuffed in his pockets and a smile plastered on his face. She started toward him and realized she would never make it there in her shoes. She bent awkwardly and stripped them both from her feet.

She ran down the stairs and into his arms.

He spun her around once before placing her bare feet back on the ground. She gripped his jacket. "What are you doing here?" She laughed and cried at the same time.

"I'm doing what I should've done ten years ago," he said, cradling her face in his hands. He bent and pressed his lips to hers and kissed her until she thought the earth might give way underneath her feet.

When he finally broke the kiss, most of the crowd was cheering. He swiped her tears away with his thumbs. "But…" she began.

He shook his head. "There are no buts. Not anymore. I'm never leaving you again."

He kissed her once more, and she wrapped her arms around his neck. She didn't need to know the details just yet; she just needed him. She had always needed him.

. . .

David was happy for Kara and Justin, but he didn't care at all about their reception. When the evening began to wind down, and the sun sank down in the cloudless sky, he offered Journey his hand. "Walk with me?" he asked.

She slipped her hand in his, lacing their fingers together as he led her along the edge of the water. The last time they had taken that walk, David forfeited six long years of his life with her. He wasn't going to make the same mistake ever again.

"What happened?" she asked as they walked.

He told her the whole story about coming home from Afghanistan and how Allie had filed for divorce. "I wasn't lying when I said I was busy. I had the divorce to take care of and the Army."

"The Army?" she asked.

He nodded. "It was time for me to re-enlist. I didn't."

She hesitated for a step.

He stopped walking and turned to face her. "I didn't want to risk disappointing you, so I decided to wait until everything was finalized before I came home." Her eyes urged him to continue. "I got Kara's invitation to the wedding in the mail, and it had her phone number on it, so I called."

"How long have you two been planning this?" she asked.

He laughed. "For three months."

Journey dropped her face onto his shoulder laughing. "I didn't know she could keep a secret for that long."

He gathered her hands up to his chest and rested his forehead against hers. "I love you, and I'll spend the next hundred years making up for the last decade if you will have me.”

Slowly, she took a step back from him and pulled her hands away. Her eyes glanced down, and he followed her gaze to where she was slipping the silver band off of her thumb. She held it up in the moonlight and showed him the inscription inside which was barely still legible.

“David Britton,” she said taking his left hand in hers. Purposefully, she slid the band onto his left ring finger. “I never let you go.”

The End.
Or Just The Beginning.

THANK YOU FOR READING!

Please consider leaving a review on Amazon!
Reviews help other readers discover new books.

If you want more of these spunky characters,
the prequel to this story is called **To Be Her
First**.

*Turn the page for a free peek at Chapter One of my
bestselling series The Soul Summoner!*

The Soul Summoner Series
Amazon #1 Best Seller
Kindle Unlimited Eligible

Book 1 - The Soul Summoner
Book 2 - The Siren

Standalone Novella - The Detective
FREE at www.EliciaHyder.com

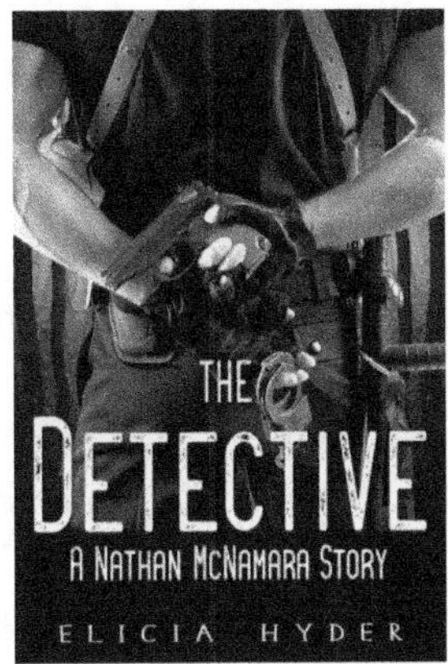

The Soul Summoner
Chapter One

Her hazel eyes were judging me again. *God, I wish I could read minds instead.*

Adrianne spun her fork into her spaghetti, letting the tines scrape against the china. I cringed from the sound. She pointed her forkful of noodles at my face. "I think you're a witch."

I laughed to cover my nerves. "You've said that before." Under the white tablecloth, I crossed my fingers and prayed we would breeze through this conversation one more time.

A small, teasing smile played at the corner of her painted lips. "I really think you are."

I shook my head. "I'm not a witch."

She shrugged. "You might be a witch."

I picked up my white wine. "I wish I had a dollar for every time I've heard that. I could pay off my student loans." With one deep gulp, I finished off the glass.

She swallowed the bite in her mouth and leaned toward me. "Come on. I might die if I don't get to see him tonight! Do you really want that kind of guilt on your hands?"

I rolled my eyes. "You're so dramatic."

She placed her fork beside her plate and reached over to squeeze my hand. "Please try."

My shoulders caved. "OK." I shoved my chair back a few inches and crossed my legs on top of my seat. I closed my eyes, shook my long brown hair off my shoulders, and blew out a deep slow breath as I made circular O's with my fingertips. Slowly, my hands floated down till they rested on my knees. I began to moan. "Ohhhhhmmmm…"

Adrianne threw her napkin at me, drawing the attention of the surrounding guests at Alejandro's Italian Bistro. "Be serious!"

I dropped my feet to the floor and laughed as I scooted closer to the table. "*You* be serious," I said. "You know that's not how it works."

She laughed. "You don't even know how it works!" She flattened her palms on the tablecloth. "Here, I'll make it easy. Repeat after me. Billy Stewart, Billy Stewart, Billy Stewart," she chanted.

I groaned and closed my eyes. "Billy Stewart, Billy Stewart, Billy Stewart."

She broke out in giggles and covered her mouth. "You're such a freak!"

I raised an eyebrow. "You call me that a lot."

"You know I'm only joking. Sort of."

Adrianne Marx had been my best friend since the fifth grade, but sometimes I still had trouble deciphering when she was joking and when she was being serious.

I picked up my fork again and pointed it at her. "It's not gonna happen, so don't get too excited."

She let out a deep breath. "I'm not."

I smirked. "Whatever."

Our waiter, who had been the topic of our conversation before Adrianne began gushing about her new crush on Billy Stewart, appeared at our table.

"Can I get you ladies anything else?" His Southern drawl was so smooth I had nicknamed him Elvis over dinner. He was a little older than the two of us, maybe twenty-three, and he had a sweet, genuine smile. His hair was almost black, and his eyes were the color of sparkling sapphires. I had drunk enough water that night to float the Titanic just so I could watch him refill my glass.

I looked at his name tag. "Luke, do I look like a witch?"

His mouth fell open. "Uh, I don't think so?"His response was more of a question than an answer.

Across the table, Adrianne was twisting strands of her auburn ponytail around her finger. I nodded toward Luke. "See, he doesn't think I'm a witch."

Luke lowered his voice and leaned one hand on our table. "You're too pretty to be a witch," he added, with a wink.

I smiled with satisfaction.

Adrianne laughed and pushed her plate away from her. "Don't be fooled, Luke. She has powers you can't even dream of."

He looked down at me and smiled. "Oh really?" He leaned down and lowered his voice. "How about you let me take care of this for you"—he dangled our bill in front of my face—"and later, when I get off, I can hear all about your powers?"

Heat rose in my cheeks as I took the check from his hand, and when I pulled a pen from his waistband apron, his breath caught in his chest. I flashed my best sultry smile up at him and scribbled my name and phone number on the back of the bill. I stood up, letting my hand linger in his as I gave him the check. "I'm in town on a break from college for the weekend, so let me know when you get off."

He smiled and backed away from the table. "I will"—he looked down at the paper—"Sloan."

I took a deep breath to calm the butterflies in my stomach as Adrianne followed me toward the front door. She nudged me with her elbow. "You should win some kind of award for being able to pick up guys," she said as we passed through the small rush of dinner customers coming in.

I shrugged my shoulders and glanced back at her with a mischievous grin. "Maybe it's part of my gift."

"Witch," she muttered.

The icy chill of winter nipped at my face as I pushed the glass door open. When we walked out onto the sidewalk, I stopped so suddenly that Adrianne tripped over my legs and tumbled to the concrete.

Billy Stewart was waiting at a red light in front of the restaurant.

Adrianne might never have even noticed Billy's official game warden truck at the stoplight had my mouth not been hanging open when she struggled to her feet. She was cursing me under her breath as her eyes followed the direction of my dumbfounded gaze across the dark parking lot. When her eyes landed on the green and gold truck, she fell back a step.

Her fingers, still coated in gravel dust, dug into my arm. "Is that…?"

I turned my horrified eyes to meet hers when traffic started moving again.

Frantically, she waved her finger in the direction of the traffic light. "That was Billy Stewart!" She was so excited that her voice cracked.

"Yeah, it was." Mortification settled over me, and I pressed my eyes closed, hoping to wake from a bad dream. When I focused on Adrianne again, I realized she had taken a pretty nasty fall. Her blue jeans were torn and her right knee was bloody. "Oh geez, I'm so sorry."

She looked at me, her eyes wild with a clear mix of anxiety and amusement. She glanced down at the gash on her knee. "Can you heal me too?" Her question had a touch of maniacal laughter.

I shoved her shoulder. "Shut up." I tugged her toward the restaurant's entrance. "Let's go to the bathroom and get you cleaned up."

Once we were behind the closed door of the ladies room, Adrianne's curious eyes turned toward me again. She hiked her leg up on the counter beside the sink.

"What the hell just happened out there?"

I ran some cold water over a paper towel and handed it to her. "I need a drink." I splashed my face with cold water and, for a moment, considered drowning myself in the sink.

She pointed at me as she dabbed the oozing blood off her kneecap. "You and me both, sister. You've got some major explaining to do."

Alejandro's had a small bar near the front door where I had never seen anyone actually sit. When we pulled out two empty bar stools, the slightly balding bartender looked at us like we might be lost. His eyebrows rose in question as he mindlessly polished water spots off of a wine glass.

"I think I'm going to need a Jack and Coke," Adrianne announced.

I held up two fingers. "Make that two."

"IDs?" he asked.

Getting carded was one of the best things about being twenty-one. Any other time, I would have whipped out my finally-legal-identification with a smile plastered on my face. But in that moment, fear of what the next conversation might bring loomed over me like a black storm cloud that was ready to drop a funnel.

I had already learned the hard way not to talk about these things.

People are scared of what they can't comprehend, and the last thing I wanted was for Adrianne to be afraid of me. Despite my unnatural propensity toward popularity, Adrianne was one of the only real friends I had.

I knew the jabs she made about me being a witch were all in jest, but there was a part of her that had been genuinely curious about me since we were kids. Adrianne, above anyone else, had the most cause to be suspicious of the odd 'coincidences' that were happening more and more frequently around me.

Summoning Billy Stewart had been a complete accident. God knows I had tried my whole life to summon all sorts of people—my birth mother and Johnny Depp to name a couple—without any success at all. Sitting next to Adrianne at the bar, I knew from the look in her eyes that seeing Billy at that stoplight solidified to her what I already knew to be true: I was different. Very different.

Swiveling her chair around to face me, she pointed to the dining table we had just vacated. "OK, I was kidding about Billy at dinner. That was some serious David Copperfield shit you just pulled out there, Sloan. Totally creepy."

I groaned and dropped my face into my hands. "I know."

An arm came to rest behind my back, and Luke appeared between our seats with a tantalizing grin that would normally make me swoon. "Did you miss me that much?" he asked.

Adrianne pointed a well-manicured fingernail at him. "Not now, Elvis," she said without taking her eyes off me.

Stunned, Luke took a few steps back.

I offered him an apologetic wink. "We need a minute."

He nodded awkwardly, stuffed his hands into his pockets, and left us alone.

When he was gone, I turned back to Adrianne. "I don't suppose you could be convinced this was all a really big coincidence?"

"Sloan, when we ran into my Gran after you said you needed to pick up some canned green beans from her, that was a coincidence. When we were talking about going to Matt Sheridan's keg party and we ran into him at the beer store, that was a coincidence. When you said you hoped Shannon Green would get syphilis and we saw her walking out of the Health Department, maybe even that was a coincidence." We both laughed.

She tapped her nails against the bar top. "Billy Stewart is supposed to be working on the backside of a mountain right now, Sloan. He shouldn't be anywhere near the city. I was joking and trying to get you to make him magically appear…and then *you did*. That's not a coincidence."

I groaned.

She lowered her voice and leaned into me. "What are you not telling me? Did you make that happen or not?"

It was too late to try and recover with a lie. I had no other choice but to tell her the truth. My legs were shaking under the table and a trickle of sweat ran down my spine. "I'm not a hundred percent certain, but yes. I think so."

She sucked in a deep breath and blew it out slowly. Her eyes were wide and looking everywhere but into mine. "I'm going to be honest. You're kinda freaking me out a little bit right now."

I nodded and pinched the bridge of my nose. "I know. I wish I had a grand explanation, but I've never had anyone explain it to me either."

I felt her hand squeeze mine. "I love you, so let me have it. Tell me everything."

My stomach felt like an elevator free-falling through the shaft. "You're going to think I'm crazy."

"Sloan, I think we bypassed crazy about twenty minutes ago," she said with a genuine chuckle.

The bartender placed our drinks in front of us, and I wrapped my fingers around the short tumbler. Adrianne drained half of her whiskey in one swallow.

I took a deep breath. I let my thoughts roll around for a moment in my head, and I tried to choose my words carefully so I didn't sound as nuts as I felt. Finally, I looked at her and lowered my voice. "You know when you're out and you see someone you really feel like you know, but you can't remember how or who they are?"

She nodded. "Sure."

I paused for a moment. "I feel that way around *everyone*. Like I already know them."

Her face contorted with confusion. She tried to

laugh it off without success. "Well, I've always said you've never met a stranger."

I looked at her seriously. "I haven't *ever* met a stranger, Adrianne."

She cleared her throat. "I really don't understand what you're talking about."

Sadly, I didn't understand what I was talking about either.

"I see people I've never met and feel like I've known them forever. I can even just see a picture of someone and know if they are alive or dead and what kind of person they are. I don't know their names or anything specific, but I have a weird sense about them before ever talking to them. It's like I recognize their soul."

She let my words sink in for a moment. "Like the time you told me not to go out with the exchange student in the eleventh grade, and then he date-raped that cheerleader?"

"Yes. I knew he had a lot of evil in him," I said.

"And you get these 'vibes' from everyone?" she asked.

I nodded. "Absolutely everyone."

"So that's why you're so good with people...why you can talk to anyone and everyone at any time?"

I nodded again. "It's easy to befriend people when it feels like you've known them for years, and I seem to be somewhat of a people-magnet."

She interrupted me. "But what does that have to

do with Billy Stewart showing up here tonight?"

"There's more."

She sat back, exasperated. "Of course there is."

"I think it's somehow related. People are naturally drawn to me, and somehow I can manipulate that."

Her eyes widened. "You can control people?" Her voice was almost a whisper.

"I don't think I would call it *controlling* people…" My voice trailed off as I sorted through my thoughts. "I know things about people, and sometimes when I talk about someone, it's like I can summon them to me."

She laughed, but it was clear she didn't think it was funny. "Come on, Sloan. Really?"

"Just think about it." I looked at her over the rim of my tumbler and sipped my drink.

She was quiet for a while. There were a thousand odd events she could have been replaying in her mind. Like, the time I said I wanted Jason Ward to ask me to the homecoming dance, and he was waiting by my locker after class. Or, when I told her I had a bad feeling about our gym teacher, and we found out on Monday he had died of a heart attack over the weekend. Finally, she looked at me again. "You know I wouldn't believe a word of this if I hadn't known you for so long."

I nodded. "I don't believe it most of the time myself."

"When you say you 'know' people. What do you know? Like, do you know that guy?" She pointed at the bartender.

I laughed. "No. It's just a sense I get. I can tell you he's an OK guy, but I'm not a mind reader."

She drummed her long nails on the countertop. "So you're psychic?"

"No, I don't think so. I just seem to be able to read people really well."

She leaned toward me and dramatically fanned her fingers like a magician. "And make people suddenly appear!"

"Shhhh!" I looked cautiously around.

Luke, who was waiting nearby, caught my eye and started in our direction.

Adrianne extended her long arm to stop him. "Not so fast, you little eager beaver."

I laughed, and the tension finally started to drain from my shoulders. After a moment, I gripped her arm. "You're not gonna get all freaked out on me now, are you? I haven't told anyone about this since I was old enough to know better."

Her head snapped back with surprise. "Old enough to know better?"

I ran my fingers across the faint scar just above my right eyebrow. "Kids can be pretty cruel when they find out you're different. When I was eight and we still lived in Atlanta, one of them threw a big rock at me during recess."

She gasped. "That's horrible!"

I nodded. "After that, Mom and Dad decided it would be best to move."

"So they know about what you can do?" she asked.

I shook my head. "Not exactly. Whatever is wrong with me can't be explained by science, so I think it scares them to talk about it. They haven't brought it up once since we moved here." I touched my scar again. "And seven stitches in the face taught me to keep my mouth shut."

She squeezed my hand, her eyes no longer judgmental. "Well, I'm not going to freak out, and I'm not going to tell anyone."

I sighed. "Thank you."

She grinned over the top of her glass. "No one would believe me anyway."

"I know."

Suddenly, she perked up with a wild smile. "What about Brad Pitt?"

I raised my eyebrows. "What about him?"

"Can you get him here?"

I laughed. "That's not the way it works!"

She crossed her arms over her chest. "How do you know?"

I smiled. "Because I've already tried."

Get The Soul Summoner Series at all major online retailers.

www.ingramcontent.com/pod-product-compliance
Lightning Source LLC
Chambersburg PA
CBHW072157130726
47910CB00010B/647